Also by Bud Fussell
From Indigo Sea Press

Destiny

Mixed Emotions

Redemption

Scoundrel

Serendipity

Shepherds

Whirlwind

indigoseapress.com

That One Night

By

Bud Fussell

Deep Indigo Books
Published by Indigo Sea Press
Winston-Salem

Deep Indigo Books
Indigo Sea Press
PO Box 67201
Winston-Salem, NC 27114
This book is a work of fiction. Names, characters,
locations and events are either a product of the author's
imagination, fictitious or used fictitiously. Any resemblance
to any event, locale or person, living or dead, is purely
coincidental.

First Deep Indigo Books edition published
September, 2018
Deep Indigo Books, Moon Sailor and all production design
are trademarks of Indigo Sea Press, used under license.

For information regarding bulk purchases of this book,
digital purchase and special discounts, please contact the publisher
at indigoseapress@gmail.com

Cover Concept by Bud Fussell
Cover design by Pan Morelli
Manufactured in the United States of America
ISBN 978-1-63066-485-5

*In **That One Night**, master storyteller Bud Fussell blends the familiar with the unique. Abandoning his use of one-word titles and his allegorical technique, Fussell ventures forth with a raw story of troubled young people facing life-changing decisions. As in the past, however, he weaves an utterly believable tale of business and morality with his splendid ability to develop characters, not just over the course of a handful of events, but over years and decades. This is the familiar literary Bud Fussell along with a powerful, well-developed new sense of destiny, possibility and will.*

Chapter One

The Skint Chesnut Mall was complete and doing an incredible amount of business. People were coming from all over to shop not only at the huge anchor stores, but the many smaller specialty stores as well. Fifteen restaurants, not counting the food court, encircled the mall, and they all seemed to be full at meal time. They consisted of fast food for those wanting that kind of food, as well as full service restaurants, serving sit-down meals. Two or three of the full-service restaurants also offered gourmet meals.

Everything about the mall was *state of the art* and tastefully done. Not only was the construction quality second to none, but it was beautiful as well. Frank Thomas, the majority owner, was blessed with exquisite taste as was Jerry Martin, the General Contractor. During construction, they both pored over catalogs and magazines, and if either saw something that they thought would be good to put in the mall, they would consult the other, and if they both agreed, whatever it was would be included.

Frank's Administrative Assistant is a lady named Melissa Morris, who is also his niece. When not chasing Jerry, her job was to sell space in the mall, and she did a remarkable job of filling it up with the better type stores. The mall currently has over two hundred and twenty-five stores and there is a waiting list to fill any space that might come open, so he is well pleased with the job she has done.

Sometimes a good deed can reap unimaginable rewards, and that's what happened to Jerry Martin. Approximately six years ago Jerry had three homes under construction, and one night three teenagers broke into one of them and pretty much wrecked it. They tore up nearly all the sheetrock and did other damage as well; enough to make it a felony rather than a misdemeanor.

The police caught them that same night, and later, when they went to trial, Jerry felt a great deal of empathy for them and he convinced the judge to let them work out their sentences by working for him until the damages were paid for rather than send them to jail. He told the judge that if they were successful in doing that until their sentences were complete, he would like for their records to be wiped clean; showing no felony, and the judge agreed.

As it so happened, that was possibly the best thing Jerry ever did. He had no idea what his act of kindness would eventually lead to. He continued his building, and the three kids held up their end of the deal. In fact; one of the boys, Stony Gray, decided he liked the building business so much he convinced Jerry to hire him full time when he graduated from high school.

He developed into one heck of a carpenter and craftsman, and his creative skills and devotion to work impressed Jerry so much that he sent him to college, and he graduated with a degree in Building Sciences. While working for his degree, he not only learned how to build things, but he learned the business side of construction as well. Currently, he's one of Martin Builders' most important members.

Three or four years before that happened, Jerry found a nice piece of land and decided he wanted to build a residential community on it, but there would be a tremendous amount of preliminary work before the first nail could be driven, not to mention the financial part of it. He was going to name it White Rock Estates.

He wanted to build between forty-five and forty-eight homes in the three quarter million to a million-dollar price range, and the cost to build that many houses at those prices would be huge. As it happened, forty-eight was the final number. Each home would have at least a three-acre property with it. He began trying to work with the county to see if they would run water and maybe pave the streets after he graded the streets in. All those things took a lot of time, but he finally got the okay from the county to do what he wanted them to do.

Next was the financing. He began talking to a fellow named John Cochran at the Cornerstone First National Bank, and when the county finally came through on his requests, he began to put the pressure on John to approve his request for construction loans. And then, when he took his figures to John, John looked at them and told him that he didn't have the authority to approve such an amount, and that he would have to talk to someone higher up than he was. The man John wanted him to talk to was not in, so he made an appointment for him to see the man the following week.

When he went back the next week, John took him upstairs to meet the man he said Jerry would have to talk to and when they walked into the man's office, the man was none other than Frank Thomas; the father of Reed Thomas, one of the kids who had broken into his house earlier.

Jerry had met Frank the night the kids were taken to the Magistrate and again at their trial, but he had no idea that he was the Chairman of a large bank. After the initial shock, Jerry made his presentation, and Frank was impressed; in fact, he was so impressed, he later inspected some of his work and gave him a job to build a high-end apartment complex for him and his partner. A little later, he gave him the job of building The Skint Chesnut Mall and some additional apartment complexes, and the good things just kept on going. Jerry got his original financing by being smart and convincing Frank of the value of financing White Rock, but Frank's gratitude for Jerry's help with Reed didn't hurt either.

White Rock was taking longer than he had planned. First of all, he put the project on hold for a full two years in order to devote his full time to the building of the mall, and then when he thought he was going to have time to work on the White Rock community, Frank would come up with a new project, and Jerry was not about to refuse him anything within

3

reason. Frank had made him a rich man with the construction of the Skint Chesnut Mall, and the apartment complexes were only adding to that. All in all, thirty-two of the forty-eight homes have been completed, and twenty-nine have been sold, with all of them meeting or exceeding Jerry's pre-construction estimates of profit. The financing of White Rock was Frank's first experience with Jerry, and he sort of went out on a limb when he approved that amount of money, but when Jerry came in with those figures, he was very gratified.

It has been five years since Tracy and Jerry adopted little B J, and he was loved just as much as he would have been if he were their own flesh and blood. He was in kindergarten, and according to his teacher, he was very smart. Frank and his wife, Marilyn, doted on him, and he called them Uncle Frank and Aunt Marilyn. Tracy and Jerry hadn't seen Tammy since the day she gave birth to B J, but Barbara, Tammy's mother, had called Jerry a few times, and when he would ask about Tammy she would say that she was doing good and had graduated from a community college there in Jacksonville.

When she called Jerry the first time, she asked him what they had named the baby and he told her John Robert, and they were going to call him B. J. She hesitated for a minute and asked, "Don't you mean J. B.?"

He answered, "Well, that would be logical, but we like B. J. the best, so that's what we're calling him." He kind of laughed and said, "He doesn't seem to care one way or the other."

One day, when he was on his way to Frank's office to go over some plans for yet another apartment complex, he was intercepted by Melissa. "Hi Handsome, "she said. "I haven't seen you in forever. Don't you love me anymore?"

"I love you the same as I loved you the last time we were together."

"That much, hunh?"

"Yep, that much."

"Seriously, where have you been? I miss seeing you every day or two."

"White Rock has been keeping me really busy, and most of my time has been spent down there. You ought to come down and see it; it's really something."

"If that's an invitation, I will. Where are you going right now?"

"I'm just on my way to Frank's office. We're going over some plans for another apartment complex. What's been going on with you?"

"Same old, same old. I was going to call you. There's something I need to talk to you about. Can I see you for a minute before you go into Frank?"

"Yeah, I guess if it won't take too long. Frank's expecting me."

"It won't take long at all; in fact, I just need for you to answer a question."

"What is it?"

"You may or may not know that I went to Delta High School. Ever since I got out and later from college, I've been active in the Alumni Association at Delta. Money is tight everywhere these days and especially in schools, and Delta is no exception. We have been trying to raise money for a new concession stand at the stadium, and I thought you might be interested in helping out some."

"What do you want me to do?"

"I want you to build it; not for free, but maybe you could take a little shorter margin than you usually do in order to help us out."

"Do you have any plans?"

"Yeah, Mr. Cuba, the head of the architectural sciences department, drew some, and I can get them for you. What do you think?"

"Boy, you come on strong in all areas, don't you? Let me think about it, and I'll talk to you later. In the meantime, get me those blueprints so I can see what you're talking about."

"Thank you, my darling. I knew I could count on you."

"Don't count on me yet. I've got to see what you're wanting and then I've got to decide whether I want to do it or not."

"Okay. I'll go out to the school this afternoon and see if I can get the plans. Maybe I can get them to you by tomorrow."

Okay. I'll see you later."

He left her and went into Frank's office where Frank had already spread the blueprints out on the conference table. After they spent quite a bit of time on the apartment complex plans, Frank asked, "Jerry, have you ever heard of the Chrisman House?"

"No, I can't say that I have. Why?"

"Well, I just bought it, and I want you and your people to completely renovate it. Are you interested?"

"Padna, you know I would never refuse you. Of course, I'm interested. Tell me a little about it."

"Well, the Chrisman House is a large antebellum mansion that sits on the Chattahoochie River down close to Austell. Do you know where Austell is?"

"Yeah, I know where Austell is."

"Well, the Chattahoochie River and Sweetwater Creek merge a few miles west of Austell, and the mansion sits right where they merge."

"What has to be done to it?"

"I don't know what all yet. I'm pretty sure all the windows will need to be replaced for one thing. The place is beautiful, but it has been empty for probably thirty years. A family used to live there, and they sharecropped, then the man died, and there was no one to take over, so the wife and their children moved out, and it has been vacant ever since. The original Chrisman family soon all died off, and there was nobody to take the place over, and finally, the county sold it for taxes, and that's how I got it."

"What are you going to do with it?"

"I don't know yet. It's such a beautiful place I felt like I had to have it. It would make a great Bed and Breakfast or maybe even a small hotel. I can't wait for you to see it. Some of the woodwork inside is phenomenal, and it has marble that was imported from Italy."

"Well, you're getting me excited. When can we go look at it?"

"Can you go sometime tomorrow?"

"Yeah, about anytime you say."

"Why don't you come here about ten o'clock in the morning? You can park your pick up here and ride out there with me."

"Sounds like a plan. Listen, I need to go if we're through. I'll see you in the morning."

When he passed by Melissa's office on the way out, she yelled at him to come in there, and when he did, she asked, "Well, did you all get things worked out on the new apartments?"

"Yeah, and in addition to that he wants me to renovate a pre-civil war mansion for him."

"What pre-civil war mansion?"

"The Chrisman House. Have you ever heard of it?"

She nearly shouted; "Have I ever heard of it. That's where my old gang and I hung out whenever we weren't in school. Have I ever heard of it? You bet I've heard of it. I've had some really good times in that old house, and nearly got in trouble a few times as well. So, Frank bought it? I didn't know that."

"I'm going to look at it in the morning. If I see any Melissa remnants while I'm down there, should I try to hide them?"

"Ha, ha; you're funny. You won't find any Melissa remnants," then she paused and smiled and said, "At least, I don't think you will."

"Well, just in case I do, what will they be; a bra or something like that?"

"You're awful. No, if you should find a bra, it won't be mine."

"How can I be sure?"

"Because I never took my bra off down there."

"Are you sure?"

"I'm sure. Now get off my case. I was a good girl then, and I'm a good girl now."

"Yeah, right."

"I don't even know why I'm talking to you. Why don't you go somewhere else? Better still, why don't you go home and see your little wife and baby?"

"Okay, I will, but you don't really want me to, do you, and B J's not a baby anymore. He's in kindergarten. Can you believe that?"

"To answer your first question; no, I really don't want you to. I'd like for you to stay with me all day, and to answer your second question; that's hard to believe. It seems like just yesterday that you got him. Now, why don't you sit down and talk to me? Maybe you can even be civil to me."

"I can't; I've got to go. I'm supposed to meet a guy down at White Rock, but maybe I'll see you in the morning. I'm coming here to meet Frank. He's going to drive when we go down to the Chrisman House. He might want you to go with us."

"You know something, Jerry?"

"What?"

"You're actually being nice to me. In all the time we've known each other, you have seldom ever been nice to me. Am I finally winning you over?"

"No, I've just decided that after seven years of fighting you off, you have finally given up and decided that you're not going to win. Being nice is a whole lot easier."

"Oh, I see. Well, I like you better when you're nice, but don't let your guard down, big boy, because I'm just as determined as ever to get my hooks in you, and when I do,

8

you'll never want to look back."

He smiled and said, "You're evil, do you know that? I'll see you tomorrow. Bye."

He was at the bank a little before ten the next morning, and he went straight up to Frank's office where Frank and Melissa were waiting for him. He said, "Good morning; are you ready to go?"

Frank answered, "We're ready. You don't mind if Melissa tags along, do you?"

"Of course not. Hi Melissa."

When they got downstairs to Frank's car, the passenger side of the car was full of some kind of furniture and some papers.

Frank said, "I'm sorry about this, but I'm just trying to keep piece at home. My wife said this has to go to Cook's Refinishing, so I told her I would drop it off. It's just a little way down the road and then we can reclaim the whole front seat. I hope you don't mind."

Jerry said, "No problem. I'll just sit back here with Melissa."

Just as soon as he and Melissa got in the back seat and Frank in the front, she reached over and grabbed his hand and interlocked her fingers with his. Surprisingly, he didn't pull away from her, and they rode that way until they got to the refinishing place.

On the way, she asked, "Have you thought anymore about the thing at the school I talked to you about yesterday?"

"Yeah, a little, but I've got to see some plans before I can tell you anything."

"I went by Delta yesterday and got the blueprints Mr. Cuba drew, and they're in my office at the bank. I'll give them to you when we get back."

Chapter Two

From the time Frank got back in the car until they got to the Chrisman House, he talked non-stop about the house and what he wanted done to it in the way of renovations. He said to Jerry, "I'm surprised you've never heard of it. Melissa, have you heard of the Chrisman House?"

"Yeah, I've heard of it."

He didn't say anything else to her about it, and in another five or ten minutes they arrived at the mansion.

It was beautiful underneath the peeling paint and rotting eaves, broken windows and scarred columns. Jerry could see why Frank would want the place. Even though it was in rough shape after sitting idle for more than thirty years, his being a builder enabled him to see in his mind's eye, what the place could look like after it was renovated.

The interior was huge, and the grand staircase itself was something to behold. Every room was graced with fine crown molding, and most of the wood trim was of solid mahogany or some other exotic wood. The master bedroom was as large as some houses, with almost twelve hundred square feet, including a dumbwaiter and a fireplace that measured seventy-two inches wide by fifty-four inches high.

After they had walked through the house and part of the thirty-two acres outside, Frank asked Jerry, "Well, what do you think?"

"I think if you restore it to its original glory, you're going to have one of the most beautiful places in the whole southeast, but I can see, from just walking around, that it's going to be terribly expensive."

"Can you give me a ball-park figure?"

"I'd rather not right now."

"Just a ball-park; I won't hold you to it."

"Well, Frank, some of the materials are going to be hard to find, and if we are able to find them they're going to be expensive. We can't just bring any jack-leg carpenter in here to do the work; we're going to have to have people who know what they are doing. I'm not comfortable guessing at a price, but since you're wanting a ball-park figure, I'd say it will run somewhere between two and three-hundred thousand dollars."

"That much, hunh?"

"It could be more. I need to come back out here and take a bunch of pictures and then go to my office and sit down with them and figure costs on everything, and after I've done that I can give you a more accurate number. My guess might be high, but I don't think so. Also, if you're planning to do something other than make it into a grand home, I will need to know just what

your plans are."

Frank said, "I'd like to move out here, but I don't know if I would ever be able to get Marilyn this far out of town, but it's beautiful, isn't it Jerry?"

"It sure is."

"What do you think about this place, Melissa?"

"It's gorgeous. I've always thought that."

"You seem to be familiar with it. When did you ever see it before?"

"Well, when I was in school. Sometimes a gang of us would come down here and hang out."

"What do you mean, hang out?"

"Hang out. That's what kids do. They hang out."

"I'm not sure I know what you mean by hanging out."

She looked at Jerry and said, "Jerry, help me out here. Will you please tell Mr. Naïve here what hang out means?"

"Frank, I think she means that she and her friends would come down here to go swimming and have picnics and things like that. Isn't that what you mean, Melissa?"

"Exactly. Thank you, Jerry."

11

Frank was dead serious, and he said, "I hope that's all you did."

"That's not all we did. We did a lot of things. For instance; sometimes Steve Ward would bring his guitar and we would sit around and sing while he played. Uncle Frank, we were good kids, and nothing out of line ever happened as far as I know. This was just a good place for us to get away from school and other things and just hang out. Okay?"

"Okay. I guess I just envisioned some untoward things going on. I'm sorry. Well, are you guys ready to go back?" Jerry noticed that she called Frank, Uncle Frank. That was the first time he had heard her call him that.

They both said they were ready, so they went to the car and started back to Douglasville. On the way back, Jerry asked Frank how long before he decided what he was going to do with the mansion, and Frank told him he hoped to make up his mind within a week or two.

"Just let me know when you decide and I'll come back with my camera. Also, I can draw plans, but if you should decide to make it into a hotel or bed and breakfast or something like that, you will probably want to get an architect or someone of that caliber to draw up some plans. You know something, Frank?"

"What?"

"That would make an incredible high-end restaurant. I bet people would drive down here from all over north Georgia, and it wouldn't surprise me if they came from as far south as Macon."

"You could be right. That's something to think about."

Jerry had been given the *go ahead* on the apartments and he had Bill Case and his men begin laying out some of the buildings without him. His people had become so knowledgeable and efficient that if they had to, they could probably start and finish a large project without him. He liked that, but he was careful to not let them know that they could do that.

He had told Melissa that he would help her and her Alumni Association build the concession stand at the Delta High School, so the temporary lull helped him with his planning of the project. The project was not an official school project and did not have to be subject to all the customary red tape normally connected to something that had to be debated and approved by the school board.

Three Weeks Later

Frank decided that he would just have Jerry and his people fix up the Chrisman House and make it into the finest antebellum mansion in the south, and that suited Jerry just fine. Frank thought he might rent it out for weddings and meetings and things like that.

Jerry met with him after he made his decision, and they laid out some extensive plans, including adding bathrooms to every bedroom that didn't already have one. Actually, none of them had a real bathroom because in pre-civil war days most plumbing fixtures had not been invented yet. The mansion did have small rooms off most bedrooms where people staying there could go to relieve themselves by use of a thunder-mug, sometimes called a slop-jar.

Once they knew where they were going, Jerry drew up some plans and then proceeded to make a materials list, which included many things that had not been manufactured in a hundred years. For those items, he was going to depend largely on Jack Richards, his father-in-law, who owned Richards Building Supply. Jack had been in the building supply business all his adult life, and if anybody could find hard-to-find items, it would be him.

After he had made a partial materials list, he went back and began pricing some of the things. When he got to the bathrooms, the costs of just basic fixtures really scared him, and he wanted to talk to Frank before he went any further on figuring the total cost in case he, Frank, wanted to go in another direction. He called him and asked if he could come by the bank to see him, and Frank told him to come by after lunch; about one fifteen.

He got there before Frank got back and sat in the outer office and waited on him. In just a minute or two he saw Melissa coming up the hall, and when she saw him she turned in and sat down with him. Even though there were several chairs, she chose to sit on the sofa with him and sat right up next to him; their legs touching. Jerry was afraid somebody was going to come by and see how close they were sitting and make something out of it. Thankfully, the way they were sitting enabled them to see down the hall, and when Melissa saw Frank coming, she scooted over a little so she wouldn't be so obvious. When he got there, Jerry stood up, and Frank said, "Hi Jerry. Come on in."

They went into his office and after they sat down he asked, "Do we have a problem, Jerry?"

He said, "No, I don't think so, but I just want to be sure that you're completely aware of how much this job is going to cost. The reason I wanted to see you today is to show you how much the bathrooms are going to run and to see if you're sure you want to have as many as you first said."

"Are they that expensive?"

"Let me show you these pictures that I got off the internet. When I was researching these fixtures, I got a kick out of the name of the company that was responsible for making the earliest versions of flushing toilets. You know what it is?"

"No, what?"

"They were made by the Thomas Crapper Company. Can you believe that?"

They both laughed and made some jokes about the word crapper, and then Jerry continued.

"Frank, you said you want twenty-six bathrooms in the house with nineteen in the bedrooms. I haven't figured the cost of all of them yet, but if you put a bathtub and toilet in each one, just those two items are going to amount to around eighty thousand dollars. That doesn't count the lavatories, and if you want showers in some of the bathrooms, that will be even more. These figures are for fixtures only. They don't count the tile floors. It looks as though the bathrooms alone are going to cost between a hundred and fifty and two hundred thousand dollars, and these figures are my cost. Labor and other things are on top of these, and I didn't want to keep going until I ran this by you."

"That's a lot of money, isn't it Jer?"

"Yep, it's a lot of money."

'Well, I want this place to be second to none in the south, so I guess I'll just have to bite the bullet and say go ahead with it.

"Okay. I'll get outa here and go back to the office and continue figuring. I was afraid you would tell me to go with contemporary stuff in order to cut costs, or maybe leave out some of the bathrooms, and I'm really glad you chose to stay authentic. I'll call you when I finish costing this thing out."

"Do you have any idea when that will be?"

"I don't think it will be too long. A lot of it will depend on how long it takes to find some of the items. If we don't run into any major delays, I should be through in just a few days."

"How many days is a few?"

"Probably three or four."

"Okay, Pal. I'll be listening for your call."

On the way out, he saw Melissa and stopped for a minute to talk to her. "Where you headed, Good Looking?"

"Back to my office. I'm working on the costs for the Chrisman House."

"When are you going to start working out there?"

"Just as soon as I finish costing it out and Frank gives me the go ahead; probably in a week or two."

"I'll be anxious to see my old hang out come back to life."

"It's going to be beautiful. It won't be a hang out any more.

I'm not going to be surprised if he and Marilyn move into it."

"It's unlikely he'll be able to get her to move that far out. If he does, I'll be shocked."

"Once she sees it, she might be the one to push him to move. I've got to run; see ya later."

As he was leaving, she yelled behind him and asked, "Are you about ready to start things at Delta High?"

He turned and said, "Just about. See ya."

With Frank's blessings on liberal costing within reason, Jerry felt good when he got back to his office and started working in earnest on the costs for the mansion. He hadn't been back long before he heard the front door open, and he just hoped it wasn't Melissa. It wasn't; it was Jack with a lot of information about some of the hard to find items they would need to make the job look more authentic.

When Jerry saw what Jack had brought, he said, "Good job, Jack. I was worried about finding some of these things, but you've really come through. Thank you for your hard work finding them."

With Jack's help and with his huge supply of catalogs and brochures, it didn't take any time for him to put together a complete estimate of the cost and call it into Frank. At first, he had guesstimated that it would cost between two and three hundred thousand dollars, but in the end, it looked as if it was going to run between five-fifty and six hundred thousand.

When Frank heard the six hundred thousand figure, he whistled and then asked, "Okay, Jer. When can you start?"

"I think we can get started on some of the preliminary work next week and then really get into it week after next."

"Good. You know, when I bought that place I knew it was going to cost some serious money to get it in shape, but I had no idea it was going to be a half million dollars, but if that's what it is, then that's what it is. What are you going to do first?"

"The first thing we have to do is clean up around the place

and then remove the things that are rotten, and pretty much strip it down to its underwear."

"I like your terminology."

"Well, that's the best way I know how to describe it."

"If you strip it down to its underwear, as you say, are you sure you will be able to restore it to its original condition?"

"Yeah, remember when I said I was coming back with my camera?"

"Yeah, I remember."

"Well, I did, and I have detailed photographs of every little nook and cranny of every room in the house, so if we're not sure about something, we have pictures to show us."

"Good man. I'll talk to you later."

The next morning, first thing, his phone rang and it was Melissa. "Hey good-looking."

"Hi Melissa, what's up?"

"I need a favor."

"Another one? What is it?"

"Jerry, I have a good friend who is a carpenter, and he needs a job."

"This is a strange request coming from you. Tell me about it."

"Well, his name is Kent Coleman, and his sister and I were in the same class in school and good friends. I knew Kent mainly from being around Natalie so much. I'm on the committee that's planning our class reunion, and we met last night, and Kent came to the meeting with another of our classmates. He has been living and working in Macon since he got out of school, and he said he just got laid off because the company he has been working for has had a major downturn in business. I told him I would mention him to you, and maybe you would talk to him. Will you do that?"

"Yeah, I'll talk to him, but listen; I'm leaving here around nine in the morning. If he wants to come in around eight, we can talk then; okay?"

"Thank you, my Sweet. I'll call him right now, and I'm sure he'll want to come talk to you."

When he arrived at his office at eight o'clock the next morning, Kent Coleman was there waiting on him. Beverly had come in fifteen or twenty minutes earlier and had made the coffee and had given Kent some. Jerry poured himself a cup and invited Kent into his office. He asked Kent the routine questions; how long have you been working as a carpenter? Where did you work before? Can you do this? Can you do that? Are you by chance a finish carpenter?

He seemed to give all the right answers and Jerry said, "Kent, I think we can use you. When can you start?"

"I can start right now."

"Really? Have you got your tools with you?"

"Yes sir; they're in my truck."

"Okay, here's what we're going to do. I have just taken a job renovating a very large antebellum mansion, and the first thing we have to do is clean up in and around it and then strip it down. You can help with that when we get out there?"

"You want me to help clean up?"

The question and the way he asked it irritated Jerry and he said, "Yeah, unless that goes against your constitution. If it does, then maybe Martin Builders is not the place for you. We all, including me, do what we have to do to get the job done."

"I'm sorry. I didn't mean that the way it sounded. I was just a little surprised by the words clean up. I'm happy to help clean up and anything else that has to be done. I'm just thankful for the job.

The way he jumped on Kent sort of scared Beverly. He was always so easy going, but this time he got right up in Kent's face when he told him that.

"Okay then; let's go." As they started out the door, he told Beverly, "We're going to the Chrisman House. If you need me, you can try my cell, but I don't know if there's any signal down there. If I don't talk to you, we'll probably be back around four thirty or so."

As they were leaving, he asked Kent if he had to go to the bathroom before they left because if he had to go after they got to the Chrisman House, he would have to go outside. That normally doesn't bother a man, but he wanted to offer anyway.

On the way down, they got more acquainted with each other, and Jerry had to say, "Melissa Morris tells me that she's a friend of yours."

"Yeah, I've known Melissa a long time. She and my sister were real good friends in school."

"Where does your sister live now?"

"I don't know. She disappeared when she was a senior in high school, and nobody has ever seen her since."

"Man, that's rough, so you don't know whether she's dead or alive?"

"That's right. My parents still hold on to hope, but I feel sure she's not still alive."

"I'm sure the police got involved, didn't they?"

"Yeah, they searched for her for several years, but finally gave up."

"Did you keep in touch with Melissa after she disappeared?"

"She came around a lot at first, and then when it looked as if they weren't going to find Natalie, she sort of tapered off her visits and then just pretty much quit coming. Last night was the first time I've seen her in several years, and it was good to see her. She was almost like my sister when Natalie was still around."

Jerry said, "You know, Melissa is pretty flirtatious. Was she that way when she was younger?"

"I never did notice it. She always liked to have a good time, but I never saw that side of her. I do know that when she wanted something, she never gave up until she got it."

"Maybe it's just me, but sometimes she comes on really strong."

19

Before they could continue their conversation, they came to the Chrisman House, and Jerry said, "Well, this is it."

Bill Case, Martin Builders' General Superintendent, had already arrived with a crew and were just getting ready to start picking up trash when Jerry got there. When they saw him, they all came over to where he was, and Jerry introduced Kent all around, and then everybody got busy and started cleaning the place up.

During the clean-up Jerry told Bill, "Bill, look at all these windows and tell me what you think. I believe we can take them out and have them redone without having to buy new ones. What do you think? These are really pretty windows."

Bill walked through the house, looking and feeling the frames on all the windows and told Jerry, "I'm like you, Boss; I think they can be reworked. Do you think that will be cheaper?"

"I'm not sure, but if we can do it and have the lites replaced with double pane glass, I think that's the way to go. That would be one way to help maintain the original appearance of the house. What do you think? Do you think we can save the old ones?"

"I believe so, Jerry. Who will you get to do it?"

"I'm not sure about that either, but I know there are companies that do such work. I'll check with Jack when we get back; he knows everything."

"I think you're right. He's amazing."

"Tell you what, Bill, let's try to finish this clean-up today, and begin removing the windows in the morning, and they're all going to have to be marked so we will know where to put them when they come back. Do you have any markers with you?"

"I don't know. I'll have to look in my truck." He went out and looked, but came back and said, "No, I don't have anything to mark the windows with. Do you want me to go see if I can find a store and buy some?"

"No, it's not that important today. We'll bring some when we come back in the morning. With five guys plus you and me, we should be able to finish cleaning up the place today. I'm going to order a dumpster to be brought down for all the trash, so we won't have to constantly be cleaning up. We can just throw all the stuff in it and have the garbage people pick it up when it gets full."

"Good idea."

The next morning the dumpster almost beat 'em there. It arrived just a few minutes after the guys did. Jerry and Bill got their heads together and decided where to put it, and when it was set, they all picked up the piles of trash they had gathered the day before and threw them in the huge container. Then, as Jerry began to mark the windows, Bill started some of the guys removing them.

Bill asked him, "Did you find a place to refinish these windows?"

"Yeah, Jack put me onto a company in Lexington, Kentucky who he says does great work. They can modernize old windows like these and make them look just like they did a hundred years ago but have a modern touch. Jack said they won the Preservation Craftsman Award, whatever that is. I just hope they're able do these. Jack gave me their number, but I haven't talked to them yet. I've got two bars on my phone, and I hope that's enough to let me call them. Before I do, I need to know how many there are and what size they are.

One of the things I haven't done is to figure out how to get them transported to Lexington. I wish they could pick them up. We might have to rent a truck or maybe ship them by truck line. In the meantime, let's stack 'em up inside the door, so we can get to them easily.

Jerry decided not to wait until they got all the windows removed. He was anxious to see if the place in Kentucky could do the work, and he could call them the measurements later. He went upstairs to the balcony to call so he could get the very best signal possible. He just hoped he would have enough signal for the call to go through. He dialed the number and after two rings a friendly female voice on the other end said, "Kentucky Wooden Window. May I help you?"

"Yeah, this is Jerry Martin with Martin Builders in Atlanta. We are needing someone to refinish forty-four windows in an antebellum mansion. Do you folks do that kind of work?"

"We sure do. Let me let you talk to Larry Freeman. Hold one minute, please."

"Hello. Larry Freeman."

"Mr. Freeman, this is Jerry Martin in Atlanta, Georgia. How are you today?"

"I'm doing great, Mr. Martin. What can I do for you?"

"My company, Martin Builders, is beginning renovations on a large antebellum mansion, and we need to get forty-four large double-hung windows refinished with double-pane glass. Can you do something like that?"

"That's what we do, Jerry. You say you have forty-four. Do you have the sizes?"

"I can have them later today. I was just wanting to see if you could do the work, and I need your suggestion on how to get them to you. Do you pick up?"

"We do, but I'm looking at Mapquest as we're speaking, and it looks like you're about four hundred miles from us. Tell you what, Jerry; I suggest you either rent a truck and bring the windows up here or put them on a freight line. We charge a dollar and a half a mile, and eight hundred miles two times will cost you about twenty-five hundred dollars, just for freight, plus our driver will have to spend the night twice. By the time we're through, it'll cost you about three thousand bucks to get the windows up here and back."

"Wow! I'm going to have to think about that. Answer this for me, Larry; you know about how big an antebellum window is. What kind of ball park figure are you looking at for each window?"

"I don't want you to hold me to this, but depending on the size and condition of the window, especially the condition, I'd say they'll run around three hundred, maybe three hundred and fifty dollars per window."

"That's pretty close to what I figured. Let me think about this freight, Larry, and I'll get back to you with the measurements later on today; okay?"

"Okay, Jerry. I'll be listening for your call."

When he hung up from Larry, he called Frank. When he answered, he said, "Hi Frank; Jerry. Listen, do you have any clients in the trucking business? I need to get the windows in the Chrisman House to Lexington, Kentucky to be refinished, and it looks like the freight is going to eat us up unless we can find a way to get 'em up there and back without paying through the nose."

"As a matter of fact, I do have a client in the trucking business. Let me call him and call you back. How much do you think they will weigh?"

"I have no idea, but tell him there are forty-four large double-hung wooden windows, and maybe he can make a good guess on the weight."

"Okay, Boy. I'll get back to you in a few minutes."

"Thanks, Frank, and oh yeah, call me on my cell."

In about fifteen or twenty minutes, he called back. "Jerry, here's the deal. T & S Transport goes to Lexington regularly and will make us a deal taking the windows up there if we promise to let them bring them back when they're ready. They normally have to dead-head back, and if we let them haul them back, then it will cut their cost and help us too. When you're ready, call Toby Russell at 770-555-9571 and you two can work out the details."

"Okay, Frank, thanks a lot. I'll call him."

As soon as he hung up, he called Toby, and they worked out the deal. T & S would pick up the windows the next day. That would give him plenty of time to finish removing, marking, and measuring all of them. When he hung up from Toby, he called Larry Freeman and told him when the truck would be there, so everything was all set about the windows.

Chapter Three

Later that afternoon, Jerry was walking through the house, making notes of different things when he noticed the tile in the very center of the foyer. It looked as if it had been broken some way and then put back down in a poor repair attempt. He just hoped it could be fixed the way it should be without having to take the whole floor up.

Continuing through the first floor of the house, he made notes of this and that, and then he went upstairs to the second floor. He began at one end and started working himself through, and when he got to the center of the upstairs, directly over where the tile downstairs had been broken, he noticed the guard-rail looked as if it had been broken. Someone had tried to replace the broken piece, but it was fairly noticeable. Making a note of it, he continued on with his tour.

The next morning, they finished removing and stacking the windows, and Bill divided his men up and had them start removing some of the old, rotten trim that was going to be replaced. It looked as if it was going to take several days to remove everything, and they quit work that afternoon at four o'clock.

Everyone knew what they were supposed to do the next morning, so they continued with the removal of the trim and other stuff. Jerry was pleasantly surprised with the way things looked where the trim had been removed. It was in surprisingly good shape, and much of it wouldn't have to be replaced; it would just be covered with new trim or paint.

Around nine-thirty, things were really humming and going well when Jerry looked out the window and saw Melissa getting out of her car. He thought to himself, *man, I don't need this today.* He noticed that she had on jeans like she had come to work, and he also noticed how well she filled them out.

25

She came in, looked around and didn't see anybody she knew, so she asked where Jerry was, and somebody pointed upstairs. When she got up there, the first person she saw was Kent, so she went over and spoke to him and asked him a few questions. Then she saw Jerry and immediately left Kent and went to him.

In a voice that only he could hear, she said, "Hey, good looking."

He said, "Hi. What are you doing out here?"

"I just wanted to come see how my old hangout was looking."

"It looks different, doesn't it?"

"It sure does."

About that time, one of the workers was trying to take out the dumbwaiter, and he skinned his knuckles and let out a yell and a few choice words. Stony Gray saw what happened and said, "You've got to have the right tools to do that job," and he went over and worked on it. In just a minute, when he did something, the whole dumbwaiter came loose and fell all the way to the basement. They were all surprised when it happened, and in a minute, Jerry said, "We need to go down to see what damage that did," so they all went down there, including the guys that were working on the first floor.

When they got to the basement, they saw the dumbwaiter and noticed that it had something in it. In looking closer, Jerry said, "That's a skeleton. Don't touch it. We need to call the police."

While they were standing there, Donny Payne said, "There's something shiny," and he went over and picked it up. Someone else asked, "What does it say?"

"It says *allergic to peanuts.*"

Kent Coleman was standing there, and in almost a yell, he said, "I think that's my sister's," and he left the group in a hurry and walked up the stairs with Melissa hollering, "Kent, Kent, come back, Kent," and she went after him.

After things settled down a little, Jerry called 9-1-1, and told them about finding a skeleton, and when he got off the phone from 9-1-1, he called Frank.

"Frank, I know you're busy, but we've encountered what you might call a situation out here, and I think you need to come."

"What kind of situation?"

"Do you remember that dumbwaiter that went from the master bedroom upstairs down to the kitchen?"

"Yeah, I remember it."

"Well, one of my guys was taking it out a few minutes ago and it came loose and fell to the basement. We went down there to see the damage, and when we got to it, there was a skeleton inside it. I just got off the phone with 9-1-1, and the police are on the way. You might want to come down here."

"I guess I'd better." Then he asked, "This is not some kind of joke, is it Jerry?"

"No, it's not a joke. There's a skeleton in the dumbwaiter."

"Okay, I'll be there in however long it takes me to get there. Thanks for calling me, Jer."

In a little while an unmarked Sheriff's car arrived and two detectives that Jerry recognized got out. They were Detective Lieutenant Ron Adams and Detective Sergeant Paul Vestal. He had met them several years ago, along with Detectives Greg Yokley and Fred Melwiki from a case he was inadvertently involved in; the Tammy Mills rape and kidnapping case.

He met them at the front door and at first they didn't recognize him until he reminded them about Tammy's case. He told them that he was the one who called and led them down to the basement to where the dumbwaiter holding the skeleton was. Looking it over very carefully, Lt. Adams picked up the skull and said, "This skull has a large crack in it, and judging from the size of it and the other bones, I'd say this is a woman or a very small man. Does anyone here have

27

any idea who this might be?"

Melissa said, "My friend, Kent, thinks it might be his sister."

"Lt. Adams asked, "Why would he think that?"

"Because she has been missing for about ten years, and when she was here, she wore a medic alert bracelet that showed she was allergic to peanuts, and we found one like that on the skeleton."

"Ten years, you say? We had a case about ten years ago where a young girl went missing, and I don't think it was ever solved, and it became a cold case. I'm going to look into that when I get back to headquarters."

Before anything else was said, he took out his cell phone and tried to call the medical examiner. He said, "Darn it, I don't have enough signal," and Jerry told him he would have to go up to the top floor to get enough, and he led him up there. When he got upstairs, he had two bars, so he called the medical examiner then and told whoever he was talking to about the skeleton and gave them the address.

By that time, everyone had gone back up to the main floor and were standing around, talking. And then, Frank arrived. He walked inside to where everybody was standing, and Jerry introduced him to the two detectives. They asked him two or three questions, and when they were satisfied that he didn't know anything about any of the situation, they turned their attention away from him. Lt. Adams singled out Melissa and asked, "If this is indeed who you think it is, did you know her?"

"Yes; she was a good friend of mine."

"What was her name?"

"Natalie Coleman."

"How did you know her?"

"We were in school together."

While he was talking to Melissa, Kent came into the room, and Melissa said, "Here's her brother. He can tell you more than I can."

Lt. Adams turned to Kent and asked, "What is your name, Sir?"

"Kent Coleman."

Just then Dr. James Powers, the Medical Examiner, arrived, and Lt. Adams excused himself from Kent and greeted Dr. Powers. They talked for a few minutes and then Sergeant Vestal took Dr. Powers to the basement where the skeleton was, and Lt. Adams returned to Kent.

"This lady says you think the deceased could be your sister. Is that correct?"

"Yeah."

"Is that because of the medic alert bracelet found?"

"Yeah."

He could see that Kent was upset, so he turned back to Melissa. "Miss, you said you were a good friend of the alleged victim. What can you tell us about her?"

"Well, like I said, we were good friends in school. She was beautiful and very popular. She was a cheerleader and went with the captain of the football team. When she was a senior, she was voted homecoming queen and seemed to have everything going for her."

"You said she went with the captain of the football team; what was his name?"

"Cliff Jackson."

"Do you know how we can find Mr. Jackson?"

"He should be in the book. He's a building contractor in Douglasville."

He wrote Cliff's name down in his little book and said, "Good, thank you."

Around noon a guy came in and announced that he was with T & S Transport and was supposed to pick up some windows. Someone directed him to Jerry who showed him the stacks of windows that were ready to go. The driver told Jerry, "Buddy, I've got a forty-eight foot trailer. Could you get some of those cars outside moved so I can get in?"

Jerry told everyone who was parked in the area of the door that they needed to move their cars or trucks to make room for the tractor-trailer, and everyone complied, including the detectives.

Bill Case assigned four men to take the windows to the truck and load them, and while they did that, Jerry and the driver filled out a Bill of Lading.

In the meantime, the detectives had gone back to talk to Melissa and Kent. Among the questions they asked, one of them was, "Do either of you have any idea who did this," and Kent said, "Yeah, it was Cliff Jackson."

"Why do you think that?"

"Because he was abusive to her."

"Do you know that for a fact?"

"Yeah."

"How do you know?"

"Because Natalie told me. Melissa, you knew how he treated her. Tell them."

"Kent, I don't know that for a fact. She confided in me that Cliff mistreated her, but she never said what he did."

After that statement by Melissa, Lt. Adams wanted to know who was at the house the last time she was there when Natalie was, and if that was the last time any of her friends saw Natalie. She gave him the names of all she could remember and what information she could about their whereabouts now. She told him that several of her high school friends had gone on to college and were now teachers, some of them at their Alma Mater, Delta High. In fact, Brad Nelson was the Assistant Principal, and Raymond King, the Guidance Counselor.

When she finished, Lt. Adams told Melissa and Kent that he wanted their numbers, and that he would be in touch, and he told them both to call him or Sgt. Vestal if they thought of anything else. Then he went downstairs to the basement where Sgt. Vestal and Dr. Powers were getting ready to remove the skeleton from the dumbwaiter.

Dr. Powers went to his car and brought in a large black bag in which to put the bones and along with the large bag, he brought a small bag into which he put the skull, saying that was because of the large crack in it, and he didn't want any more damage to happen by carrying it in the same bag with the rest of the bones. Forensics would have to examine the crack to try to find out what caused it. Normally, much more information can be found in the skull than in the bones of the rest of the body unless there are obvious signs of trauma.

Just as soon as the Coroner and Detectives left with the skeleton, all the workers resumed what they were doing before the dumbwaiter fell except for Kent, and he continued to talk to Melissa. Jerry was very patient with him, but they still had a job to do, and after about thirty minutes, he went over to the couple, and as tactfully as he could say it, he said, "Kent, I'm really sorry if this turns out to be your sister, but we have a tremendous amount of work to do. Would you like to take the rest of the day off?"

"No, thank you, Jerry. I'll be all right. Sorry for taking so much time away from work."

And with that, Melissa said, "I've got to get back to work, too. Sorry for hijacking Kent, Jerry. I'll see you later."

Jerry was relieved when she left and didn't realize that Frank was still there. He had been upstairs, mentally going over how he thought the house was going to look when the renovations were all done, and when he saw Melissa through the window, leaving, he came down and told Jerry he would see him later. He hurriedly went outside and yelled at Melissa, but she already had her car radio on and was pulling out and couldn't hear him. Jerry wondered what he wanted.

At mid-afternoon, Jerry left the mansion and went to his office. As soon as he arrived there he told Beverly about finding the skeleton in the dumbwaiter.

She said, "That's crazy. Do you have any idea who it is?"

"Do you remember Kent Coleman, that guy that came in the other day looking for a job?"

"The one you got mad at for asking about cleaning up?"

"Yeah, that's the one. Well, he thinks the skeleton is his sister."

"Why would he think that?"

"Because she's been missing for ten years, and when she was alive, she wore a bracelet that said she was allergic to peanuts, and there was a bracelet like that on the skeleton."

"Oh my. What's going to happen now?"

"The police are investigating, and hopefully it won't affect our work too much."

Three days later, they finally got most of the old, rotten stuff stripped out of the mansion and were ready to start rebuilding. Speed would be slow for a while because a large part of the materials was no longer readily available and had to be special ordered, but there was still enough to keep everybody busy.

Chapter Four

While things were moving slowly at the mansion, Jerry took time to go to the school and help get things started there. He was assigning the job of Construction Superintendent to Bobby Kunkle, his longtime supervisor.

As soon as he got the approval, he called Jack and ordered the lumber and roofing, and then he called Rich Ingle with Ingle Electric to schedule the electric work, and finally, he called Mid-Georgia Plumbing to set up their part in the project.

He and Bobby and Tony Sutton, the president of the alumni association made measurements for everything and then snapped a chalk line at the places where the stand would be. Other than drive a few stakes to mark the corners, that was all they could do until the plumbers did their work and the materials came in, so he let Bobby leave. Since Kent was needing the work, he let him stay and drive in the stakes.

Tony and Jerry had just met, and Tony already felt a strong attraction to Jerry; maybe because of his positive attitude about everything he did. When they were finished marking out the concession stand, he invited Jerry up to the school for a Coke. Melissa was still there, so he invited her to go with them, and of course, she jumped at the chance to be anywhere with Jerry.

Jerry mostly listened as Melissa and Tony carried on much of the conversation. Delta High was projected to possibly be state champs in football in the upcoming season, so the air was filled with positive thinking and excitement. Delta had a quarterback that everybody was sure could take them to the championship.

While the three were still drinking their Cokes, none other than Cliff Jackson came up. Cliff was, himself, an All-State quarterback when he was at Delta, and he still loved to hang around the school quite a bit in order to try to keep his legend alive. When Melissa saw him, she said, "Hi Cliff, what are you doing out here?"

He had not met Jerry and didn't even acknowledge his presence, and when she asked him what he was doing out there, he answered in his normal, arrogant way, "Actually, I was looking for Tony. I understand they're going to build a new concession stand, and I thought they would like for me to build it, since I'm an old Delta jock."

Uncomfortable with his answer, Tony introduced him to Jerry and told him that they had already worked the deal with Martin Builders to do the job.

Sort of taken aback, Cliff said, "Oh, I see." And then, he asked Jerry, "Jerry, are you new to this area? Are you experienced with building things? What are some of the things you've built?"

With that, Melissa squinted her eyes, put her hands on her hips and asked him, "Cliff, have you ever heard of the Skint Chesnut Mall?"

"Yeah, I think so."

"Yeah, I think so my foot. Your mouth probably watered every time you saw it under construction because you weren't included in it. Well, my man Jerry here is the one who built it. Does that answer your question about has he ever built anything?"

Looking a little sheepish he said, "I knew that. I was just trying to get a rise out of you guys."

Melissa answered, "Well, you succeeded, you arrogant S.O.B. Now, why don't you go back and work on that chicken coop or whatever it is that you're building?"

"Whoa, lady. Calm down. Can't you take a joke?"

"Not that kind. Jerry and his company are one of the most recognized and successful building contractors in the whole southeast, and they're going to build this at their cost. You need to grow up and respect your betters."

"Wow, I really hit a nerve, didn't I? I'm sorry. Okay, I'll get outa here," and he started to leave without even telling Jerry he was glad to meet him, but before he could leave, Kent Coleman came up, and when he saw Cliff, he went berserk.

He charged Cliff, grabbed him by the neck of his shirt, and along with a string of expletives, pushed him backwards, causing him to fall over a chair. He told Cliff he was going to kill him, but first, he was going to kick his butt.

Cliff was taken by complete surprise, and before he could react, Jerry grabbed Kent and Tony grabbed Cliff. Kent tried to break free from Jerry, but Jerry had a good hold on him and wouldn't let him loose.

In his shock, Cliff's voice came out in a yell, and he asked Kent, "What in the hell is your problem?"

Kent, in a yell, answered, "You killed Natalie. We found her body where you hid it at the Chrisman place, and you're not going to get away with it."

"I didn't kill Natalie. What makes you think I did?"

"Because of the way you treated her."

Cliff, still in a yell said, "You're the one who killed her. I heard you two fussing that night before she went missing, and you were mad enough to do it. I've thought that all along."

The two stood there yelling at each other, and a crowd began to gather. Each man was accusing the other of killing Natalie until J.D. Tabor, the principal of Delta, came over and told them to break it up. Things had cooled off a little by then, and Jerry asked Kent if he would be cool if he turned him loose and Kent said he would. When he turned him loose, he didn't say a word; he just walked away from them and went to his car.

Cliff said, "Man, that guy is a certified nut. I'm going to call the police and file assault charges against him."

Tony said, "Cliff, why don't you just try to forget this? Kent's hurt and is trying to find out what happened to Natalie

35

the only way he knows how. After all, she was his sister."

"I don't care. I'm going to file charges. Nobody does to me what he did and gets away with it. If you guys hadn't kept us apart, I'd a killed him."

Melissa, trying to be an arbitrator, asked Cliff, "Cliff, what time did you leave Chrisman that night? I know when I left, Natalie was still there."

"I left before everybody else did, Melissa. Natalie and I had broken up two nights before that, and I didn't want to be there."

Surprised, she asked, "Well, if you two had broken up, why were you down there that night?"

"Because she called me that afternoon and said she wanted to bring my letter jacket and class ring back, and that she would be at Chrisman that night if I wanted to get them, so I went down there to get my things and left after I got them."

"Wow; I didn't know you two broke up."

"Yep, we did," and then he looked at Tony, as if nothing had happened and said, "So, you don't want me to build the concession stand. I'm very disappointed. I've got to go. I'll see you. Bye Melissa; see ya J.D."

Melissa and Tony both said, "Bye," and J.D. said, "See ya," as he left them.

After he left, Jerry said, smiling, "Do you all have this kind of excitement over here very often?"

"No, thank goodness," Tony said.

"Good; I was afraid I might have to outfit my workers with armor when they come out here to work on the concession stand." Then he said, "Well, I need to go. Tony, if they get the plumbing in tomorrow, my men will be out the next day to start building." He reached in his pocket and pulled out one of his business cards and gave it to him and said, "If you need me for anything you can reach me at one of those numbers. It was good to meet you, Tony. I'll see you later. Bye Melissa."

He debated whether to go to White Rock or to go home,

and after he decided to go home, he thought of something and went to his office, instead. Beverly was still there when he got there and she gave him the slips for his calls, which he began to answer when he got to his desk. He had three calls to answer, and when he had finished, he called for Beverly to come into his office.

When she went in, he said, "Bev, I've been thinking about something. What would you think about our having a cookout sometime for our employees and their families. They work hard, and I would like to recognize them for it. Do you think that's a good idea? We could have it at my place; there's plenty of room, and everybody could bring their families."

"I think that's a great idea. You mentioned a cookout; do you intend to cook or are you thinking about maybe having it catered?"

"I haven't thought that far yet. I'd like to do the cooking, but it will probably depend on how many people there will be."

"What are you thinking about the food; burgers and dogs, barbeque, or something else?"

"I'd like to have barbeque with a whole hog and all the trimmings."

"Can you cook a whole hog?"

"I don't know. I figure I can if I put my mind to it."

"Do you mind if I make a suggestion?"

"Of course not; what is it?"

"There are people that travel around doing that, and from what I hear, they do a great job. I'm sure you can do it yourself, but if you do that, you're going to lose a lot of the one on one personal contact with your people, and you don't want to do that. There will probably be two hundred or more people, and I just feel that if you hire someone to come do the cooking, it will eliminate a lot of headaches for you. Just a suggestion."

He smiled and said, "I knew there was some reason I kept you around here. That's a fantastic idea, Bev. How about seeing who you can find to barbeque for two hundred or more people."

"Okay, I'll get on it first thing in the morning. When do you want to have this shindig?"

He thought for a minute and then said, "How about one month from this coming Saturday with a rain date one week after that?"

"Sounds good. Are you going to do anything besides eat?"

"What do you mean?"

"Do you want a band? Are you going to have a bar? Things like that."

"I don't know. I just thought about this about five minutes ago, and I don't know what all we'll have. I can tell you this; we will not have a bar. It's not that I'm against someone having a drink; I have one myself sometimes, but I just don't think a barbeque party at my house is where I want a bar. As for the other things, I'll have to talk to Tracy and see what she suggests."

"Okay, Boss. Just let me know. Do you need me for anything else?"

"No, that's all. I just wanted to run that by you. You're a good sounding board. Thanks. Listen, I think I'll take off. I'll see you in the morning."

"Okay. Have a good evening."

His casual thought about a cookout was now something important that he wanted to do, and on his way home he began to get excited and was anxious to run it by Tracy to get her input. As soon as he got home, Tracy greeted him with a kiss and wanted to know how his day went. He told her and then asked if she would like to have a Margarita. She said she would, and while he was making them he told her about his idea for a company cookout and asked her what she thought. "I think it's a good idea. Have you thought about where you're going to have it, what you're going to serve, when it will be and all the other details?"

"Right now I'm thinking about a month from this coming Saturday with a rain date the following Saturday. I want to have it out here, and I want to have a whole pig barbeque. Beverly is going to try to find somebody who goes around doing that. As far as what else we're going to serve, I need your help on that. We definitely won't have a bar, but we may offer beer in addition to cokes and drinks like that. Most of the time, when people serve barbeque they serve baked beans and slaw with it, and I guess we'll probably have that, too. We can have that or anything else you can think of."

"Are you going to have any dessert?"

"What do you think?"

"I think you should have something."

"What do you suggest?"

"I don't know. Let me think about it."

When she had said that, Jerry said, "Come and get it," and he held out a Margarita for her. She took it, and they both sat down in the den and enjoyed them. He told her about the upset at the school earlier, and she wanted to know all about what was happening concerning their finding the skeleton at the work site.

Jerry had made a little more than one Margarita for each of them, so they split the remainder, making each of them have about another half. When they finished, they had an early dinner, watched part of a TV movie and went to bed.

The next morning, Jerry went straight to White Rock since he couldn't do anything at the school until the plumbing was done, and he hoped it would only take the plumbers about a day to do their job.

While he was driving, he thought, *I hate to take Bill Case or Bobby Kunkle off their jobs to look after the concession stand. I think I'll give Stony Gray a crack at being a supervisor. The concession stand will be a good trial for him. If he does a good job on that, I might give him a chance to be the assistant* supervisor *on the new apartments. I told Bobby*

39

he would be in charge of the concession stand, but I don't think he'll mind at all if I give the job to Stony. Stony needs to put that new education to work, and I want to see what I paid for. While he was still thinking about Stony, he arrived at White Rock and pulled up in front of one of the houses that was just getting started.

There were still sixteen of the forty-eight houses left to finish in the community, and it was neat the way he had things planned. There were currently eight in various stages of construction, and barring any unforeseen holdups, he planned to complete one house every other week. He would also begin construction on one house every other week, giving Martin Builders a completion date for the total White Rock community thirty-two weeks from then. He could double up on them, but he figured that by doing it the way he had planned, there would be a semi-quiet continuity to it rather than such a big splash of vacant houses all at once, and he felt that the owners of the other twenty-nine homes would appreciate it. Also, there were still three homes that hadn't been sold yet, and he didn't want to have so many sitting vacant all at the same time. He had contracts on two of those, so when he finished the next two, there would still be only three that were vacant.

Bobby Kunkle was his main foreman out there, so he went to find him as soon as he got there. Bobby showed him where they were, construction wise, in each home, and after they had gone through all eight, Jerry left to go to the Chrisman House.

About forty-five minutes from White Rock, he noticed a sign he hadn't seen before; a *For Sale By Owner* sign offering two hundred and forty six acres, plus or minus. He pulled over, backed up and then wrote down the phone number. He then turned up a dirt road by the sign and rode through part of the land, thinking, *man, this could be another White Rock. This land is beautiful. Wonder what they're asking for it.* After seeing it, he really got excited. He tried to call the number with his cell phone, but there was no signal, so he would have to wait until he got to civilization to call. It was about twenty minutes from the Chrisman place and they hardly had signal there, so he decided that it would be better if he waited until he got back to his office later that afternoon.

All sorts of thoughts were running through his mind. At first, he thought he would ask Frank if he wanted to go in with him and buy and develop it, and then he decided that he would rather do it alone like he did White Rock. He felt that he could make a lot of money either way, but he convinced himself that if he got the land that he would do it alone and hope that Frank would finance it.

When he arrived at the Chrisman House, Bill Case had his men tearing out some of the rotten trim on the second floor. A stranger was downstairs looking at and measuring some things, and when Jerry asked him who he was, he said his name was Mac Rosser with the CSI in Douglasville. He was a criminalist doing some work on the murder case of Natalie Coleman. Not too long after Jerry arrived, Detectives Grey Yokley and Fred Melwiki showed up and looked around.

Grey told Jerry, "Fred and I are going to take over the case from Ron Adams and Paul Vestal. They've been working on another case for a while and they asked the captain if we could take this one."

Jerry told them, "Fellas, I want to cooperate with you and will do everything I can to help you, but this thing is something that I nor any of my people had anything to do with, and we need to be able to get into the complete house in order to do what has to be done. Do you have any idea when that will be?"

Grey said, "Yeah, when Rosser gets through after while, you should be able to have free rein on everything. I'm sorry if we've been a problem, but these things do have to be investigated, and I know you understand."

"Do you all have any concrete leads on who killed Natalie?"

"Not yet, but we're hoping that DNA will reveal something. You've got to remember that this happened ten years ago, and there were a lot of people around her that day or night. We're in the process of talking to everyone that we know was there with her, and we feel pretty sure that we'll come up with the killer once we get all the facts. We're collecting DNA from everyone who we know was there, and if we get a match on that, that was on the victim's clothes, we'll have our killer."

"Well, good luck."

Chapter Five

The whole time he was at the Chrisman House, his mind was on the pretty land he had seen on his way over there, and he could hardly wait to get back to his office, so he could call about it.

Before he left, he found Stony and told him that he wanted him to be in charge of building the concession stand at Delta High School and to come by his office the next morning instead of coming down there. Stony took the news with a mild case of shock and grinning from ear to ear, he told him he would be there.

Jerry could hardly wait to get to his office, so he could call about the land. As soon as he walked in, Beverly handed him some sheets with calls to return, and he took them and hardly slowed down on his way to his office.

He dialed the number he had written down and waited on an answer on the other end. Finally, after four rings a woman answered, and Jerry told her he was calling about the land they had for sale. She said, "Just a minute. You'll need to talk to my husband."

"Okay, thank you."

After a long pause, a voice on the other end said, "Hello."

"Hello. My name is Jerry Martin, and I saw your For Sale sign out on Kapps Mills Road. It says there are two hundred and forty-six acres. Is that correct?"

"Yes sir. That's right."

"Well, I guess since the sign is still standing, the land is still for sale."

"Yes sir, it is. Are you interested in buying it?"

"Well, I might be. It depends on several things; mainly the price. By the way, what is your name, sir?"

"My name is Clarence Cummings. What are you going to

43

do with the land if I sell it to you?"

"I'm a building contractor, and if I were to be able to get the land from you, I would build fifty or so million dollars homes. It would be a full neighborhood with a swimming pool, tennis courts, and other things. Have you by chance ever seen the White Rock neighborhood?"

"No, I don't believe I have."

"Well, it's has similar homes to what I'm thinking about for your land, should I be able to get it. How much are you asking for your place?"

"I'm gonna have to think about selling it to you before I talk money. I've been hoping I could find somebody to farm it. This farm has been in my family for over a hundred years, and I really don't want to see it turned into a housing project."

"Housing project? I'm not talking about a housing project. Did you hear me say that I want to build some million-dollar homes? That's hardly a housing project."

"Tell you what; let me think about it for a day or two, and you call me back."

Starting to feel desperate, Jerry said, "How about we do this, Mr. Cummings? How about I come to your place to meet you in person, and then we can talk more about it. I'd like to take you out to my White Rock neighborhood, if you would like to go, and that way you can get some idea of the type houses I build. Could I do that?"

"I suppose so. When do you want to come?"

"How about early tomorrow afternoon?"

"That ought to be alright, but I'm still going to have to think about selling it to you."

"Wonderful. Do you live there on the land?"

"No, I live close to it, though. You know where the sign is, right?"

"Yes sir."

"Well, there's a road straight across the road from the sign, and it leads up to a patch of trees where there's a big two-story house sittin right in the middle of them. That's where I live. Early afternoon you say?"

"Yes sir. If that's alright with you, or I can make it later if you want me to. I just can't come in the morning. You tell me when it's best for you."

"Early afternoon is okay; what time is that; about twelve-thirty or one o'clock?"

"Yes sir. Why don't I get to your house as close to one o'clock as I can?"

"Okay. I'll see you."

As soon as he hung up from Mr. Cummings, he called Frank Thomas. "Frank Thomas's office."

"This is Jerry Martin. May I speak to Frank please?"

"One moment."

When he answered, Jerry asked, "Frank, what's going on?"

"Just trying to make a living, Jer. What are you doing?"

"Same old, same old."

"What can I do for you?"

"Frank, I've found a beautiful piece of land that would be perfect for a development similar if not nicer than White Rock. I don't know if the guy will sell it to me yet, but if he will, do you think you'd be interested in helping me out with the financing?

"How much land are you talking about, and where is it?"

"Two hundred and forty-six acres, and it's on Kapps Mill Road between the Chrisman House and White Rock."

"I know where that is. Who has the land?"

"A man named Clarence Cummings."

"Really? I know Clarence, and I'm familiar with his farm. He has a lot more than two hundred and forty-six acres. I wonder why he's selling that part."

"I don't know. He's not sure he wants to sell it to me for what he calls a housing project, but I'm going out there to meet with him tomorrow afternoon. My reason for calling you is just to see if you're interested in financing it for me."

"You don't know how much he's asking for it?"

"No. He says he wants to think about it. Just in case he will let me have it, how much do think it's worth?"

"I'd try to get it for around three thousand an acre. Land in that area runs anywhere from three to almost seven per acre, and I think Clarence's place is closer to the three figure. I don't think he has any creeks or ponds or anything like that on it. I think it's just land. If he decides he will sell it to you, why don't you offer him three and see what he says. You can always come up if you have to. To answer your question; yeah, I'll finance it for you. By the way, when do you plan to start on my apartments?"

"I'm planning to start next week. I promised Melissa I'd build a concession stand at her school, and unless I'm completely wrong, it shouldn't take but two or three days to do it. The plumbers are supposed to be over there today, so we can start in the morning, and oh yeah, Frank; you'll be interested to know that I'm putting Stony in charge of building it."

"Really? That's great. He's made you a good man hasn't he, Jer?"

"He really has. I haven't fully made up my mind yet, but I'm thinking about making him the assistant foreman on your apartments."

"Wonderful. Reed will be happy about that, too. You know, they're just like brothers."

"I know. I haven't seen Reed in a while. Is he doing okay?"

"Yeah, he's doing great."

"Please tell him I asked about him. He's a good boy."

"I'll tell him. You know, Jer, he's still a little embarrassed when he's around you."

"Tell him not to be. He made a mistake when he was a kid and he stood up and paid for it like a man, and as far as I'm concerned, he has nothing to be embarrassed about. If any or

46

all three of those kids ever need me, I'll be the first in line to help them. Tell Reed that for me, will you?"

"I'll tell him. Thanks, Jer."

When he hung up from Frank, he took a sheet of graph paper and tried drawing proposed layouts of the new neighborhood, but since he didn't know how the land laid, he couldn't do too much. Being an optimist, he was already thinking down the road on the project; not letting himself think that he might not even be able to get the land in the first place.

It was five o'clock, and Beverly stuck her head in the door and said, "Good night."

Surprised at the time, he answered, "Good night. I'll see you tomorrow," and he got up, turned off the lights, and locked up.

As he was getting ready to leave, the phone rang, and since Beverly had just left, he answered it. It was Bobby Kunkle. "Hi Boss, Bobby."

"Whatta ya say Bobby?"

"I'm good. Listen, the reason I'm calling is to tell you that it seems like we spent half the day today running people out of the Chrisman place."

"Who were they; do you know?"

"They said they were friends of the girl you found in the dumbwaiter. Don't we have some signs that tell people they are not allowed to be in the work area?"

"We do. We had a lot of them around the mall when we were working on that, but I'm not sure where they are now. Bill should know. I'll call him and tell him to call you. Where will he find you?"

"Just tell him to call my cell. I'll have it with me."

"Okay, will do. You all work it out, will you?"

"Ten-four. See ya."

"See ya."

When he pulled in the driveway at home, B.J. saw him and was waiting at the door for him to come into the house. When he opened the door, B.J. jumped up in his arms and said, "Daddy, let me show you what I did at school today," and led him into the den and showed him a little figure he had made out of popsicle sticks.

Jerry went on over the project and told him how much he liked it which seemed to satisfy B.J., and he immediately left him and went into his room and started playing with something else. As soon as he left, Jerry kissed Tracy hello and asked about her day.

She had had a typical day for a mother of a five-year old and asked him about his day. He told her about the land he found, and she could see that he was extremely excited about it. They spent time in the kitchen while she fixed supper, and soon it was time to call B.J. to come eat. After they finished and cleaned up the kitchen, they spent some time playing with B.J. before putting him to bed, and then they spent the rest of the evening while Jerry talked about the possibility of building the large new neighborhood he hoped to build.

When they were getting ready for bed, Jerry told her, "Honey, if I'm able to get that land, I'm going to need to come up with a name for the development, and since you're good at things like that, how about helping me decide on one, will you?"

"I'll see what I can come up with."

The next morning, he took time to have coffee with Tracy before he left and then went through the drive thru at Hardees on his way to Delta High. When he arrived, he didn't see Stony's pick up, but Stony was there at the job site. They greeted each other, and Jerry asked him, "Where did you park?"

Stony answered, "I parked in a visitor spot around close to the main entrance."

"Well, while we're working on this job, you can park down here, and that'll save you a lot of walking. I told Bill Case to send you enough men to build this stand; are they here yet?"

"Yes sir. There are four."

"Perfect. I'll stay for a little while to help you get started, and then I'm going to meet a man who has some land that I want to buy to build a large neighborhood kinda like White Rock."

He took the plans from his truck and went over them and checked the plumbing that the plumbers did the day before to make sure everything was according to the plans. Everything checked out, so he called all the men together and showed them the plans and told them that Stony would be in charge of the job. He then told Stony what needed to be done in the order that they needed to be done. All the men that Bill had sent were experienced and they knew pretty much what to do without being told, and once they began hammering and sawing and putting the concession stand together, Jerry saw that he wasn't needed any longer. He was confident that Stony could handle it, so he told him he was leaving and to call him if he needed him.

It was too early to meet Clarence Cummings, so he decided to run by the Chrisman House before he went to meet him. When he got there, Bobby was driving signs in the ground that said that due to insurance regulations there could be no entry beyond that point. While he was still there, he noticed two people drive up, who looked familiar, and when they saw the signs, they left, so he hoped the trespassing problem was solved.

He estimated that it would take about twenty-five minutes to get to Clarence Cummings, and he would need to leave around twelve thirty if he were to get there at one o'clock, so he shadowed Bobby until Bobby broke for lunch at noon, and then he went to his truck and headed down the road toward Clarence's, thinking it wouldn't hurt if he was a little early.

He went to the house in the grove of trees where Clarence said he lived, and when he pulled up to the house, Clarence was waiting for him on the front porch. Jerry got out of the truck and went up to the porch where he and Clarence spoke and shook hands.

Clarence said, "Pull that chair over here," and Jerry dutifully obeyed. When he sat down, the two men engaged in small talk about the possibility of rain, how dry the crops were, and other important subjects. Clarence was a man of few words and didn't say very much other than the few small talk sentences. Jerry was anxious to find out about the land, so he asked.

"Mr. Cummings, have you thought about selling me your two hundred and forty-six acres?"

"I thought about it after we talked yesterday, but I haven't made up my mind yet. I just don't want to see it become a housing project."

"Well, like I told you yesterday, it will definitely not become a housing project. I'm finishing up a development similar to what I want to do with your land, and I'd love for you to see it."

"I'd like to see it sometime."

"We can go see it now if you have the time. Would you like to? It'll just take thirty to forty-five minutes to get there, and I think you'll be impressed."

"Would it be alright if my wife went with us?"

"Absolutely. I'd love to have her."

"Wait here a minute." He got up and went to the door and yelled, "Mother, come here."

In a minute, a mildly attractive middle-aged woman came to the door and Clarence said, "Mother, this fellow wants to take me to see some houses he's built, and said he'd like to have you go with us. You wanna go?"

Before she could answer, Jerry said, "Mrs. Cummings, I'm Jerry Martin."

She answered, "It's very nice to meet you, Jerry Martin. I'm Stella Cummings," and with just those few words, Jerry could tell that she was more than likely much more educated than Clarence.

And then Clarence asked again, "You wanna go with us?"

"Yes, I'd like to, but I need to freshen up some."

"No you don't. You look fine. Just go get your pocketbook, and we'll go."

"Alright. Just give me a couple of minutes."

She disappeared into the house and while they were waiting on her, Clarence said that they had been married for thirty-two years, and that they had three grown sons.

Jerry asked him, "I figure you've got a lot more than two hundred and forty-six acres; why are you trying to sell just that many?"

"One of our son's wife has some serious medical problems that costs a lot of money, and they don't have enough, so me and my wife want to help them, and in order to do it, we need to sell part of our farm."

"I'm so sorry."

Stella came out in a few minutes and they got into Jerry's pickup. Jerry and Clarence in front and Stella in the back. They drove out the driveway and turned right onto Kapps Mill Road and headed toward White Rock Estates.

While Clarence was a man of few words, his wife was just the opposite. From the time they started their trip, Stella talked constantly. She talked about her and Clarence's family, their background, and every time she would tell something about the Cummings family or background she would ask Jerry questions about his.

Jerry was finally able to talk to Clarence without being interrupted, and he asked him to tell him about his farm; how many acres were there, total. Why was he selling only two hundred and forty-six acres and some other things he wanted to know in case he would be able to buy it.

He had been genuinely entertained on the forty-five-minute trip, and before he knew it, they had arrived at White Rock. He turned onto White Rock Road, and the beautiful white, four- rail, split-rail fence made the drive look as if it were a fantasy-land. The first house was a couple hundred yards after they turned on to White Rock Road, and Stella commented on how beautiful it was. They continued to drive through the neighborhood, and in a couple of minutes they came to one of the houses that was still vacant, and Jerry asked if they would like to go in and see the inside. Stella jumped at the idea while Clarence just nodded, so they got out and went in.

Stella went crazy when she saw the kitchen. She said to Clarence, "Look at these cabinets, Honey. They would look good in our house."

Clarence answered her with the only amusing thing Jerry had heard him say. "Yeah, they're pretty alright, but putting cabinets like these in our house would be like putting silk stockings on a pig."

She answered, "You're such a kill-joy."

Jerry continued to walk them through the house, and when they were through, he wanted to know if they wanted to go through another one, and Clarence answered, "No, I think we've seen enough. They're nice, though."

"What did you think of the whole neighborhood?

Clarence said, "It's nice."

Stella said, "Is that all you can say: it's nice? I think these are the nicest houses I've ever seen. How much do these houses cost, Jerry?"

"When we're finished, there will be forty-eight houses, and they will all run between seven hundred and fifty thousand to a million dollars. The ones I want to build on your two hundred and forty-six acres will all cost a million dollars or more. Do you remember the three we saw at the top of the hill where the people were mowing at one of them? Well, those three were all a million dollars."

He looked at Clarence and asked, "Now, Mr. Cummings, do you still think a development like this is a housing project?"

"No, it's more than that, I guess."

From the back seat, Stella said, "Boy, Clarence, you're something else."

With that, Jerry asked Clarence, "Since you've seen the kind of houses I build, do you think now that you might want to sell me that acreage?"

"I'm thinking about it."

Feeling more at ease talking with him, he asked, "Do you know what you will have to have for it?"

"Well, we've been thinking that we would like to get forty-two hundred an acre. How does that sound?"

"It sounds pretty high, based on what I've been told about the property values in that area."

Sounding sort of indignant, he said, "You've been talking to the wrong people. Who told you that's too high?"

"I called my financial man, and he said he was familiar with your land, and he said he would finance it for me, but he won't go nearly that high."

"Who's your financial man? I don't know of any financial people that are familiar with my land. Who's your man?"

"Do you know a man named Frank Thomas? Frank and I are partners on several things, and he told me that he's familiar with your place."

Clarence looked down and sheepishly said, "Oh." Then he asked, "Did he say how much I should sell it for?"

"Yes sir, he did, but it's so much lower than what you said, I don't know if we can ever get together or not."

"How much did he say?"

"He told me I should offer you three thousand an acre; that that's pretty much the going price on plain land that doesn't have creeks or ponds or anything like that. Yours doesn't have any of that does it?"

"No, but three thousand's out of the question."

Then Jerry said, "Tell you what; you think about it overnight, and I will, too, and we'll talk again tomorrow. Does that sound alright?"

"Yeah, that sounds alright, but I'll tell you right now; I'm not selling my land for three thousand dollars an acre. It's worth a lot more than that."

They had reached the Cummings house, and Jerry pulled up to the house just as they finished talking, and Clarence and Stella got out. Jerry said, "It was sure nice spending the afternoon with you folks, and I look forward to seeing you both again."

Clarence said, "See ya," and Stella said, "We enjoyed it, too, Jerry. Your houses are beautiful, and maybe you and Clarence can get together, so you can build some over here. Bye."

Chapter Six

Jerry was encouraged as he drove back to his office. Obviously, Clarence was willing to sell him the land; price was the only obstacle, and he felt that that could be worked out. As soon as he arrived at his office, Beverly gave him his messages, and he went to his desk and began drawing up scenarios to present to Clarence in hopes that he would sell him the land. He didn't even return any of the calls on the slips of paper. The more he worked at it, the more excited he became. Finally, he came up with two scenarios that he thought would work if Clarence would just go along with them. When he put them on paper, he called Frank Thomas.

When the bank operator answered, he asked to speak to Frank, and then when Frank's secretary answered, he said, "Hi Sandra. Is Frank in?"

"Hi Jerry. Yes, Just a minute."

"Hi Jerry. What's up?"

"Frank, I spent most of the afternoon with Clarence Cummings and his wife, and I think there's a good chance that he's going to be willing to sell me his land."

"Great! How much are you going to be able to get it for?"

"I don't know yet. He's asking forty-two hundred an acre, and I offered him three thousand. We agreed to think about our positions overnight and talk again today."

"Sounds promising. You say you spent time with him and his wife?"

"Yeah. He was afraid I was wanting to build a housing project, so to convince him I wasn't, I took him and his wife down to White Rock to show them the kind of houses I want to build. I have been putting some ideas together, and hopefully we can come to an understanding tomorrow. I just wanted to keep you in the loop. Tell me what you think about this; I think he's wanting to raise a million dollars because his son and his wife are head over heels due to some medical problems. I think I'm going to tell him that I will give him a million dollars, but I want three hundred acres instead of the two hundred and forty-six. A million dollars for three hundred acres will bring my offer up to thirty-three hundred dollars an acre instead of three thousand. What do you think? Do you think he might go for that?"

"Well, if he's really needing the money, he might."

"I'm going to call him as soon as I can in the morning, and I'll let you know what happens."

"Okay, Buddy. Good luck."

While he was working on different scenarios to present to Clarence, and idea popped into his mind that involved Tracy, and that gave him something else to be excited about, so he finished what he was doing and headed home to tell her what he was thinking.

He almost ran from his pickup to the house when he got home. He yelled for Tracy, and she answered from the bedroom where she was changing the sheets on their bed.

He scared her the way he came in yelling, and when she got into the den she asked, "What's wrong, Honey?"

"Nothing's wrong. I've just come up with a way to make you a millionairess. Are you interested?"

"The way you came in yelling, I thought something was wrong. Do you seriously think you have to ask me if I want to be a millionaress? Of course, I do. How do I go about it?"

"Well, you know that I'm trying to buy a tract of land to build another development similar to White Rock, don't you?"

"Yeah, you told me."

"Okay. I think I'm going to be able to get it, and if I do, I plan to build around fifty homes, and possibly as many as sixty, and each home will sell for a minimum of a million dollars. Here's my idea; if you get your real estate license and sell the homes, I'll pay you the standard rate for selling them, which is currently six percent. If you sell a house for a million dollars, and you get paid six percent, you will make sixty thousand dollars. Multiply that by fifty, and you're talking three million dollars."

Tracy didn't say anything for a minute, and then she asked, "Okay, what's the catch?"

"No catch. Think about it. You can make a ton of money if you want to. You know Sheila Higgs, the lady that sells the White Rock houses. She has become rich selling my houses. Most of them sell for around eight-hundred thousand, and at six percent, you do the math. So far, she's sold twenty-nine with contracts on two more. If she's averaging forty-eight thousand per house times thirty-one, she's made almost a million and a half so far, and there are still seventeen more to go.

"This is what I'm hoping you will do. What do you think?"

"I think it's a no-brainer, but I don't have a license to sell real estate. How do I go about getting one?"

"You have to take a real estate course that lasts seventy-five hours, and they offer it at the Community College. You can call them to find out all the particulars.

By the time he finished telling her about how she was going to be rich, she asked, "Is your name Santa Claus?"

They both laughed and Jerry asked, "How about a Margarita?"

Jokingly, she said, "Yeah, that sounds good. When I get rich, instead of a Margarita, we'll have Champagne."

He replied, "You may, but I'll stick with the Margarite. I don't like Champagne."

"Honey, let me ask you a serious question."

"Okay, shoot."

"What would you think if I asked Wendy to partner up with me?"

"I think you'd be making a huge mistake. For every house she would sell, it would take at least sixty thousand dollars out of your pocket. Maybe I should say our pockets. You will need to think very carefully about it before you do anything."

Jerry finished making the drinks and it pretty much ended the subject. They went out on the front porch and drank them while B.J. played out in the yard, and they talked about each other's day.

The rest of the evening was typical; play with B.J., have dinner, get B.J. ready for bed, watch T.V. and go to bed.

The Margarita helped, but Jerry was still so keyed up he had a hard time going to sleep. Finally, he drifted off, but didn't sleep very well. Every time he woke up, the Cummings land was on his mind.

At last, it was time to get up. He was groggy from lack of sleep, but he knew he had to shape up because it was going to be an exciting day. He dressed and left early for the small project at Delta High School. He was anxious to see how Stony fared the day before on his first day as a foreman, and he was very pleased when he asked one of the veteran workers about it, and was told that he thought he did a really good job.

He talked to Stony and asked when he thought they would be through with the concession stand, and Stony told him he thought it would run into the next day. That was okay with Jerry because he thought from the beginning that the project would take two or three days, and if it had to go into the next day, that would only be three days.

While he was at the concession stand, he told Stony, "We're going to be starting the new apartments next Monday, and I want you to be prepared to go there to work. It's going to be a large project, and I have a surprise for you."

"You have a surprise for me? What is it?"

"Before I tell you, I want to tell you just how proud of you that I am. You've worked hard and have caught on to everything that you've been asked to do without complaining, and I think you're becoming a very valuable member of the Martin Builders team, so here's the surprise; beginning next

Monday, you're going to be the assistant foreman of the apartment project. You'll be working closely with Bill Case, and if Bill has to be away for something, you will be in charge, and with that job comes a change in pay. Unless you have an objection, you will no longer be on an hourly basis; beginning Monday and from then on, you will be paid a salary.

"Now, just in case you're not familiar with how a salary works, you will be paid the same thing regardless of how much or how little you work. For instance; let's say you go to work Monday and something happens to make it impossible to work more than an hour or two. And then the problem gets cleared up and it takes you twelve hours for each of the next two days to catch up what you lost Monday; you will be paid X amount for Monday and the same X amount for the next two days. In other words, you will be paid the same every week, regardless. Salary is the best deal, however, if you would rather stay on an hourly basis, we can do that; it's up to you. What do you think?"

Stony turned his head away from Jerry for a minute, and when he turned back around to face him, tears had welled up in his eyes, and he said, "I don't know what to say, Mr. Martin. I did something terrible to you, and you repaid that terrible thing with something good, and now this. I don't know what to say except thank you so much. I won't let you down."

"I know you won't, and now that we're going to be working closer together, how about calling me Jerry."

"Jerry, can I hug you?"

"You sure can," and with that Stony went over and gave him a sure enough bear hug. When he put his arms around him, he said, "I love you, Jerry," and when he said that, Jerry's eyes welled up.

He pulled away and said, "Enough of this. We've got to get to work." He gave Stony a pat on the back and walked up to the school.

When going to the office, he had to pass by the gym, and when he got to the doors to the gym, the school's cocky quarterback was bullying a young fellow that one could tell could not defend himself. Jerry stopped and told the boy to turn him loose and to leave him alone.

"Who are you to try and tell me what to do, Ace?"

"I'm someone who will stomp a mudhole in your butt and wade it dry, and my name is not Ace; it's Mr. Martin to you."

"Well, MISTER MARTIN, do you know who I am? I'm the quarterback for the current and next State champion football team. You don't have any call disrespecting me."

"Then act respectful instead of like such a jerk."

At that moment, Kevin Hollingsworth, the Head Football Coach walked up and said, "Is there a problem here?"

Before the kid could answer, Jerry said, "No problem. This so-called person was bullying a little boy when I came in, and I stopped it. He acts as if he's untouchable just because he's the quarterback of your football team."

"Well, he does have a certain amount of status because he's the quarterback of the State champions."

"That's bull, Coach. I used to play a lot of high school football, and then I played four years at the University of Georgia, starting three of those four years, and in all the years I played, I never ran across anyone with an attitude like this guy has." He looked Coach Hollingsworth in the eye and said, "Maybe his attitude comes from higher up," and he walked away, leaving the boy and the coach standing there.

When he got to the office, he asked to see J.D. Tabor, the Principal. When J.D. came out, he and Jerry shook hands and he asked Jerry what he could do for him, and Jerry said, "Nothing. I just wanted to tell you that if everything goes well today, we should have your concession stand completed sometime tomorrow."

"Wonderful. Maybe, if we can get everything organized, we'll be able to use it at Friday night's game."

"I'll tell my foreman to come tell you the minute they finish it."

"Great. Thank you."

Jerry then left the Principal's office and went to his pickup to call Clarence Cummings. When he called, Stella answered and was bubbly as usual. Jerry asked to speak to Clarence and she said to wait a minute. In a minute, Clarence answered with his naturally gruff voice, "Hello."

"Good morning Mr. Cummings. Jerry Martin here. How are you doing this morning?"

"Fine."

"I wonder if you would have time to see me this afternoon if I come out there. I've got some things to talk to you about. Have you thought any about what we talked about yesterday?"

"Yeah, some."

"Can I come out about one again?"

"Yeah, that'll be alright."

"See you then," and he cranked up his truck and headed toward the Chrisman House."

As he was walking into the house, Bobby met him at the door, and he had something in his hand. "What have you got there?" Jerry asked.

"Jack found this while he was moving a large dresser in one of the bedrooms."

"What is it?"

"It's a diary, and we think it belonged to the dead girl. It was taped to the back of the mirror over the dresser."

"Wow! We had better get this to the police. Did you read any of it?"

"No, not really. I just flipped through the pages and determined that it is a diary, but I didn't read any complete pages. Here, you take it," and he handed it to Jerry.

Jerry took it and turned around and took it to his truck. He laid it in the console and would give it to one of the detectives whenever he saw them. He didn't think he needed to make a special trip to deliver it because it had been there for ten years, and he didn't feel that another few hours would make that

61

much difference. While he was at the truck, he flipped through some of the pages in the diary, and while he didn't read anything in detail, he did see many of the names that he was familiar with; Sean, Mac, Cliff, Travis, Tommy, Denise, Ray, Brad, Melissa and others that he wasn't familiar with.

He went back in the house to see how they were progressing. Several of the special-order items had come in, and they were installing them. He was particularly anxious to see the Italian Marble that he ordered to repair the foyer where a large piece was cracked.

Plumbers were everywhere. Frank wanted so many bathrooms in the house that nearly all the plumbing had to be installed from scratch because antebellum buildings were built, for the most part, before plumbing was available for residences.

Two of Martin Builders finest finish carpenters were working on the grand staircase bannisters, and Jerry was extremely proud of the way they were shaping up. He thought, *if the rest of the house comes out looking as good as those bannisters, this is going to be a certified showplace. Boy, they look good.*

He spent another hour or so at the Chrisman House, then told Bobby he had to go, and left for the Cummings place.

When he got there, he got out of the truck and walked up to the house and rang the doorbell. Stella came to the door and in her bubbly personality said, "Hi Jerry. Come in. Clarence is in the other room waiting for you. Come on, and I'll show you."

She led him into a room that looked as though it was the place where they stayed most of the time. Clarence was sitting in a large leather chair and didn't bother to get up when Jerry entered the room.

Jerry walked over to him and held out his hand to shake hands and said, "How are you today, Mr. Cummings?"

He held up his hand to shake hands with Jerry and said, simply, "Fine."

Clarence was so rude and unfriendly that it sort of stopped Jerry from saying anything else for a good seven or eight seconds, and then he said, "You said you had thought a little about selling your land to me. What have you come up with?"

Clarence said, "If you will remember, I told you yesterday that I want forty-two hundred dollars an acre. I thought about it after you left and decided that maybe I can let it go for four thousand. Will that make it look better to you?"

"Well, knocking off a couple hundred dollars makes it look better, but you're still at four thousand an acre and I don't think I can get that much financed. I don't know how well you know Frank Thomas, but I know him pretty well, and I know that you will have a hard time finding any other lender that will loan any more than he will."

"So, you're saying that you won't buy it for four thousand an acre?"

"Let me run this by you. You haven't said this, but after talking to you yesterday about why you're wanting to sell the land and the total price you're wanting to get for it, it looks to me that you're wanting to raise a million dollars. Now here's what I'm prepared to do, and I think you'll be foolish if you don't accept it, and I think Frank will go for it. I'll pay you a million dollars for your land, but for a million dollars, I want three hundred acres; not two hundred and forty-six. That will give you the money you want, and for another fifty acres that you won't even know is gone, you'll be able to help your son and his wife through this hard time. What do you say?"

"How much is that an acre?"

"It figures out to thirty-three hundred and thirty-three dollars an acre, and Mr. Cummings, I'm pretty sure that that's about all anybody can pay you for it."

"Is that the best you can do?"

"Yes sir, it is. We're talking about a million dollars here for land that you're not even using. That's really the best I can do, and I hope you'll accept my offer."

Without saying anything else to Jerry, he yelled, "MOTHER, come in here, will you?"

In a minute, Stella came in from wherever she had been, and Clarence said, "Mother, this fella has made an offer on our land, and you and me need to talk about it."

She said, "Okay, what do you want to talk about?"

He said, "Let's go in there," and he looked at Jerry and said, "Me and Mother need to talk. Just have a seat, and we'll be back in a few minutes."

Jerry said, "Take your time. I'll be right here."

He could hear them talking from where he was sitting. He heard Clarence tell her what he offered him, and then he heard him say, "I think he's trying to rob us," then he heard Stella say, "I don't think so. Remember what that Appraiser told you? He said you'd be lucky if you could get thirty-two hundred dollars an acre. What does Jerry's offer amount to per acre? And he heard him say, "He said it was thirty-three hundred and thirty-three dollars," and then she said, "See? That's more than the Appraiser said. I think you ought to take it. And another thing; this will take a big load off of us, and we can help Ron and Cathy. I know it will be a big relief to them. Don't you agree?"

"I suppose; okay, I'll tell him we'll take his offer."

They both walked into the room where Jerry was sitting, and Clarence said, "We talked about it, and we think we'll accept your offer of a million dollars for three-hundred acres. When do you want to do the transfer?"

"The sooner the better. After I leave here, I'll call Frank Thomas and start the ball rolling. I'd say we might can have everything done in about a week. Does that sound alright?"

"Yeah, that sounds alright."

"Now don't hold me to that. I don't have any control over these financial people, but I know in my dealings with Frank, he has always been pretty fast in getting things done. After I talk to him, I'll call you and let you know what he says."

"Okay."

Then Jerry said, "Since we're talking about fifty-four acres more than the original two-hundred and forty-six, would you like to show me where that will be?"

"I can show you pretty close, but it'll have to be surveyed before we can set the actual boundaries."

"That's right. I'll have to get Frank to step on it because I don't want to hold you up any longer than we have to. We can go look at the approximate boundaries, though, can't we?"

"Yeah. You ready?"

Jerry said, "I'm ready. You wanna go, Stella?"

She looked at Clarence and asked, "Is that alright, Honey?"

"Clarence said, "Yeah, come on."

They piled into Jerry's pickup and drove out the drive, crossed Kapps Mill Road and went through the land Jerry saw when Clarence showed him before. When they got to the end of that, Clarence said, "Now here's where we begin the extra fifty-four acres that you want. We'll just have to guess at it since it's not surveyed."

They drove for a little ways and Jerry noticed a fairly good-sized stream flowing. He made a mental note and thought, *if that stream is on the fifty-four acres, it might just become a lake.*

They only stayed out there a few minutes and then they went back to the house. Jerry had forgotten some papers he had taken in when he first got there, so he had to go in to get them. After he got them, he was telling the Cummings goodbye, and as he was getting ready to walk out of the house, Stella came over to him and hugged him and said, "Thank you, Jerry. You've been a Godsend. Then she looked at Clarence and asked, "Don't you think he's been a Godsend, Honey?"

And in his own excitable way, he said, "I guess."

As he was walking out, he turned around and said, "I'm going to call Frank Thomas right now and tell him to get the surveyors out here just as soon as he can. I'll call you when I find out something. I'll see you all."

He forgot that there was no signal that far out, so he would have to wait until he got to somewhere where there was enough to make a call. The first thing he had to do was to stop by Delta High to see if Stony had finished the concession stand, and when he got there, he saw several people at the stand stocking it with cups, plates, napkins, and everything needed to operate a concession stand during a football or soccer game. He got out to look it over and was well satisfied with the way it was built.

He drove up to the office area and noticed a police car parked there. He got out and went in and ran into detectives Yokley and Melwiki in the office. They spoke and talked for a couple of minutes and then Jerry said, "Fellas, I'm glad I ran into you. I've got something I want to give you. Wait just a minute and I'll go out to my truck and get it."

He hurried to his truck and retrieved the diary that his men had found at the Chrisman House. He went back in and the detectives were in J. D. Tabor's office, so he went in and handed the diary to Detective Yokley. He said, "Here's something I'm sure you will want."

Detective Yokley asked without looking, "What is it?"

Jerry answered, "It's Natalie Coleman's diary. My men found it at the Chrisman House this morning."

Then Detective Yokley began to slowly thumb through the pages, and in a few minutes said, "Thank you, Mr. Martin. This seems to have just about everybody in it. He went on to say, "You know, I haven't had time to digest all that's in this, but from what I have read so far, the last page would indicate that there might be another one. It could be out there as well. Mr. Martin, please have your men keep an eye out for it, will you?"

"Yes sir. I'll tell them. Well, gentlemen, I've got to run. I'll see you all later."

Most of them said they would see him later.

When he got to his truck, he took out his cell phone and called Frank. When Frank answered, Jerry said, "Frank, I did it."

"You did what?"

"I bought that land from Clarence Cummings, and I need to come see you."

"Good. What did you have to pay?"

"Well, before I tell you, let me tell you this. If you remember, I told you that he wanted to sell two hundred and forty-six acres for forty-two hundred dollars and acre. I offered him three thousand and he refused to sell at that price, then I went back and offered to pay him a million dollars, but for that price I wanted three hundred acres. I had the idea that he was needing to raise a million bucks, and that's why I made him that offer. After he and his wife talked about it, he accepted my offer, and oh yeah, Frank; the first two hundred and forty-six have already been surveyed, but the additional fifty-four have not, so how do we go about getting that part surveyed?"

"I can take care of that for you. When do you want it done?"

Being silly, Jerry said, "In the morning."

"That quick, hunh?"

"Yeah, I would like to get it done ASAP, and get the financing done so I can pay the Cummings. They need the money as quick as they can get it. I think I told you that it's for their son and his wife who have some serious medical expenses."

"Okay, Jer; I'll get somebody on it right away, and I'll have to look at the land before we sign off on the loan. When will be a good time for you?"

"Anytime you say."

"Well, tomorrow's Friday, and I'll be in meetings most of the day, and I hate to ask you to work on Saturday, but

Saturday would be better for me. I'm tied up all next week. Will Saturday work for you?

"Sounds good to me. I'll pick you up at what time?"

"Is nine o'clock good for you?"

"It's perfect. I'll see you then."

Chapter Seven

Frank was waiting in his car when Jerry arrived at the bank to pick him up. "Good morning, Jer."

"Good morning. How are you?"

"I'm fine, and I know you are."

"Yes, I am fine. Listen, we have to pass close to the Chrisman House on the way to the Cummings. Would you like to stop and see what's been done so far?"

"Yeah, that would be great. You know, I've been so busy lately, I haven't had a chance to get by there as much as I would like to, so yeah, I'd like to see it."

In a little while they came to the mansion and got out. The first thing they noticed was the beautiful bannisters on the grand staircase. They went from room to room on the first and second floor and then they went down to the basement. When they got down there, there was a light burning on the floor, and Frank said, "Why is that lamp on the floor and why is it on?"

Jerry said, "I have no idea. Bobby Kunkle is always careful not to leave anything on. In fact; most of the time, he turns off the power when the men leave."

The two men stood there looking at the thing and noticed that not only was a light burning on the floor, but there was a bucket full of something sitting in the middle of a large area that had been soaked with what smelled like kerosene, and the bucket was up against the light bulb. After a closer look, they found the bucket was full of kerosene.

Jerry got down in the floor and found that whoever rigged up the contraption had put a one-hundred-and-fifty-watt bulb in an extension cord socket that was only rated for sixty watts. There were two more sixty-watt extension cards attached to the first one, and they ran to the breaker box, and when he looked, someone had rigged the breaker with a wire that would have prevented it from flipping. The first thing he did was disconnect the extension cord from the light bulb, but he left the wire on the breaker. It was a good thing that he and Frank went by there because there was a good chance the house would have caught fire if the breaker had flipped, and the way it was rigged, it would have been soon after the time they found it.

Frank said, "I wonder who could have done such a thing."

And Jerry answered, "I don't know but it looks like God is on our side, doesn't it?"

"It sure does. I'm sure thankful He sent us in here when He did."

"Me too. God is good, isn't He frank?"

"He really is. Not only could the house have burned down, but you and I could have been killed. Jerry, would you mind if we said a prayer to thank Him for what He did?"

"I think we should," and the two men took turns thanking God for letting them find the booby trap when they did and for sparing their lives.

"Frank, at the risk of getting held up for a while, I think we should call the police. What do you think?"

"I think you're right."

"I'll go up to the top floor to see if I can get a signal, otherwise, we might have to ride up the road until we can find one."

When he got upstairs, luckily, there were three bars.

He figured the detectives were off since it was Saturday, but if they were, they could tell him who to call, He had Greg Yokley's cell number and he called that. Surprisingly, Greg answered.

Jerry said, "Good morning, Greg. Jerry Martin here. How're ya doing?"

"Fine, Jerry, how about you?"

"I'm fine now, but I might have just escaped a close call,

70

and that's why I'm calling. Frank Thomas and I are at the Chrisman House. You remember Frank don't you; he's the owner of the Chrisman House."

"Yes, I remember Frank."

"Well, we came in to see the progress my men have made on the renovation, and when we went down in the basement, someone had rigged up a booby trap down there, I guess with the intention of burning the house down. If it had gone off when we first came in or before we found it, we could have been killed as well as the house being burned. I thought you would want to know this because there must be a dangerous somebody out there. Tell me what to do, and I'll do it."

"Wow, Jerry. It looks as if the tentacles of a ten-year-old murder have come forward to today, doesn't it?" Did you touch the booby trap?"

"Yeah, I had to. I unplugged one of the extension cords and took a wire off the breaker box, but everything is still down there."

"Jerry, if you don't mind, stay there. I'm going to call Fred and we'll come down there."

"Greg, do you think I need to put a security guard down here?"

"I think that would be a good idea. We sure wouldn't want that beautiful place to go up in flames."

Jerry asked, "Is there any way we can get the county to do that?"

"I'm afraid not. That's private property, and we can't guard private property."

"Okay. I'll get one. You never know unless you asked, do you?"

He hung up and told Frank that they need to put a security guard on duty until whoever did this was caught, and the first thing Frank asked was, "Is the county going to pay for it?"

"No. I asked Greg that same question, and he said this is private property and they can't guard private property. Are

71

your bank guards your employees or are they with a security company?"

"They're with Mid Georgia Assured Security."

"Can you have them assign someone to guard this place for a while?"

"I guess I'll have to. It looks as if there's no end to the money I'm having to spend on this place."

While they waited for the detectives to arrive, they spent their time closely examining all that had been done. There were so many bathrooms, it looked as if they were the primary things being built, but of course, they weren't. Although the fixtures were modern, they looked like they had been made pre-civil-war, down to the claw-foot bath tubs.

After they looked at all the bathroom, Jerry took him to the foyer and pointed out the place where it looked as if something had fallen on the marble floor, and then was poorly patched. Next, he took him up the stairs to the center of the grand staircase and showed him where it looked like the bannister had been broken directly over the patched floor in the foyer, and again, had been poorly repaired; probably by someone in a hurry.

"I feel that these places in the foyer and the bannister were possibly where Natalie's murder took place."

Frank asked him, "Did you show these places to the police?"

"I'm not sure."

"Well, they need to see it if they haven't already. Show this to them when they get here."

"Okay, I will."

After about an hour had passed, the two detectives arrived at the mansion, and Jerry went over their discovery. Then they went to the basement where he showed them the wire in the breaker box and the light-weight extension cord that he unplugged. Fred took numerous pictures of everything from all angles.

After they took the pictures, they wanted a statement from Jerry, and he told them everything he had found, and then he told them about the foyer and the bannister over it. They had already been told about it, but they wanted to see it again, without a lot of people around. Jerry carefully pointed out the damages and apparent attempts to repair them.

He and Frank were pleasantly surprised by the short time the detectives kept them. It was only a little after noon, and they still had plenty of time to go to the Cummings', but before they left, Jerry asked Greg, "Did you find anything interesting in the diary I gave you.?"

"Yes I did. It seems that the group was pretty close. The diary had several names in it, but it was mostly just who did this and who did that in their daily lives. There wasn't really any meat to it. By the way, I need to get a statement from you, if you don't mind. It shouldn't take but a few minutes.

"Okay; let's do it. Frank and I need to get out of here just as soon as we can. We have to go about tewnty-five minutes down the road to look at some land."

Greg said, "Okay, I'm ready if you are," and he started by asking some questions, and then asked him to tell how they found the skeleton. When he finished that, Greg said he would have the statement typed up, and whenever he could, he could come sign it.

While Jerry was giving the detectives his statement, Frank went up to the top floor and called the security company and ordered a guard to come to the mansion, and if he would be there when they said he would, he and Jerry could stop by and give him his instructions on their way back from the Cummings place.

The four of them left the mansion at the same time; the detectives going back to Douglasville and Frank and Jerry turning onto Kapps Mills Road.

When they arrived at Clarence Cummings' farm, Jerry turned into the house to tell them that he and Frank were going to drive over the land he was going to buy. When he rang the doorbell, Stella answered it and he told her, but she wanted him to tell Clarence, so she called him to come in there. Jerry told him, and when he mentioned Frank's name, he wanted to speak to Frank, so he came outside to the truck to see him, and when Frank saw him coming, he got out and not only shook hands with him; they embraced.

Frank told him that Jerry had told him about his son's wife, and he wanted him to know how sorry he was. They talked for a few minutes and Frank said they had to go, because they had to get back. He congratulated Clarence on selling Jerry the land and assured him that whatever Jerry built out there would be an asset to the area, and that he felt that the price he sold it for was an excellent price for that part of the state. He told Clarence that when Jerry got the neighborhood built, it should make the price on the rest of his land go up in value.

After they got back in the truck and started driving across the road to Jerry's future land, he told Frank, "I know you said you knew Clarence, but I didn't know you two were blood-brothers."

"Is that what it looked like?"

Smiling and looking at him, Jerry said, "The only thing missing was you two cutting yourselves and mixing your blood."

"Oh, come on; it wasn't like that. I've just known Clarence for a long time, and I was glad to see him. He's a good man when you get to know him."

They drove pretty much all over the three hundred acres, and when they got to the part that was not surveyed, Jerry showed him the creek and told him he was thinking about damming it up and creating a small lake, to which Frank said, "That's a good idea. How large do you think it will be?"

"Oh, I don't know; probably eight or ten acres."

"That will increase the value. Have you thought how you're going to use it? Are you going to build houses around it?"

"I don't think so. I think I'll stock it with fish and make it available to everyone who lives in the community to use with canoes or small boats with no more than a trolling motor."

"That will be a good selling feature for the rest of the land. How many homes do you think you will build out here?"

"I've got to sit down and do some figuring, but if I figure the same way as White Rock, I think I can get eighty houses. When you add the roads, pool, tennis courts and everything else, each house at White Rock took three point sixty-four acres. If you deduct ten acres for the lake from the three hundred acres out here and figure three point sixty-four acres per home, it comes out to eighty, and at a million dollars per home, you're talking about eighty million dollars. How does that sound?"

"It sounds like you're going to be a rich man."

"You want to know something else?"

"Yeah, what?"

"I told Tracy she needs to take a real estate course and get her license, and she can sell the houses and we can make the six percent we're having to pay another realtor. Do you think that's a good idea?"

"I think it's a great idea. Boy, you're going to have it all covered, aren't you?"

"I hope to. Padna, I think we need to head back to the Chrisman place, don't you?"

"Yeah. I hope the security guy is there so we won't have to wait on him."

There were two men there when they got there. One of them explained that their company would require two people to do the job because there were too many hours for one shift. After Frank okayed it, Jerry walked them through the entire mansion. When they got back to the front door, Frank took over and let them know exactly what he wanted them to do. He also told them they would have to go to the top floor to get enough cell phone signal to make or receive a call. He told them they could work out their shifts, but to remember that he would only pay for one at a time. If they both stayed the whole time, he would still only pay for one man, and they understood. When he finished explaining things and got them settled in, he and Jerry got into the truck and headed back to the bank to pick up his car.

On the way back, Jerry told Frank that he planned to start on his apartments Monday, and Frank was very happy about that. He said, "I don't remember if I told you or not, but I'm making Stony Gray the assistant superintendent of the apartment project."

"Yes, you told me, and I'm very pleased. Stony is a good man."

"Yes, he is, and I think it's time he found himself a good woman."

Soon, they reached the bank parking lot and Frank got out, but before he walked off, he turned and told Jerry, "Thanks for the day, Jer. I'm glad we got to the Chrisman place when we did or else it would be in ashes right now, and I'm very impressed with the three hundred acres you're buying from Clarence. I think it will make an outstanding neighborhood. I'll call first thing Monday morning and see how fast we can get the surveying done, and I'll let you know. You have a good weekend and give Tracy a hug for me."

"I sure will. I'll talk to you next week. See ya."

Before he got home, he thought that he needed to talk to Bill Case about something, so he called him from his truck. "Hello Bill, I'm sorry to bother you on Saturday, but I wanted to tell you that when you get to the apartment site Monday morning and get ready to start laying out the buildings, I want you to teach Stony Gray how that Lay Out Pro thing works. Stony's going to be helping you, and I want him to learn everything he can about all our equipment. You may get there before I do, but I'll see you fairly early."

"Okay, Boss. I'll do it. See ya Monday."

Finally, he made it home after a very trying day, and he and Tracy were very glad to see each other. He asked, "What would you like to do tonight; anything special?"

"Nothing special, but maybe dinner and a movie would be good."

"Then let's do it. It was getting late, so he went in and took a shower.

At dinner, Tracy wanted to know what Jerry had been doing all day, since it was Saturday and he didn't usually work all day on Saturday. He told her about meeting Frank with the intention of going to the Chrisman House and the Cummings land and right back, but how they got held up at the Chrisman place after nearly getting killed by a booby trap.

She was aghast at that and wanted to know every detail.

"There's not a whole lot to tell."

"That's just like you, Jerry Martin; always closed-mouthed. Now you tell me what happened and don't leave out a single thing."

"Okay, Miss Inquisitive. Frank and I stopped at the mansion on our way to the Cummings farm because he wanted to see how much we had done on the renovation. We went over everything on the first two floors and then went to the basement. As soon as we got down there, we saw a light burning, and I knew it wasn't like Bobby to leave a light on. When we got closer to it, we found a large watt light bulb screwed into a light weight extension cord, and the extension cord was run into the breaker box where someone had wired the breaker where it wouldn't flip when the light and cord shorted out. Another thing; someone had poured kerosene all over the floor and put a full bucket of kerosene right next to the light bulb, so when it shorted out, the kerosene would catch fire and burn the house down.

"It didn't scare me at first, but later, when I thought about it, it scared me because what if it had shorted out while I was down there? I would likely have been burned up."

"Wow!! That was a close call, wasn't it?"

"Now that I think about it, I'd say so."

"Did you call the police?"

"Yeah, and they came out and looked everything over. They didn't find any clues, so they'll probably go back next week."

"Do you think it's tied into the murder of that girl in the dumbwaiter?"

"Probably. Let's get off that subject; what about this movie we're going to; is it supposed to be good?"

"Wendy and Tom went to see it the other night, and she said they both really enjoyed it."

"I'm ready for some good entertainment; right now, I'm ready for some good food."

They had a delicious dinner and afterwards, they went to the *Rockin' 8* theater and saw a very entertaining movie.

Sunday was good; Church, lunch out with Jack, and a *stressful* afternoon of napping between watching ball games.

First thing Monday morning, Jerry went to the apartment site to be sure there were no problems getting started on laying out the first building. Bill and Stony were already there, and Bill was explaining some of the points of operating the Lay Out Pro.

This was going to be the largest apartment complex he had built for Frank, so far. All the others, except one had been eight buildings with eight apartments in each building making a total of sixty-four units per complex. That one was nine buildings with eight apartments, making a total of seventy-two. This one was to be twelve buildings with eight units in each building, making a total of ninety-six apartments for the complex. In the others, he concentrated on two buildings at a time, but on this one he was planning to concentrate on three and possibly four at a time, and that would let him complete the entire ninety-six units in basically the same time it took to complete sixty-four units in the others. This project was large enough that he had his trailer/office parked at the site. There's a large difference between an eight building complex and one with twelve buildings.

It was obvious to Jerry that Bill had studied the plans and building surveys because he knew exactly where to go on the vast property to start laying out the first building. When Jerry asked him where the second and third buildings would be, all he had to do was to take a quick glance at the surveys in order to tell him.

Jerry asked, "Bill, when do you expect to have all twelve buildings laid out?"

"Well, a lot of it will depend on how quick our sharp, young friend here catches on. I think we can lay out a building a day. I know I can do that, but Stony has never seen this program, so I don't know. From what I've seen of him, he's pretty sharp, and these young people catch on to electronic gadgets much faster than you and I do, so it could be that once he gets into it, he might lay out two in a day. We'll just have to see."

"Okay; I'm going to leave it up to you to train him well. I've got big things in mind for him."

He spent another hour or so at the site watching Bill and Stony, and when he was convinced that Stony could handle the Lay Out Pro almost with no help from Bill, he left for the Chrisman House.

When he pulled into the parking area, the first thing he noticed was a car with the words *DOUGLAS COUNTY* on the door and the letters *CSI* under them. The detectives must have conveyed the information about the booby trap to them, and they were apparently concerned enough about it to come out and investigate.

He went in and introduced himself to the two investigators, and they asked him to tell them the story. He was getting tired of telling it because he not only had hashed it over in his mind several times, he had told the detectives, and then told it to

Tracy Saturday night, but he did what they asked and told them the whole story. When he finished telling them his story, he asked, "When do you fellows think we can clean up the mess in the basement and get back to work?"

One of the men told him, "We hope to be through out here by this afternoon, but we need to leave everything in place, until at least tomorrow, in order to be sure we've got everything we need."

"Okay, but do you think we can clean it up tomorrow?"

"I feel sure you can. We'll call you and tell you for sure."

Bobby Kunkle found Jerry and told him they needed to ask him something on the second floor, so he excused himself from the CSI guys and went with Bobby upstairs. While he was upstairs, his cell phone rang, and surprisingly, he had enough signal to answer it. It was Larry Freeman with Kentucky Wooden Windows. "Hi Larry. How're ya doing?"

"Hi Jerry. I'm doing great. Are you ready for some windows?"

"Yeah. We were wondering when you were going to have them ready."

"Well, we're planning to ship them tomorrow, and they will be at your place either Wednesday or Thursday."

"Great. We'll start hanging them the minute they get here. You've got my office address, haven't you, for the invoice?"

"Yeah, we've got it, so we're all set. The windows look great. I hope you like them."

"Good; thanks for calling, Larry."

"Bobby, that was Kentucky Wooden Windows. They're shipping our windows tomorrow, and we'll have them Wednesday or Thursday."

"Good. I need them to keep some of my men busy."

"When do you think they're going to finish the bannisters on the staircase?"

"They still have some sanding and recoating, but I'd say they'll be finished by Friday."

"How about the marble in the foyer?"

"That'll probably be done by Friday as well."

"So, when we get the windows in and the foyer and staircase finished, the main things remaining will be the bathrooms and finishing the trim in several rooms, right?"

"That's right. I'd say we'll be finished with everything in two or three weeks. Then it will be up to the carpet layers to do their magic on the grand staircase."

"Boy, that will be good. Did I tell you about the land I bought?"

"No. Where is it?"

"It's between here and White Rock."

"What are you going to do with it?"

"Build a neighborhood like White Rock; only bigger and more expensive."

"Wow! How many houses are you planning?"

"It hasn't been surveyed yet, but there are three hundred acres. White Rock has a hundred and seventy-five. I'm guessing that we might get eighty out of it if we allot the same amount of land per house that White Rock has."

"Do you think I'll be working on it?"

"I'm sure you will, but I haven't thought that far yet. I want you to finish up here at the mansion, and then I need for you to go back to White Rock; we've still got several houses to build out there. If the new development is anywhere like White Rock was, it'll be several months before we can clear all the red tape. And then, it'll take a while after that to run water lines, that is, if we can get the county to run them. If they won't, then we'll have to run them ourselves. If we have to run them ourselves, we'll probably have to set up our own water company, and that will mean drilling enough wells to supply eighty homes."

"What if you just don't have water lines; what if you just drill wells for each house?"

"That's a possibility, but I just don't know if a person

81

buying a million dollar home wants a well house sticking up in their yard. I don't know; we'll just have to see what shakes out when we get into it. In the meantime, if you're planning to stay with Martin Builders, you've got some pretty good job security for a long time to come."

Smiling, Bobby said, "That's good to know."

He left Bobby and went downstairs to where the CSI guys were, and in a few minutes, Detectives Yokley and Melwiki came in. "Good morning," he said. "I thought you guys were through out here."

"We thought we were, too, until your little booby trap episode came up, Saturday."

"Are you through questioning everybody about the murder?"

"Not everybody. Some don't want to talk to us, and without good cause, we can't force them to. Some of them are on the staff at the school, so we'll have to question them over there, if we can catch them between classes and other things."

"Can I make a suggestion?"

"You certainly can; what is"

"You said you got the names of most of your people of interest from the diary that was found, right? Well, why don't you set up a roundtable discussion that would include all the people on your list, and they would all more than likely be there because they would be afraid that somebody else might finger them for something, if they weren't there. Besides, they would be curious about what's in the diary. You could set it up as a discussion of Natalie's diary."

"That's a great idea, Jerry. We'll see if we can set something up."

He finished up and found Bobby and told him he was leaving and would be back Wednesday to see the windows. After he told Bobby bye, he headed for White Rock.

There were three homes at White Rock still vacant, and he had contracts on two of them. As he was driving up the road to the construction sites of additional houses, he saw a moving van unloading furniture at one for which he had a contract. His real estate lady was showing the last of the three, and hopefully, she would get a contract on it.

They were finishing two houses every two weeks, so two more should be finished anytime. They had been moving so fast, and with the upcoming new neighborhood getting ready to start, he decided to speed up the construction on the remaining White Rock Homes. If by chance things went smoother than he anticipated in the new start-up, he would need all his workmen at the new project.

He spent an hour or an hour and a half out there and then left to go back to his office. He didn't realize that the day had passed and on his way back, he noticed that it was five o'clock, so when he got to the place to turn, he turned and went home.

The next morning at the office, he played *catch up* most of the morning. He had been running so much in so many directions, he had fallen behind on some of his things. He happened to glance at his calendar and saw that the company cookout was scheduled for the end of the following week. He mentioned it to Beverly and she assured him that everything was lined up and she wanted to know if he was going to send out invitations because if he was, they should go out this week.

He asked, "Do you think we should send invitations?"

She said, "You don't have to, but it would be a nice touch. You've attained a status that not many contractors have, and an invitation from Martin Builders to attend a function at the home of Jerry Martin would be quite an honor."

"Come on Beverly; I'm just an average guy who God has blessed with good fortune."

"Okay, but that's not the way most people look at it. Now, you need to answer my question; do you want to send out invitations?"

"If you think we should, then send them."

In a few minutes, Beverly rang in and said Detective

Yokley was on the phone. "Good morning, Greg."

"Hi Jerry. I just wanted to tell you that we're taking your suggestion and setting up a roundtable discussion tomorrow with everybody mentioned in the diary. I don't know if we should include anybody else or not, but these people may be all we need. Thanks for mentioning it."

The windows arrived Wednesday morning and Bobby put several men to installing them immediately. They worked really hard and finished at mid-morning Friday. Bobby was so pleased that at noon on Friday, he gave the men the rest of the day off.

The week was pretty much routine until Saturday morning when Detective Yokley called. Jerry answered the phone and Greg said, "Jerry. I don't know what we've gotten into here, but Cliff Jackson was assaulted last night."

"Really? What happened?"

"Somebody hit him in the head with a large pipe wrench that has MARTIN BUILDERS engraved on it."

"You're kidding!!!"

"No, I'm not kidding."

"Is he going to be alright?"

"Yeah, he's in the hospital, but it looks as though he's going to be okay. Jerry, we need to talk."

"I'm sure we do. When and where?"

"Can you be at my office at eleven o'clock?"

"If not right at eleven, it shouldn't be but a few minutes after. I'm a long way from you, and I have to shower and other things."

"Okay. Just make it as soon as you can."

He actually made it to Greg's office at ten fifty-five. He went in and was directed to Greg's desk. "Good morning, Greg."

"Geed morning, Jerry, have a seat. Would you like a cup of coffee?"

"Are you having one?"

84

"Yeah, I am."

"Then I'll have one, too; one sweetener and no cream."

Greg said, "Come on. You can get your own," and they walked down the hall to the coffee pot. They poured their coffee and doctored them the way they wanted them and then went back to Greg's desk.

As soon as they sat down, Greg picked up a very large pipe wrench and asked Jerry, "Does this look familiar?"

Jerry took it and looked it over and then turned it over, and on the other side was engraved *MARTIN BUILDERS*. "This must be ours. We engrave our name on all of our hand tools and attach engraved plates on all our large ones such as compressors, etc.. Where did you find this?"

"It was next to where they found Cliff Jackson."

"And where was that?"

"Between the athletic department and the parking lot at Delta High School."

"I don't know what to say, Greg. The wrench is obviously mine, but I don't believe for a minute that any of my people attacked him, and I certainly didn't do it. Do you have any idea who might have hit him?"

"We had our roundtable meeting on Wednesday, and there were nine present, so I guess we have nine suspects until we can eliminate some of them. Do you know if any of your people had any connection to any of the people in the diary?"

"Well, Natalie's brother works for us, but of course you knew that, and you've met Melissa Morris, one of Natalie's good friends and the executive assistant to Frank Thomas, the owner of the mansion. I'm sure you can eliminate both of them from the suspect list."

"Maybe after we check their alibis and their DNA."

Jerry said, "For the record, I was in my office all day yesterday. Beverly, my secretary can vouch for that."

"Thanks, Jerry. You're not a suspect. We just had to talk to you because the attack weapon belongs to you, and it apparently happened on one of your projects. You can leave whenever you want to."

"Okay. Thanks. Are you at liberty to tell what happened at the roundtable?"

"I think I can. Some of them didn't say a word the whole time, but some of them wouldn't shut up, like Cliff. He spent half the night accusing people of killing Natalie, especially her brother. That Cliff is a real piece of work."

"What all did he say at the meeting?"

"Most of his accusations were toward Natalie's brother, Kent. They nearly came to blows when he first started talking. I had to get in between them, and I made Kent sit down. Then I told Cliff to tell his story of the night Natalie went missing."

Cliff said, "Yeah, I was at the Chrisman the night Natalie disappeared, but I didn't kill her. I saw her and Kent having a huge fight, and that's why I think he killed her. Natalie and I had been dating for over a year, but we broke up two days before she went missing."

"I interrupted and asked him why he was at the Chrisman if they had broken up."

He said, "All of you know that I was a great football player. I was all everything; All-City, All-State, All-Conference, and second team All-America. I should have been All-America, but one of the judges didn't like me for some reason. While Natalie and I were dating, I gave her my letter jacket, some of my jerseys, and my class ring to wear around her neck. Two days before she went missing, we broke up, and the day she went missing, she called me and wanted me to go to the Chrisman so she could give back the things I had given her, and that's when I saw her and Kent having that big fight."

"I asked him if he knew why they were fighting and he said he didn't know."

He said, "I don't know why they were fighting, but I know they were. They were talking low, and I couldn't hear what they were saying, but it looked like a real donnybrook. When

86

they finished, I went over to Natalie and she gave me back all the things she had brought. I thanked her and told her bye, and I left."

"Then I asked him if Kent was there when he left."

"He said, "I guess he was. I didn't see him leave, but I know he was so mad at her that he must be the one who killed her.""

"Then I called on Kent to tell his side."

He said, "Cliff was right. Natalie and I had a huge fight that night, but I sure didn't kill her. She was my sister, and I loved her dearly."

"I asked him to tell us why they were fighting, and he said, "I don't like to tell things that are personal, and my fight with Natalie was nobody's business until now. I went to Chrisman that night to try to talk Natalie out of leaving. You see, our parents had just told us that they were going to get a divorce, and Natalie was so upset, she was going to leave home. I was upset, too, but I wasn't going to leave. When I heard her say she was leaving, I had to try to stop her, and that's why I went to Chrisman that night. She got mad at me when I tried to get her to change her mind, and we had a big fight, arguing about it. I stayed until most of the other kids left, and then I left, and Natalie was still alive when I left her.""

"I asked him if he had any idea who might have killed Natalie."

He said, "Cliff's the only one I can think of. He mistreated her the whole time they dated, and I think he did it.""

"Cliff got up again and was going to mix it up with Kent, but I was able to get him to sit back down. I then asked the whole group if they had any idea who did it, and two or three said they thought Cliff was the only one who might have done it because of the way he treated her, but they stopped short of accusing him."

Then Jerry asked Greg, "Where do you go from here?"

"We're not sure. We have to wait on the CSI folks to wrap up their search for clues, and then we'll try to put together a scenario that will lead us to a suspect and consequently the killer. Fred and I both think that whoever assaulted Cliff is the one who killed Natalie."

"Did her diary not help you?"

"Not really. We've now talked to all the people listed in it except for one, and we hope to find out for sure who that is and to talk to him within the next day or two,"

"Who is that?"

"We're not absolutely sure. At the end of the diary, she mentions someone named Jay, and she seemed to be kind of nervous about him."

"Why? What did she say?"

"Not too much. She just talked about how he was weird, and he scared her. She said he always wanted to come back and take her home when she didn't have her car, or he wanted to do something else for her.

"How do you plan to find out who he is if you've already talked to everybody on the list?"

"I didn't say we talked to everybody on the list. I said there were nine at the roundtable, but there were a couple that were not there. We only talked to each person about themselves. We didn't mention anybody else when we questioned them. We'll just have to go back now and question the people again and ask each one if they know who he is."

"I'm anxious to find out more about this case. When do you plan to talk to the folks again?"

"One day this week. I'd try today, but I've got to go out to the Chrisman House when we finish here. "I'll let you know what we find out."

"Thanks. Speaking of the Chrisman House, I'm on my way out there now. The windows came in, and I want to see how they look."

"Okay. We'll probably see you out there."

Jerry had called Frank Friday afternoon and told him about the windows, and he wanted to see them, so they agreed to meet at two o'clock, and that's why he was going out there on a Saturday.

When he arrived at the Chrisman, Frank was already there and had Melissa with him. They were sitting in his car waiting for him.

When he got out, they got out, and they all went in together. Jerry asked, "Why were you all sitting in your car? You could have come in."

And Frank answered, "We didn't want to come in with the police here. We were afraid we might disturb them."

They went in, and before they went to any of the rooms to see the windows, they noticed how the sun was casting an unbelievably pretty hue on the grand staircase and the foyer in general, and they just stayed there for a couple of minutes taking it in.

Then Jerry led them to the first room, and when Frank saw the windows, he was very excited. "Jerry, are you sure these are the same windows that you sent to Kentucky?"

"Yep. They're the same windows. They did a good job on 'em, didn't they?"

"I'd say. They look like new windows. Do all of them look this good?"

"Yeah. Come on; you can see for yourself."

"About two thirds of the way through the walk-thru, they came upon Detectives Yokley and Melwiki. Jerry spoke first, and jokingly said, "It seems like I have already seen you one time today."

"Detective Yokley said, "I was thinking the same thing. Hello, Mr. Thomas; Hello, Ms. Morris. How are you folks today?"

Melissa didn't say anything, but Frank answered for both of them, we're fine, thank you. I hope you fellows are having a good day."

"We are; thank you. Mr. Thomas, you sure have a beautiful place here."

"Thank you. I'm looking forward to getting the renovations completed. I just hope it doesn't continue to attract violence the way it has."

"Yeah, that's unfortunate, but I don't think it's this place. It just so happened that the incidents were here, but the violence would probably have happened somewhere else if it wasn't here."

Jerry said, pointing to Melissa, "Here's somebody that might can help you find out who Jay is."

"That's right; Ms. Morris, would you mind if we talked to you for a minute. We just need to ask you one question."

"No, I don't mind. What do you want to know?"

"I think you know that we have Natalie Coleman's diary."

"Yes, I know."

"There are several names listed in the diary, but one seems to have had some special meaning to her, and that name is Jay. Do you know who Jay is?"

"Yeah; that's easy. It's J.D. Tabor. Before he started calling himself J.D., he went by Jay. He's now the principal of Delta High School."

"Natalie described him as being weird. Did you think he was weird?"

"Very. He's better now, but back then weird was a good description for him. He was older than we were and out of place, and since he didn't fit in very well with our group he might have just acted weird, trying to fit in. I know he had had his eyes on Natalie for a long time, but he was afraid of Cliff and didn't make any moves on her because of that."

"Was he out here the night Natalie disappeared?"

"I think so. You know, it has been ten years, and it's hard to remember everybody that was somewhere on a particular night that long ago, but if Natalie was here, I'd say he was, too."

"Well, thank you, Ms. Morris. You've been a big help."

"You're welcome. Let me know if I can help you anymore."

"Will do; thank you."

Jerry and Frank and Melissa continued walking through the mansion, and when they got back close to the front door, Jerry asked," Do you want to see anything else, or are you ready to go?"

Frank said, "I'm ready to go. Are you ready, Melissa?"

"Yep; I'm ready."

"After they got outside, Melissa said, "You know, I had forgotten about Jay. Now that they have found him in Natalie's diary, I'm not going to be surprised if they find that he did something to her."

"That's pretty strong," Jerry said.

"Maybe not strong enough."

Before they parted, Jerry asked Frank, "Have you found out yet when the surveyors are going to start on the Cummings land"

"They started on it Thursday. Didn't Melissa call you?"

"No, she must have gotten busy, but that's okay; as long as they're out there."

"They're out there, and I'd say they'll be finished by the end of next week." Glaring at Melissa, he said to him, "Sorry you didn't know."

"That's okay. When should you and I get together?"

There's no hurry. We'll just have to get the paperwork done before you start anything."

"How about one day next week?"

"Maybe. I know I have several meetings next week. Give me until Monday morning to check my schedule, and I'll let you know. Is that okay?"

"That's fine. I think I'll go to the Douglasville Douglas County Water and Sewer people Monday morning and start working on getting water to the development. I need to go to Georgia Power, too."

Melissa asked, "What's the name of the new development going to be?"

"Don't know yet. I haven't come up with anything so far. Well. I'm gonna take off. Frank, I'll call your office Monday to see when a good time would be for us to get together. Melissa, I'll see you."

Frank said, "Okay partner, I'll probably see you next week," and Melissa said, "Okay, see ya."

As they were going to their cars, Jerry remembered something and turned and ran to catch up with Frank and Melissa before they left. Frank lowered his window and Jerry said, "I almost forgot; next Saturday, we're having a pig-pickin out at my place, and I would like for you all to come. Frank, please bring Marilyn, and Melissa, you can bring someone, too."

Frank asked, "What's the occasion?"

"It's sort of an appreciation party for everyone in my organization, and I consider you two in my organization, so I hope you will come."

"I'm sure we'll be there," Frank said.

"Good, I'll see you next week."

As they drove away, Frank said to Melissa, "That's a good man, right there."

And Melissa answered, "He sure is. I wish I could have found him before Tracy did," and Frank stared at her for several seconds.

Chapter Eight

The rest of the weekend was good. After Church, Sunday, they stopped and got some fried chicken on their way home and went down to the lake and had a picnic. Tracy took some quilts and pillows, and after they ate, they laid back and talked for a while and then went to sleep.

The next morning, Jerry got up and went to his office, and Tracy told him before he left that she was going to the community college to get the details on taking a real estate licensing course because she was pretty sure that she wanted to sell the homes in the new development that he was going to build.

He contacted the water and sewer department as well as Georgia Power and did all he could until the surveying was finished, and the land transfer had taken place. He went over the upcoming pig pickin with Beverly just to make sure everything was all set, then he called Frank to try and set up an appointment. Frank was in a meeting, but he had told Sandra, his secretary, to ask him if he could come on Wednesday around nine o'clock. He agreed to that time and then went to the apartment complex site to see how they were progressing. Finding everything good, he left for the Chrisman Mansion. He was hoping they were going to be finished with it within the next two weeks.

On his way, Melissa called him on his cell. When he saw her name on the caller ID, he answered, "Hi Melissa."

"Good morning, handsome. How are you this morning?"

"I'm fine."

"Are you going out to the Chrisman House today?"

"I'm on my way right now."

"I've been thinking a lot about Natalie's diaries, and I feel sure there is another one somewhere in the house. Would you mind if I came out there and looked for it? I promise I won't get in the way."

"I guess that'll be alright, but how do you think you'll be able to find anything? My men have been working in there for several weeks, and if there's anything in there, one of them would more than likely have found it, but you can look. When are you coming?"

"I'll leave the bank in about an hour. Is that okay?"

"Yeah, I'll see you when you get there."

The bathrooms were holding up the completion of the rest of the mansion, and that's what Jerry was going to concentrate on for the rest of the week. All the fixtures were new, but many of them were pseudo versions of the originals, and the modern-day plumbers were having a hard time with some of them.

He was having a hard time doing any one thing because every time he started on something, someone would yell for him or go into the place where he was to ask a question, and then, after a while, Melissa arrived. He tried to ignore her, but she came to speak to him and to tell him where she would be in the house, in case he needed her.

He told her, "Okay, thanks, but I doubt that I'll need you. Have fun with your treasure hunt."

"Thanks," and she left him to start her search on the second floor. There were a few pieces of furniture left from when the last people lived there, and she thoroughly searched each piece without success. Time was getting away, and the workers were getting ready to leave, and she still hadn't found anything, so when Jerry got ready to leave, she left, too.

Before she left, she told him, "Jerry, I just know Natalie's diary is here somewhere, and I'm not going to give up until I find it. If you don't mind, I'll come back whenever I can or whenever my *slave-driving* uncle eases up on my work load. I'm sure I can find it. Natalie and I always thought alike, so I'll just think like I know she would, and I betcha I find it."

She had to aggravate Jerry one more time before she left. She asked, "Jerry, everybody has gone now. You wanna stay; just you and me, for a while?"

He smiled and asked, "What would you say if I said Yes? It would scare you to death."

"Yeah, right. Why don't you try me and see?"

"I've gotta run, Melissa. I'm going to work tomorrow and Wednesday, and then I'm going to take off and get ready for the pig pickin, Saturday. Are you coming?"

"I wouldn't miss it."

"Are you going to bring a date?"

"What; and two time you? I should say not."

"Okay, but sitting around the lake and the horse pasture at sunset can really be romantic. You could be missing something special by being alone. Think about it."

"I'll think about it, but I can't think of anyone I would want to bring. I don't know anybody like you."

"Whatever. I'll see you Saturday. Bye. Actually, I may see you Wednesday. I've got an appointment with Frank at nine o'clock Wednesday morning.

"What are you 'all up to?"

"I'm buying a piece of land, and he said he would finance it, so I'll be at the bank to sign my life away."

"What are you going to do with the land; build something?"

"I want to build a large high-end development."

"Like White Rock?"

"Yeah, only a lot bigger and more expensive."

"Wow! You're something else. Do you know that?"

"No. I'm just a poor carpenter that got lucky with God's help."

"Okay, I'll see you Wednesday morning. Why don't we have lunch together?"

"We'll see. Bye."

Jerry got to the bank a little before nine, Wednesday

morning, and he went straight to Frank's office. When he got to the outer office, Sandra told him that Frank would be right with him, so he took a seat and talked to her until Frank came out and invited him in to his office.

After some small talk, Frank asked, "Jer, are you about ready to start building?"

"Not hardly. I've talked to the water people and the electric power people and I hope it won't be long before we can start seeing water lines put in. Of course, we have to get the surveys and all that before we will know where the roads and everything will be, so it'll be a good while yet."

"Do you have blueprints for all the houses?"

"Not all of them, but I probably have about half. I'm working on getting the rest now, and I'll probably build a few of them like some of the houses at White Rock. These will be forty-five minutes from White Rock, and if I make some changes to the exteriors, no one will know that they're alike."

"That's smart. When have you talked to Clarence?"

"Not since that day that you and I were out there."

"Did you all agree on one million dollars?"

"Yes."

"I thought that was the amount. When do you want the money?"

"Just as soon as I can get it. I want to pay Clarence as soon as possible. He seems to need it as soon as he can get it."

"We'll try to get everything done today, but as you know, there's always paperwork to do. If we can get it done, you can get it today. If we can't, it might be tomorrow, Is that a problem?"

"No problem. Tomorrow will be fine."

Okay then, do you want it deposited into your account?"

"That will be fine, then I can just write Clarence a check."

"Okay. Now what about the financing on the houses that you're going to build? Are you going to have to borrow money on them?"

"Frank, I may have to borrow some, but I'm hoping that I won't have to. Thanks to you, I made some money on the mall, White Rock, and the apartments, and I've got that. If I play my cards right and don't get reckless, I may be able to build the houses with my money; at least that's what I'm hoping."

"I hope you can, too, but if you need to borrow some, you know where I am. You've established a fine track record here, so there won't be a problem if you need some."

He called Melissa to come into his office, and when she got there, he said, "Melissa, our friend here is borrowing a million dollars, and I want you to fix up the paperwork and deposit the funds into his account. When can you have that ready?"

"I should be able to have it tomorrow sometime."

"You can't do it today?"

"No sir. I'm working on the rush project you gave me yesterday afternoon, and it will take me until the end of the day today, or possibly in the morning to finish it. If you want me to, I can stop working on that and do Jerry's. It's your decision."

"Jerry is tomorrow okay?"

"Yeah, that's fine."

"Finish the rush job, but do Jerry's as soon as you can."

"Alright; I'll do it," and she left to go back to her office.

As he was getting ready to leave, Jerry told Frank good bye and said he hoped to see him at the pig pickin Saturday, and Frank said they would be there. On his way out, he stopped by Melissa's to see what time his papers would be ready the next day, and she told him around noon, which meant she would plan to have lunch with him.

He got to the bank at eleven-thirty the next day and went to Melissa's office. "Good morning. Have you got my stuff ready?"

"Not quite. It'll be a few more minutes. Sit down, and I'll have it ready in a little bit. And then, you can take me to lunch."

97

He said, "Since I'm the one who's having to wait, it doesn't look as if I should have to pay for lunch."

"I guess you're right. Alright, I'll take you."

When she finished the paperwork, he signed what seemed like a hundred papers, and after he got everything signed, she gave him a deposit slip for one million dollars. When she handed it to him, she said, "Don't spend all this in one place."

"He said, "I'm going to do just that. I've got to write a check for the whole thing this afternoon."

"Alright, I'm going to take you to lunch now. Where do you want to go?"

"How about the Steak and Shake?"

"The Steak and Shake it is." They got into Melissa's sexy new BMW and headed to lunch. Her last BMW was a pretty grey, but the new one was Melbourne Red with an Oyster interior.

After lunch. She drove back to the bank where Jerry got his pickup and thanked her for lunch. His parting words were, "You're coming to the pig pickin aren't you?"

"I wouldn't miss it."

"Great. I'll see you Saturday."

The invitations read that the festivities would begin around five o'clock, and pickin the pig would begin around six. Cars began arriving right at five, and there was a steady stream of them until after five thirty. Two or three didn't arrive until right at six.

Jerry had designated one of the pastures as a parking lot, and it was a good thing. There were so many cars, it would have been impossible for all of them to park in the driveway.

Tracy acted as hostess while Jerry mulled around among the people. He knew his employees, but not their families, and he enjoyed meeting them. Stony Gray brought his mom and dad with him, and while Jerry had met them before, he was really glad they came.

An area was set up near the barn the way it was for Tracy

and Jerry's wedding, complete with a small dance floor. A country band was playing country classics as well as some favorite, easy listening tunes, and some of the folks danced. He and Beverly had estimated that there would probably be around two hundred people attending, and there were at least that many, although no one counted. He just hoped one pig was going to be enough for everybody, and when he mentioned it to Beverly, she assured him there would be enough. She had ordered enough food for two hundred and sixty.

He was so busy mixing with the people, that he didn't see Frank and Marilyn Thomas come in. At one point he looked up, and they were talking to Tracy, and right beside them was Melissa. She must have ridden with them.

True to his word, he didn't have an open bar, but he did have beer for those who wanted it, and of course, plenty of soft drinks. He didn't think beer would offend anyone, but he knew that liquor could cause problems.

Stony had been mixing with everybody ever since he got there, and in a little bit, he saw Bill Case come in with his wife and daughter. He went over to speak, and Bill said, "Stony, I see you made it. I'd like for you to meet my wife and daughter. This is my wife, Janet, and this lovely lady is Judy. Janet, Judy, this is Stony Gray. Stony is working with me."

"It's sure nice to meet you ladies. Glad you could come."

Tracy came up about that time and introduced herself and told them how glad she was that they came. She talked with them for a few minutes, then moved on with her hosting duties.

Stony was the hit of the party. His outgoing personality made all the women just love him, and made the men enjoy being around him. He could dance like nobody's business and was on the dance floor with a different woman just about every dance, beginning with Judy Case, and then with Tracy.

The band played without a break until six o'clock, when

the eating started. Stony hadn't had a chance to talk to Bobby Kunkle, he had been so busy, so he made it a point to go over and see him and his family when the break came. "Hey Bobby. I'm glad you could come."

"Hi Stony. I'd like for you to meet my wife and daughter. This is Kitty, and this is Deena. Girls, this wild man is Stony Gray."

Stony said, "Did you say Kitty?"

"Yeah. Kitty."

"Kitty Kunkle; that's the coolest name I've ever heard."

She laughed and said, "I'm glad you like it. I like the name Stony, too."

Deena looked to be around Stony's age and she was a knockout. Since it was the time when everybody was beginning to get their food, Stony stayed with the Kunkles, and when they had filled their plates, he sat with them and got better acquainted. He seemed to like Deena, and she seemed to like him as well.

As it usually happens, things got quiet while everyone was eating, but it didn't last long. The band started about the time most people were finishing and Stony was *chompin at the bit* to get back on the dance floor. He looked at his table companions and asked, "Kitty Kunkle, would you like to dance?", and she said, "I'd love to." He liked to say Kitty Kunkle.

They went out on the floor and Stony had no idea she could dance as well as she could, and they really put on a show. As he was walking her back to the table she said, "I don't know when I've ever had so much fun. Thank you, Stony."

And Stony said, "I know. I had a lot of fun, too. Thank you so much. Maybe we can get back out there before this shindig is over."

"I'd love to."

The next song was a fairly slow one, and he asked Deena if she would like to dance. She said, "You probably won't

100

want to dance with me. I'm not a very good dancer."

Kitty said, "Go on out there. You're a great dancer."

She got up, and Stony took her by the hand, and in his inimitable way, he turned around to Bobby and said, "You're next, Papa."

"Bobby just smiled and said, "I can hardly wait."

When he finished his dance with Deena, he went over to Marilyn Thomas and asked her to dance. She said, kidding, "Well, I thought you were going to overlook me."

And he said, "You should know better than that. I couldn't overlook my substitute mom."

"You look like you're having a good time."

"I am. You know, Jerry Martin is just about my favorite person in the whole world."

"He's a winner; that's for sure."

Jerry and Tracy were sitting at the table with Frank and Marilyn and Melissa, and Jerry and Tracy went to the dance floor, and everybody was surprised by the way they could dance. They really cut a rug. When they finished the dance, they returned to their table, and Tracy excused herself. When she left, Melissa asked Jerry, "Do you think you could dance like that with me?"

He said, "I'll bet I could. Do you want to see?"

"I absolutely do."

"Okay, let's go."

They went to the floor and while Melissa was not as good as Tracy, she was good. They finished the first dance, and the next one was a slow one. "Let's stay out here," Melissa said, so they stayed on the floor and danced a romantic slow dance.

While they were on the floor, Tracy came back, and when she saw them dancing close, the look on her face was unmistakable. She didn't like it at all.

She sat down, and soon the song ended. When Jerry and Melissa returned to the table, Jerry asked her if she wanted to dance, and she said, coolly, "I don't think so." After an uncomfortable pause, she said, "Why don't you ask Marilyn to dance?"

He glared at her for a couple of seconds and then asked Marilyn if she would like to dance. She said she would, and they went to the dance floor. While they were out there, Tracy got up and went around, mingling with the crowd and left Frank and Melissa sitting at their table.

After a while, things started to wind down, and Stony gravitated to the Kunkle table once again. He danced with Kitty and then with Deena. The first one he danced with Deena was pretty fast, and then the second one was slow. It was ultra-romantic and they danced very close. When it was over, they stayed on the dance floor and talked until the band started another song, then they danced to it as well.

Before they left the dance floor, Stony asked, "Deena, would you like to go grab a movie sometime?"

"I'd love to."

"Are you seeing anybody?"

"No. Are you?"

"No, I'm not. When we get back to the table, why don't you write down your number, and I'll call you, and we'll set something up, if you want to."

"I won't have to write it down. You can remember it. It's *D-KUNKLE.*"

"*D-KUNKLE?* That's a really neat number. Yeah, Even I can remember that. Thank you."

The party soon wound down, and people began leaving. Most of the carpenters and laborers left, but Bill Case and his family and Bobby Kunkle and his family stuck around. Beverly and her husband and Frank, Marilyn, and Melissa stayed for a while as well. When Stony saw that Deena and her family weren't leaving, he told his folks he wanted to stay for a little while, and that gave him and Deena a little more time together.

While they were all standing around talking, Jerry asked

Stony, "Stony, are you alright?"

"Yes sir. Why?"

"Well, I watched you on the dance floor, and you had moves I'd never seen before. I guess I thought you must have pulled something. Where did you learn how to dance like that?"

"In college."

"In college? How in the world did you learn to dance like that in college?"

"Well, there was always something going on in the commons, and every chance I had, I went in there, and if they were playing music, someone was always dancing, so I did too. It's not something you learn; it's just something that comes naturally if you feel the music."

"Well, I enjoyed watching you," and some of the others added their agreements.

Beverly had asked a few of the employees if they would like to stay and help gather up the tables and chairs and other things, and when she told them Jerry would pay them, she had no trouble getting enough help.

Chapter Nine

On Monday morning, Detectives Yokley and Melwiki decided that enough time had passed without talking to J.D. Tabor, they didn't intend to let him get by any longer without answering their questions. They gave him time to get school started and to get the new week smoother out, and then they went into the school office to talk to him.

When they got into the office, they told one of the student volunteers that they wanted to see Mr. Tabor, and she went into J.D.'s office to tell him. In what seemed to be a very long time, he finally came out and said, "Good morning. What can I do for you fellows this morning?"

Fred said, "Good morning, Mr. Tabor. We want to ask you some questions this morning."

"I'm sorry. I've got a meeting coming up in just a few minutes. I'm afraid you'll have to wait until some other time."

Fred said, "No, not this time. We've tried three or four times to talk to you, and you've always had some excuse. We'll give you time to get on the phone to cancel or postpone your meeting, but we are going to talk to you this morning."

"Alright, what do you want to know?"

"Can we go into your office?"

"Yeah, I guess."

When they got into his office, there were two chairs across from his desk, but he didn't offer to invite them to sit down, so they stood while he sat behind his desk. Fred asked, "Mr. Tabor, when you were younger, did you go by the name Jay?"

"Yeah."

"Why did you change?"

"I was like a lot of guys. A lot of boys go by Bobby and when they get older they change it to Robert, or some go by Billy and change to William when they get older. I went by

Jay until I got out of college and then changed it to J.D..
Actually, my name is Julian David, but I don't like that, so
J.D. is it."

"Do you recall the night Natalie Coleman disappeared?"

"No, I don't think I was there."

"We have reason to believe you were. Think hard. Are you
sure you weren't there?"

"It has been ten years. Do you remember where you were
on a certain night ten years ago? I'll bet you don't. I don't
think I was with Natalie that night, but if someone says they
saw me, then maybe I was."

"What was your relationship with her?"

"There was no relationship. I barely knew her. As best as
I can remember, she was a good deal younger than I am."

"Did you have a crush on her?"

"Of course not. As I said, she was much younger than me."

"Mr. Tabor, we were told that you had a crush on Natalie,
but you were afraid of Cliff Jackson since he was her
boyfriend. Is there anything to that?"

"Absolutely not. I've already told you that I didn't have a
crush on her, and I certainly wasn't afraid of Cliff."

"Finally, where were you the night Cliff Jackson was
assaulted?"

"I was at home."

"Were you alone? Yes, my wife was at bridge club until
about eleven o'clock."

"Can anyone vouch for your being there?"

"I guess not."

"Oh, there is one more thing. Mr. Tabor, would you
consent to giving a sample of your DNA?"

"Yeah, I'll give you a sample. I don't have anything to
hide."

"Great. Thank you." Fred swabbed his mouth, bagged the
swabs, and they left.

The Delta High Alumni group had met a few days earlier,

but they were planning a large fund raiser, and they didn't accomplish everything they needed to when they met, so they were going to meet at the school again that afternoon; after school let out. Some of the group got there early and hung around outside the office.

Cliff Jackson had sustained a concussion and a serious gash on his head when he was assaulted, but he appeared to be alright, and he was there. Melissa was also there along with Tony Sutton and a couple of others.

While they waited on the others and time for the meeting to start, they talked about various things, and since they were so closely connected to Natalie Coleman, Melissa and Cliff talked about her and her case. Melissa mentioned that even though they had found her diary, she felt strongly that there was another one, and she intended to find it. Cliff said he thought there was one, too, and he would be glad to help her find it.

Cliff said, "I remember when we were going together, she would write down everything in that diary. If you wanted to find out something on any day, if she was around, it was in her diary. She recorded everything, almost religiously."

Melissa said, "I know she did. That's why I feel like there's another one out there because the diary they found didn't have a thing in it about the day she went missing, and the book was full. If that was the last one she wrote in, there would be something about that day."

The student volunteers that worked in the office heard all that and didn't have any idea what they were talking about, but J.D. and the school secretary overheard it all and knew exactly what they were saying.

Soon the rest of the group showed up, and they all went into the teachers' lounge for their meeting that lasted about an hour. After they finished and were leaving, three or four of them stopped outside the school office to talk. The office was located about the center of the building, and among the ones who stopped to talk were Cliff and Melissa.

Cliff asked Melissa, "When are you planning to go back out to Chrisman to look for the diary?"

"I don't know for sure; maybe tomorrow afternoon."

"Would you care if I went, too?"

"No, I don't care. The more the merrier, but we can't get in the way of the workers out there. I'll have to call Jerry Martin to see when we can go. Call me sometime in the morning, and I'll let you know."

"Okay, I'll talk to you in the morning."

When Melissa called Jerry the next morning to find out when she and Cliff could come out to look for the diary, he told her, "You can come anytime you want. We're not working tomorrow. The painters are supposed to finish somewhere around noon, and that's too late for my men to start. I'll be there, though."

When Cliff called her the next morning, she told him she was going out to the Chrisman around one o'clock. "I'll see you out there," he told her.

She had thought a lot about where she wanted to look for the diary since the last time she was out there, and when Cliff got there she told him where she was going to start and suggested that he go to another spot that she thought might also be a possibility, the whole time making sure they stayed out of Jerry's way.

When Jerry saw Cliff, he remembered the rocky start they got off to earlier, so he didn't say too much to him.

Melissa went into the room where the dresser was in which they found the first diary and began her search there. She reasoned that if Natalie thought the dresser was a good hiding place for one, then it would be a good hiding place for more than one. The dresser was sitting in the middle of the room, so she didn't have any trouble looking over every inch of it. The first one was taped to the back of the mirror, so she examined all the outside surface without finding anything. Then, she started on the drawers. Each drawer fit inside what could best be described as another drawer. In other words; if a drawer was pulled all the way out, nothing could be seen where it was except two sides, a top and bottom, and a rear panel, making a drawer inside a drawer.

She ran her hand over every inch that she could reach without success, and then she turned the dresser over on its back so she could look it over from the bottom. The way the dresser was built, nothing could be seen from the outside, but the bottom was covered with some kind of fabric, and she noticed that the fabric had a small tear on the right side.

She rubbed the bottom from front to back and from right to left, and when she got near the torn place in the fabric, she felt something that was different from the rest of the bottom. She pulled the torn piece up and reached her hand inside, and when she did, she found a small book that had been taped to the bottom of the bottom drawer. It was the diary she was looking for.

She let out a yell and Jerry heard her and came running, as did Cliff. He thought she had hurt herself or had gotten hurt some way, and when they got in there, she said, "I found it. I found Natalie's diary."

Jerry said, "Good girl." Pointing to the torn fabric on the dresser, he asked, "Is that where you found it?"

"Yeah, isn't that incredible?"

He said, "I'm surprised that somebody hasn't already found it, since they've looked so hard for it."

"Me too, but here it is."

Jerry said, "We need to call the police and turn it in."

She said, "I will, but I'm going to read it first."

"That's none of your business, Melissa."

"It's not the police's business either."

"No, but it's tied into Natalie's murder, so let's turn it in."

Melissa said, "I'll tell you what; you call the police and tell them I found it and see what they want to do. They might just want to come get it now, and they might not come until tomorrow, since it's already so late today. I don't mind giving it to them; I just want to read it first."

"Okay, I'll go upstairs and see if I can get a signal."

"Bless your heart. You go call them, and I'll go out to the car and start reading."

As usual, in order to get a signal for a cell phone, it was necessary to go to the top floor, and then, there wasn't always one there, and as luck would have it, there wasn't one that time.

Melissa and Cliff were sitting in her car, reading Natalie's diary, and Jerry came out and told them, "There's no signal. I'll have to drive up the road a couple of miles before I can get one, so you all keep reading, and I'll be back in a few minutes."

He got in his pickup and left them in the car, reading.

As soon as he got out of sight, a hooded figure stepped out from around the building with a gun. When they saw him, they got out of the car, and Cliff asked, "What do you want?" Thinking they were being robbed, he reached in his back pocket and pulled out his billfold and said, "Here, take it, and leave us alone."

Without a word from the hooded man, he shot Cliff in the chest, and Cliff went down.

Melissa then bolted and ran toward the house. The man shot at her twice as she was running and missed. She made it to the house and ran to the basement. The man was several yards behind her, so she was able to find a place to hide. It was very dark in the basement, but there was a small beam of light from the master bedroom, shining down through the unfinished dumbwaiter. She stood up as straight as she could and tried to become part of the wall.

She could hear him coming down the stairs, and her heart was beating up into her mouth. Of course, he couldn't see anything either, but he knew she was down there, and he wasn't about to let her leave. He walked slowly through the basement and stopped every now and then to see if he could hear anything, and when he couldn't, he slowly moved on.

Melissa held her position and at one point she moved her hands across the wall she was standing against and felt what felt like a two by four. She grabbed it and pulled it to her. She guessed that it was about up to her waist, and she took it with both hands and stood in what she thought was a good defensive position.

The hooded man took off his hood because it was so dark, he couldn't see anything, besides, if he was successful in his mission, there wouldn't be anybody to identify him. In what seemed like forever to Melissa, he continued his stalk, and she could tell he was getting closer. In a couple of minutes, it was almost as if he was right up against her, and she said a little prayer and tightened her grip on the board and swung at him with all her might.

She could feel the contact, and it stunned him. She heard him fall backwards, and at that point, she found the stairs and ran up to the first floor, closing the door behind her. There was no lock on the door, but she had taken the board she hit the man with upstairs with her, and she wedged it under the door knob, in hopes that it would keep him from getting up there to her.

In the meantime, Jerry drove in from his trip up the road to call the police. He saw Cliff lying on the ground and he ran over to him. Cliff was seriously hurt, but he was awake and told Jerry that Melissa and the hooded man were in the house. He said the man had a gun, so be careful.

Melissa didn't know what to do, so for a minute or two, she just stood at the top of the stairs, trying to decide what she should do next, when all of a sudden, at the top of the unfinished dumbwaiter was the man pointing a gun at her. The frame of the dumbwaiter was built almost like a ladder, so the man took advantage of the small ray of light and climbed up to the first floor.

Melissa was horrified, and when she looked at the man, she saw that it was J.D.Tabor. "J.D., what are you doing?"

J.D. said, "Shut up. You've caused me enough trouble."

"How have I caused you trouble?"

"By insisting there was another diary, and I can't afford anyone seeing it."

"JD., did you kill Natalie?"

"I said, shut up. I'm not going to talk to you anymore," and he lifted the gun higher and took careful aim at her.

Jerry had been silently slipping up on him, and when he got close enough and saw him raising the gun and aiming it at Melissa, he lunged at the gun and knocked it out of his hand, causing it to fire, and sending J.D. falling down into the basement.

At that instant, Detectives Yokley and Melwiki pulled in next to Melissa's car. They immediately saw Cliff lying in the grass and then they heard the shot. Fred Melwiki went over to check on Cliff, and Cliff said the man with the gun was inside with Melissa and Jerry. Greg pulled his gun and carefully entered the house.

When Melissa saw Jerry and saw him knock the gun out of J.D.'s hand, she ran over to him and threw her arms around him and squeezed him for all she was worth.

Fred radioed for an ambulance, and after making Cliff as comfortable as he could, he drew his gun and entered the house to join Greg. By that time, he heard talking and knew things were alright, so he holstered his gun and joined the others.

When they reached the master bedroom, they saw Melissa still holding on to Jerry. "What happened here?" Greg asked.

Jerry said, "Well, we had a little excitement. Did you see Cliff Jackson outside?"

"We did. An ambulance is on the way. Now tell us what happened?"

"Is Cliff still alive?" Jerry asked.

"Yeah, I think he'll be alright. Now, what happened?"

Jerry pulled away from Melissa and said, "I really don't know the whole story. Melissa can tell you more than I can."

Greg asked, "Ms. Morris, do you feel like telling us what happened?"

She reached over and took Jerry's hand and said, "Yeah, as long as my hero is here to support me."

Chapter Ten

Then Greg said, "Good. Can you start at the beginning?"

Jerry interrupted, "Excuse me. Before you get started, if you'll go down to the basement, you'll find Natalie Coleman's killer."

The detectives looked shocked, and Greg asked, "What did you say?"

"I said if you'll go downstairs, you'll find J.D. Tabor. He killed Natalie Coleman."

They immediately left Jerry and Melissa, and after going to their car to get flashlights, they came back in and went to the basement where they found J.D. Tabor with a large contusion on the left side of his face and other cuts and bruises from the fall.

Greg told him he was under arrest while Fred put the handcuffs on him, Greg read him his rights, and then they led him upstairs. After they got up there, Greg, said, "Jerry, Ms. Morris, too much has happened this afternoon to handle out here. We're going to need for you to come to the police station to answer questions and to give a statement. The ambulance should be here any minute to take Mr. Jackson to the hospital, and we'll wait on them to get here. You can wait and go as we do, or you can go on to our office now if you want to."

Melissa said, "I'm so shaky right now, I don't know if I can drive. Jerry, can I ride with you?"

"Yeah, get your keys, and you can leave your car here until tomorrow."

While she was going to her car, they heard the ambulance' siren, and in a minute, it pulled into where they and Cliff were. After they gave a quick check of Cliff's vital signs, they put him on a stretcher and put the stretcher in the ambulance and took off for the hospital. He had lost a lot of blood, and the

EMT's put an IV in his arm before they left.

Greg told Jerry, "You all can follow us to our office. One of us will have to book our prisoner, but one of us can work with you all. I'm sure glad you all are alright. This looks as if it could have gotten real hairy."

Melissa said, "If it wasn't for my hero here, I would be dead right now."

Greg said, "Well, I'm glad he was here for you."

They got in their car, and Melissa and Jerry got in Jerry's truck, and they all headed for the police station. Melissa tried to hold Jerry's hand, but he pulled it away, so she finally settled on just resting her hand on his right arm as he drove. She said at one point, "Thank you for saving my life, my darling."

Trying to lighten things up a little, he said, "Think nothing of it. It's all in a day's work."

She said, "I'm serious. If it weren't for you, I'd be dead right now."

"I know. I'm just glad I was there."

On the way to the station, Jerry called Tracy to tell her a little about the happenings at the Chrisman House and told her he didn't know what time he would be home because he had to go to the police department, and then he told Melissa that she should call Frank and tell him what happened, which she did.

When she hung up, Jerry asked, "What did he say?"

"He said he was going to come to the police station."

"I thought he might."

When they arrived at the police station, they all went in and instead of going to Greg or Fred's desk, they went into a room which was private. Before they got started, Frank arrived, and the desk sergeant escorted him back to where they were. After he was seated, and Greg briefly explained to him why they were there, he turned to Melissa.

"Ms. Morris, do you feel like talking to us now?

114

"Yeah, I'm okay now, and will you please call me Melissa?"

"Okay, Melissa, can you start at the beginning? Why were you at the Chrisman House today, and why was Cliff Jackson there?"

"I felt sure that there was another one of Natalie's diaries hidden out there, so I went out there to look for it."

Greg asked, "Why was Cliff Jackson there?"

"We had talked about it and he offered to help me look for it."

"Okay, go ahead, but first, why did you think there was another diary?"

"Well, Natalie and I were best friends and we knew each other really well. We even thought alike and sometimes even finished each other's sentences. When I saw the first diary that was found and saw that it was finished all the way to the end, I knew that wasn't the end of the story, and there wasn't anything in it that suggested that it was written on her final night, so I knew there had to be another one.

"I heard that the first one that was found was taped behind the mirror to a dresser, and I went out to Chrisman one time, but didn't find anything, and then I got to thinking that if Natalie thought the dresser was a good hiding place for one diary, it would be a good place to hide another one, so that's where I started today. After going over the whole thing completely, I turned it over and that's when I found it. There was some kind of fabric covering the bottom of the dresser and it was torn on one corner. I felt all over the bottom and when I got near to the torn place, I felt something, and it was the diary.

"I let out a yell, and Jerry came running. He thought I had hurt myself some way, and when he saw that I was alright, he said we had to call you guys. He couldn't get a phone signal out there, so he drove up the road until he got one. That's when J.D. appeared. Cliff and I were out in my car reading the diary before you all came to get it, and when we looked up, this man with a hood was staring at us. We got out of the car, and Cliff took out his wallet and offered it to the man because he thought that was what he wanted, but the man shot him without even saying a word.

"When he shot Cliff, I ran, and he was right behind me. He shot at me two or three times and missed, but I made it to the house and ran down into the basement. It was dark down there, but I found a place to hide and found a board to use as a weapon. When he got down there, he took off the hood so he could see a little, and after a while, he caught up to me, and I hit him in the head with the board and ran upstairs. The blow must have stunned him because I had time to get upstairs ahead of him. I wedged the board under the doorknob, and he couldn't get the door open, but he went back down and found the dumbwaiter and climbed all the way to the top where he held the gun on me. That's when I saw that he was J.D. Tabor.

"Jerry came back from calling you guys and found Cliff lying outside. Cliff was conscience and told him what happened and that I was in the house with the man. Jerry slipped in and heard us talking, so he knew where to come. He slipped over to where we were without making a sound. From where he was, he couldn't actually see J.D., and J.D. couldn't see him, but he could see the gun, and when he saw J.D. raise the gun and aim it at me, he lunged and knocked the gun out of J.D.'s hand, and J.D. lost his balance and fell down into the basement. Since you had already been called, we just waited on you to come, and that's the end of the story."

"Tell us a little about the diary. Were there any names in it that weren't in the other one?"

"No, the same ones and maybe not as many."

"If we hadn't got J.D. today, is there anything in the diary that would have lead us to him?"

"I don't know. I know it confirmed why Kent and Natalie were fighting that night."

"Why were they?"

"Because their parents had just told them that they were getting a divorce, and Natalie made up her mind to leave home. Kent went out there to try to talk her out of leaving, and they got into it."

"Why would he go out there to talk to her about that, instead of doing it at home?"

"Because he was afraid that she was going to leave from there."

"Did it not say anything about J.D.?"

"Yeah, it did. She said Jay kept pestering her and wanted to come back later that night to take her home, and she had decided to let him."

"Is there anything else you want to tell us, Melissa?"

"No, I've told you all I know."

"Jerry, could we get your statement now?"

"Greg, I really don't have a statement. Melissa covered everything in her statement, and if I tell you anything, it will just be a duplicate of what she told you."

"Okay. I'll accept that."

"Thanks Greg."

"Mr. Thomas, it seems that if your Chrisman House could talk, it could tell some really good stories, doesn't it?"

"It looks that way, doesn't it? I just hope this is the last chapter in this ten year old mystery. I'm going to tell him another time, but I want to say in front of you gentlemen right now how thankful I am for Jerry Martin. The very first time I met him, he was in the process of doing our family a great service, and he didn't even know us, and now he saves the life of my niece. God sent a great man when he put Jerry on this earth, and I'm so very thankful for him. Jerry, God bless you," and he wiped tears from his eyes."

Melissa was crying, and when she looked at the two detectives, they had tears in their eyes as well.

Jerry said, trying to lighten the mood a little, "Enough of

this serious stuff. I'm thankful that I was there to help, but I didn't do anything that someone else wouldn't have done. Let's get outa here. These detectives have a killer to question." He shook hands with the detectives and then with Frank. Melissa came up to him and hugged him and said, "You've been my hero ever since I met you, but now, I really don't know what to say except, thank you. I owe you my life."

Still trying to lighten things up, he looked at her and said, "I had to save you or else there wouldn't be anyone to aggravate me."

She smiled through the tears and said, "You're awful," and she hugged him again.

He looked at Frank and said, "Melissa left her car at the Chrisman House. If you need for me to take her out there as I go tomorrow, I'll be happy to. Just give me a call."

"Okay. Thank you, Jerry."

As they were leaving, Melissa told Jerry, "If your offer to let me ride with you to get my car still stands, I'd like to do that. What time will you be going out there in the morning?"

"Not too early. I have to go to the office first. It might be ten o'clock. Is that too late?"

"That's just right. I'll be ready to go at ten."

Frank said, "Jerry, I'll bring her to your office to keep you from driving all the way to the bank. Okay?"

"No, you don't need to do that. You're too busy to act as a chauffeur. I'll pick her up at the bank. Don't even think about coming all the way to my office."

"Are you sure?"

"I'm sure. I'll be at the bank about a quarter after ten."

"Okay, if you're sure. You ready, Melissa?"

"I'm ready. I'll see you in the morning, Jerry."

"You all have a good night. Melissa, be sure to say your prayers tonight."

"Don't worry. I've already started and you're in them."

"Good. Good night, folks."

They both said good night and they all left.

Inside the police station, Greg asked Fred, "Fred, it's pretty late. Do you want to question J.D. Tabor tonight or wait 'til in the morning?"

"I'd just as soon get started tonight. If he has all night to think about it, he might just lawyer up in the morning, and we'll be delayed closing out this case."

"Alright, I'll have him brought up." He picked up the phone and dialed a number, and when they answered, he said, "Gordie, bring that new prisoner up to I.R.-Two, will you?"

"Fred, do you want a cup of coffee to take back with us?"

"Yeah, 'cause we might not get any supper," so they stopped on the way to IR2 to get a cup.

When J.D. was brought into the interrogation room, they asked him if he wanted anything to drink, and he declined. Okay, J.D. we're having a hard time understanding why a person of your status and intelligence would get yourself in such a mess. Do you want to tell us your side of the story, beginning with the murder of Natalie Coleman ten years ago?"

"I didn't kill her."

"You were there."

"I was there, but I didn't kill her."

"Who did?"

"I don't know. I heard that Cliff Jackson did."

"No, Cliff has been cleared, in fact; everybody has been cleared except you."

"I also heard that her brother, Kent, might have killed her."

"Nope. He's been cleared, too. Listen, J.D. I want to help you if I can. You seem like a straight up guy, but what you did this afternoon; shooting Cliff Jackson and trying to kill Melissa Morris are very serious charges, and you'll have to pay for them, and then, if we add murder to that, you may never get out of prison, but if you cooperate, we can put in a good word to the District Attorney for you, and it will help."

"How much will it help if I cooperate with you?"

"I can't say, but I'm sure it will save you several years."

"Okay, what do you want to know?"

"Tell us about that last night at the Chrisman House."

"You've got to remember that it's been ten years, and I don't remember a lot about that night, but I'll tell you what I can recall. Whoever told you that I had a crush on Natalie Coleman was right. I did have a crush on her, even though she was younger than me. She usually drove out there, but that night, she rode with someone else, and I thought that might give me the chance to take her home in my car. I asked her two or three times, and she said no, but I kept on, and she finally said she would let me. I remember I had to leave for something; I don't remember why, but I told her I would come back to get her.

"When I went back, everyone had left, but Natalie was still there, waiting for me to take her home. I misread things at that point because I thought since she waited for me after everyone left that she really wanted to be with me. She was getting her things together, and I thought I would kiss her, but when I tried, she pushed me away. I thought she was just playing with me, so I kept trying, and she ran from me. We ran up the stairs from the foyer to the second floor and when we got up there, she tripped and fell through the bannister down to the floor in the foyer. She must have hit her head.

"I ran down to see if she was hurt, and when I got down there, she wasn't breathing. I tried everything I knew to revive her, but it was too late; she never did start breathing again. I panicked, because I didn't want anybody to know I went back, and I didn't know what to do, so I started trying to figure out what I could do with her. I didn't have anything to dig a hole with, so I couldn't bury her, and I was afraid that somebody might see me if I carried her down to the river.

"Since she was dead, I went upstairs to try to fix the bannister, and without the proper tools and know-how, I just did a mediocre job, but at least it was put back together. Maybe nobody would notice it. And then, I went downstairs to see about the floor in the foyer. Her fall broke the marble, and all I could do was try to put it back together the best I could. The whole time I was trying to make the repairs, I was trying to think of some place to put Natalie, and when I walked through the bedroom, it came to me to put her in the dumbwaiter. I went into the foyer and picked her up and took her to the dumbwaiter and stuffed her in it. It was hard to get her in it, but I finally did it, and I cranked it down and stopped it in between the floors. Then I found a small board and wedged it in between the dumbwaiter and the wall to keep it from coming loose and falling.

"I admit that I did all that and tried to cover it up, but I didn't kill her. She died as the result of a terrible accident."

Greg asked him, "Why did you go after Cliff Jackson and Melissa Morris this afternoon?"

"Because I knew that both of them were so close to Natalie that when they said they thought there was another diary, I figured they were right, and I was afraid that if there was one, it would say something about me going back out there that night. I just couldn't take a chance on another one being found and made public."

"Did you set up the booby trap in the basement of the Chrisman House?"

"Yes."

"Why?"

"Well, the diary hadn't been found at that time, so I figured if the house burned down, it would burn any diary that might be in it."

Fred asked, "Why do you think the diary would say something about you going back if she was already dead? She didn't write anything after you got there, did she?"

"No, but she knew I was coming back because I told her I was."

Greg then asked him, "Did you assault Cliff Jackson with a pipe wrench?"

"No, I didn't do that."

"Do you know who did?"

"I think so, but I'm not saying anything about that."

Greg asked him, "J.D. was all this worth it?"

He hung his head and said, "No, I don't guess it was. I don't know why I was so afraid of somebody knowing I went back to Chrisman that night, and looking back, I would have done things differently. I've managed to totally ruin my life and the life of my wife, and I'm so sorry for that. Now that I've cooperated with you, what do you think is going to happen?"

"Well, we're going to do what we told you we'd do. We're going to talk to the District Attorney and recommend that he be lenient with you. Is there anything else that you need to tell us?"

"No. You know everything. Maybe I'll be able to sleep at night now."

Greg called the jailor to come get J.D. and take him back to his cell, and then he told Fred, "You know, that fellow is very intelligent and seems to have a lot on the ball, and it's a shame that he's ruined his life the way he has."

"Let's wrap this up," Fred said. "I guess we need to make a list of charges to give the D.A. before we leave, don't we?"

"Yeah, write these down and I'll call them out to you."

"Okay, shoot."

"The first one is concealing a body. I'm glad it's that instead of murder. Second; two counts of attempted first degree murder, and third, Criminal attempt to commit first degree arson."

The next morning, the Atlanta Constitution had it on the front page, under the fold. The headline was 'PRINCIPAL ARRESTED and under the headline it told how the principal of Delta High School in Douglasville, Julian David Tabor, was arrested the day before. It said that he was charged with concealing a body, and that additional charges included two counts of attempted first degree murder, and one count of attempted first-degree arson were to be filed, and he was currently in the Douglasville jail under one million dollars bail.

The next morning, a lady walked into the Douglasville Police Department and asked to see Detective Greg Yokley. The Desk Sergeant asked, "Could I tell Detective Yokley what it's about?"

"I committed a crime, and I want to talk to him."

"What's your name, Ma'am?"

"My name is Denise Tabor."

"Just a minute." He picked up the phone and dialed Greg's number, and when he answered, the Desk Sergeant said, "There's a Denise Tabor up here to see you."

"Did she say what she wants?"

"She said she committed a crime and wants to talk to you."

"Okay, send her back."

The sergeant directed her back to Greg's desk, and Greg greeted her when she came in. "Good morning, Mrs. Tabor. What can we do for you this morning?"

"I want to confess to a crime."

"And what crime would that be?"

"I'm the one who hit Cliff Jackson with a wrench."

He didn't know whether to believe her or not, so he said, "I see. Tell me about it."

"You probably already know, I'm J.D. Tabor's wife. I'm a teacher at Delta High, and the day I hit him, I saw Cliff at the school in the Athletic Department. I knew he probably parked in the parking lot, so I went out there to wait on him to come out. I had planned it for several days, and when they were working on the concession stand, I stole the wrench and waited for the right time to use it. When he left the Athletic Department and went to the parking lot, I accidentally on purpose dropped a little notebook and hoped he would stop to pick it up for me. He did, and when he bent over to get it, I hit him as hard as I could with the wrench. He went down, and I ran to my car. There was no one around, so nobody saw me."

"Mrs. Tabor, why did you come in here today?"

"Because I was afraid you might try to pin this on my husband. He has enough against him right now, and he certainly doesn't need to be accused of something that he didn't do."

"Mrs. Tabor, were you aware of the Natalie Coleman situation."

"Yes, but not for a long time after she went missing. I suspected that Jay had something to do with it, and one day when we were talking, he told me what happened."

"Why did you assault Cliff Jackson?"

"Because he was Natalie's boyfriend, and I thought that if he saw the diary and figured things out, he would turn Jay in."

"Mrs. Tabor, I'm afraid we're going to have to hold you. You will be charged with assault

with a dangerous weapon. Do you have a lawyer?"

"No. Do I need one?"

"Yes ma'am, I'm afraid you do. Do you know any to call?"

****

Jerry was at the bank the next morning almost exactly at ten-fifteen, and Melissa was standing outside waiting for him. "Good morning," she said.

"Good morning. Did you sleep well?"

"I'm afraid not. Yesterday was stuck in my mind, and I had a hard time relaxing. I like to have never gone to sleep, but when I finally did, I slept like a log until the alarm went off at six o'clock."

"Well, things should be much better now that the mystery about Natalie has been solved, and J.D. is no longer around to set fires and shoot people."

"I know, but you know what, Jerry? Things will never be

124

the same for me at the Chrisman House the way they were before."

"Maybe they will. Did you see the Constitution this morning?"

"No, I didn't see it."

"Well, it has the whole story. Now that Frank owns it, things should be much better. It won't be a hangout for kids anymore, but it should be a place where anybody would enjoy being there, whether for a wedding or a dance. Do you think Frank and Marilyn will move out there?"

"I doubt it. I haven't heard either one of them say a word about it, and knowing Marilyn the way I do, if she was planning to move, then that's all she would talk about."

Chapter Eleven

That's all that was said about the Chrisman House. The rest of the way, she asked, and he answered questions about the new development he was planning at the Cummings farm. Soon, they arrived, and Jerry pulled in next to Melissa's car, where they both got out of his pickup.

Jerry said, "Well Melissa, I hope you have a good day today. I'll see you."

She walked around the truck and said, "Thank you, and thank you again for saving my life." She put her arms around him and said, "If there's ever anything that you want, just tell me, and I mean anything. I love you."

Putting his arms around her, he smiled at her and said, "I'll keep that in mind."

Standing on her tip toes, she tried to kiss him, but he turned his head, causing her to have to kiss him on the cheek.

He said, "Melissa, I've got to get to work." Again, he told her, "I hope you have a good day. You'll feel better when you get to work and get your mind off yesterday."

He spent some time at the Chrisman, and then went out to White Rock and finished out the day. On his way home that evening, Frank called him on his cell. "Hey Frank; what's up?"

"Hi Jer. Listen, the reason I'm calling is to tell you that Marilyn and I would like to take you and Tracy out Saturday night. Are you interested?"

"Of course, I'm interested. What have you got in mind?"

"We'd like to take you to the Atlanta Athletic Club unless you'd rather go somewhere else."

"No, the Atlanta Athletic Club is the ultimate in my opinion. We'd love to go there with you."

"Great, I'll have Sandra make reservations."

"Okay, Padna. I'll look forward to it."

The gathering at Jerry's last Saturday did wonders for the moral of his employees. Not that the moral was not already good; it just seemed that the comradery between the workers and between the workers and their supervisors was at a higher level. Bill Case told Jerry that Stony had caught on to the Lay Out Pro like he had been operating it for years, and Jerry was real happy about that because that would expand the abilities of Martin Builders to take on more jobs simultaneously, thus, more business.

Stony was at work early every day and stayed late, making a huge favorable impression on Bill. He caught on quickly to just about everything he was shown, and Bill felt kinda like he was on vacation. On Monday, after the pig pickin, Stony put in a full day's work, and then could hardly wait to get home to call Deena Kunkle.

He wanted to find his own apartment, but until he found one, he was living with his parents. When he got home, he went into his room and had to think for a minute about her number. *She said it is DKUNKLE, so let me figure out what that is.* He took his phone out of his pocket and began dialing the letters. It turned out to be 770-358-6553. The phone rang several times, and finally the voice mail answered. "This is Deena. I really want to talk to you, but I can't right now. Please leave your number and a short message, and I'll call you back as soon as I can. Have a blessed day."

Stony said, "Hey Deena. It's Stony. Call me if you get this before I find you." Then he called Bobby's house because she lived at home with them. Deena's mother answered. "Hello."

Stony asked, "Is this Kitty Kunkle?"

"It is. Who's this?"

"This is Stony. I'm glad you answered because I love to say Kitty Kunkle."

"Well, I'm glad I could give you some pleasure. How are you Stony?"

"I'm doing great, and I hope you are. I'm trying to find your beautiful daughter; is she there?"

"No, Stony, she's not. She went to the mall with one of her girlfriends and hasn't got home yet? Can I have her call you?"

"Yes, please, if you don't mind. Listen, I sure enjoyed meeting you guys at Jerry's last weekend. I especially enjoyed dancing with you both. I hope we can do that again sometime."

"I enjoyed it too. Maybe we can. Well, I'll have Deena call you. Bye, Stony."

"Thank you. Bye."

He had just hung up when his phone rang. The caller ID said D KUNKLE. "Deena, Hi."

"Hi Stony. I'm sorry I missed your call. I left my phone in the car while we shopped. What are you doing?"

"I just got home from work and wanted to call you. Did you have a good day?"

"Yeah, it was great. I finished my Clinicals this morning and went to the mall this afternoon."

"What are clinicals?"

"That's something that you have to do when you're trying to become a doctor or a nurse. It's part of your course, but you do it in the hospital instead of a classroom."

"That's right! You're going to be a nurse, aren't you?"

"Yeah, hopefully in about six months."

Being Stony, he asked, "If I get sick, will you take care of me?"

She said, "I will. What are you going to have wrong with you?"

"I don't know. Whatever will require a nurse."

"Okay, you let me know when you start feeling bad."

"Don't worry. I will. Listen, would you like to go to a movie one night this week?"

"Yeah, I'd love to. What do you want to see?"

"I don't know. Whatever you would. How about tomorrow night?"

"Okay. That sounds good. Do you want me to meet you?"

"No, I'll pick you up. If we go to the seven o'clock show, I'll get you at six-thirty. Is that too early, or would you rather go to the nine o'clock?

"Six-thirty is fine. I have to get up early every day, so the early show is best for me."

"Me too. Great. I'll see you tomorrow night."

He went to work whistling the next morning, he was so excited about having a date with Deena. Bill noticed as soon as he got there that Stony was in an extremely good mood, and he asked him, "Boy, you're in rare form this morning. What did you do; win the lottery?"

"No, but I won something just as exciting."

"What's that?"

"I've got a date tonight."

"Who with? She must really be a prize."

"Do you know Bobby's daughter, Deena?"

"I've met her, but I really don't know her. I'd say that if she's as sweet as she is good-looking, you've got a right to be excited."

"I don't know her either. I only met her at Jerry's the other night, but I've got the feeling that she's a keeper."

Bill smiled and asked him. "What are you going to do if Bobby comes to the door with a shotgun?"

"Oh, that's easy. I'll just say, "Sorry, I'm at the wrong house."

Bill laughed and said, "Stony, you're one of a kind; did you know that? We had better get to work."

Since the complex was going to consist of twelve eight-unit buildings, Jerry had decided that since all twelve buildings were laid out, he would go ahead and dig and pour the footings for all twelve at one time, rather than do two at a time the way he had done on Frank's other complexes. He planned to build four buildings at a time on this complex, and he thought by doing it that way, he could save Frank money in the long run. It didn't hurt that Stony was there to help, either.

He had ordered the excavators to come that morning, and the truck carrying the large excavator arrived about eight o'clock. After they unloaded the big machine, Bill showed them where to dig, and after they got started, he left Stony in charge from that point on. He was not at all uncomfortable leaving him in charge because in the short time Stony had been given more responsibilities, he had proven himself.

Thankfully, all twelve of the buildings had been laid out, so the excavator didn't have to slow down at all. When they finished one, they went to the next one, and by the end of the day, footings had been dug on seven of the twelve.

About three o'clock Jerry called to see how things were running, and Stony told him that it looked as if they were going to finish seven that day. Jerry was very pleased and told him that he was going to go ahead and order the concrete for the next morning. He told him, "I don't know how many they can pour in a day, but the way the excavator is going, he'll be through by the time the concrete people get to the ones he did today. How're you liking it, Stony?"

"I'm loving it. I can't wait until they start on the framing and other things. This is a dream."

"Good. I'm going to send Bill out in the morning to get the concrete people started, and then, you'll probably be by yourself again tomorrow. Do you have a problem with that?"

"No sir. I can handle it. Thank you for your confidence in me, Jerry."

Soon after the excavating guys left, Stony got his stuff together and left as well. He was really looking forward to later when he would be with Deena. He went home, showered, and put on clean clothes and grabbed a bite to eat. His parents were going to have a big meal, but it wasn't ready when he had to leave, so he just snacked on some cheese and crackers, and left so he wouldn't be late. He had never been to the

Kunkle's, but judging from the address he had for them, it was going to take thirty to forty-five minutes to get from his house to theirs.

When he got there, he went to the door and rang the bell. Bobby came to the door and Stony said, "Hi Bobby. I see you're unarmed. Bill said you might come to the door with a shotgun, and I'm glad you didn't. Is Deena ready?"

"Come in Stony." Kidding with him, he said, "I didn't bring my gun this time, but depending on how you treat my daughter tonight will tell me whether I will bring it next time."

About that time, Kitty walked in and said, "Hi Stony."

"Hi Kitty."

"Is Bobby giving you a hard time?"

Without missing a beat, he said, "I think he's just mad at me because I didn't dance with him at Jerry's the other night," and they all laughed. "Listen, we're going to the seven o'clock movie. Would you all like to go with us? I hear it's a good movie."

Stunned by the invitation, Kitty said, "That's so sweet of you to ask, but you two kids go and enjoy yourselves. We old people will stay here and rest. Maybe we can all do something another time."

"Did you say old people? You're not old. No old person could dance the way you can, and I've seen how Papa here can work. He can outwork most of the young guys, so don't say you're old."

"Thank you for that, Stony, but maybe we'll go another time."

He said, "Okay", and then he looked at Deena and asked, "Ready to go?"

"I'm ready."

They went to the movie, and after they got inside, and the movie was playing, they held hands, and that made Stony feel good. When it was over, he asked her, "Would you like to go somewhere and get something to eat?"

131

"If you would."

"How about a burger and shake or a burger and coke or something like that?"

"That sounds good. I got home too late to have dinner."

"Wow! How about we go somewhere and have a full dinner then?"

"No, no. A burger sounds just right."

"Okay. Sounds good to me, too."

They went to the Steak and Shake and got their food and sat there and talked for a long time. They both had questions about the other, and they felt comfortable with each other.

"How old are you, Deena?"

"Twenty-two. How old are you?"

"Twenty-three."

They continued to talk until almost eleven o'clock, and then Deena said, "We need to go, Stony. I've got to get up early in the morning."

"I do, too. Can I see you again?"

"I sure hope so."

"When?"

"Is tomorrow night too soon?"

He laughed and said, "I was hoping you'd say that. No. Tomorrow night is perfect."

When they got to Deena's, Stony walked her to the door and gave her a kiss on the cheek. He said, "Deena, I hope you have enjoyed tonight just half as much as I have. I can't wait 'til tomorrow night."

"Me neither. I really had fun."

"You be thinking about what you'd like to do tomorrow night. What time can I call you?"

"I get out of school at two o'clock tomorrow, so you can call me any time after that."

"Great, if I can, I'll call you a little after two, but just in case I can't, don't worry. I'll call you the minute I can. Jerry has given me a lot more responsibility, and I want to do him a good job, so I may be really busy until quitting time, but like I said, don't worry, I'll call. I'm not going to let you get away from me."

"Don't worry. I'm not going anywhere."

When she went into the house, Bobby and Kitty were already in bed, but she slipped into their bedroom and tapped Kitty on the shoulder. When she woke up, Deena motioned for her to get up. She got out of bed and went with her into the kitchen and asked, "Did you have a good time?"

"Oh Mama, I had the best time. We went to the movie and then to the Steak and Shake to get something to eat. Neither one of us ate before we left, so we were both kind of hungry. We ate and then just sat and talked. Mama, I like him so much. I know this is only the second time I've seen him and our first date, but you know what Mama? If he were to ask me to marry him right now, I'd say yes."

"Deena! Aren't you a little carried away?"

"No, Mama, I mean it. I don't know how strongly he feels about me, but I hope I can hold onto him. We're going out again tomorrow night."

"Did he kiss you?"

"On the cheek as he was getting ready to leave. He was a perfect gentleman. Oh, and we held hands in the movie."

"It sounds to me like Cupid was sharpening his arrows."

"I think he was. Mama, I really like him."

"I like him, too. He likes to call me Kitty Kunkle, and I get a kick out of the way he says it. Honey, this was your first date, so just play it cool and see what happens. If it's meant for things to happen, I'm sure God will let you know."

"Do you really mean that?"

"I mean it with every ounce of my being. You should pray about this, Deena."

"I'm going to. I'm sure I won't sleep tonight, so I will probably have plenty of time to pray."

When Stony got home, both of his parents were in bed, and

he hated that because he was every bit as excited over Deena as she was him. He didn't want to wake them, so he had to deal with his excitement by himself. One time, he almost picked up the phone and called her, and then he thought that if he did, he might wake her parents up, and he didn't want to do that, so he turned on the TV and laid in bed watching it until he finally drifted off.

Chapter Twelve

The next day was good. The excavators finished digging the footings for all the buildings in the complex, and the concrete people poured and finished the footings for six of them. They told Stony they would finish the next day, and since it took all day to do six that day, he looked for it to take the whole day the day after.

Bill went to the complex the day after and told Stony they could start building on the first four buildings while the concrete people finished the footings on the final six. Stony had been working as a carpenter ever since he started with Martin Builders and learned quite a bit in his college courses, but he had never started a building from the footings up, so he was excited about doing that. He had a thirst for learning and starting a building would certainly teach him something.

On Wednesday, he watched every move that Bill made and took mental notes of everything. They were starting on four buildings, so if he forgot something on the first or second one, he could pay close attention on the third and fourth ones and become adept on how to start a building by the time he got through the fourth one. His quick understanding was not lost on Bill.

They worked hard and Stony kept looking at his watch after they ate lunch, and when it got to two-thirty, he told Bill he was going to use the phone, but wouldn't be on it very long. He dialed DKUNKLE(358-6553), and she answered on the second ring. "Hey, Stony."

"Hey Pretty Lady. How are you?"

"I'm wonderful, now that I'm hearing your voice. How are you?"

"The same way. Do you still want to go out tonight?"

"Yeah. I can't wait. Where are we going?"

"Well, I thought we might go somewhere where they have good food and music. Have you ever been to Olivers?"

"No I haven't."

"I haven't either, but one of the guys that works with me said the food was real good, and they play a lot of slow music. That sounds good to me. Would you like to go there?"

"That sounds good to me, too. Are we going to eat there?"

"I thought we would unless you don't want to. I thought we could just make it a complete package."

I would love to go there, and yes, I want to eat there, too. What time?"

"How about I pick you up at seven o'clock? I don't think it's too far from where you live, so we could get there pretty early and eat and then have the rest of the night to dance and talk, that is, if you like to dance that much."

"I didn't used to be much on dancing, but I love to dance with you, Stony. I can hardly wait to go tonight. I'll be ready when you get here."

"Okay. I'll see you at seven. Listen, I've gotta go. See you tonight."

"Okay, Hon. I'll see you."

When he hung up, Stony thought, *did she call me Hon? Man, this might be better than I expected. I hope she meant it.* He went back to where Bill was, and Bill saw that his face was flushed.

"Is everything alright," he asked.

"Yeah, it's better than alright."

"Oh, okay. I won't ask what you're so happy about."

"I don't mind telling you. I had a date with Deena Kunkle last night, and it went so good that we're going out again tonight. Bill, I think she's a keeper."

"Well, if she's anything like her parents, she is."

"I can't wait to see her again."

"Boy, she sure must be something else."

"She is. Enough of this. We've got work to do."

Bill thought to himself, *boy, this kid is something else. Here he is telling me that we've got to get to work. I'm supposed to be the one to tell him that. Jerry's got a prize here. I just hope he sticks around.*

They worked until five o'clock and then took off. Some of the guys wanted to go to the neighborhood bar about a mile from the complex to get a beer, and they invited Bill and Stony, but Stony thanked them for the invitation, and told them he had to go. He promised to do it another time. Bill went with the guys, and explained that Stony was smitten with the love bug.

Stony went home and when he got there, his mother and daddy were both there. He got home late the night before and left before they got up that morning, and his mom was anxious to talk to him.

"What time did you get in last night?"

He said, "I think it was about eleven-thirty."

"Did you have a good time?"

"I had a wonderful time."

"Who did you go out with?"

"Do you remember meeting the Kunkles at Jerry's pig pickin?"

"Yes, I remember. That was that real pretty girl, wasn't it?"

"Yes ma'am. Her name is Deena, and that's who I was with, and I'm going out with her again tonight."

"You must really like her. You never have gone out with the same girl two nights in a row."

"I do. Mom, I think I'm going to marry her."

"You don't mean it. You've only had one date with her."

"Have you ever heard the saying, 'Love at first sight'? Well, this is that."

"You don't know anything about her."

"I know she comes from good stock. I've worked with her daddy for about seven or eight years, and I know that he and his wife, Kitty, are top notch people. They say the apple doesn't fall from the tree, so I'm sure Deena is a chip off both blocks. I'm anxious for you and dad to meet her."

"I'm anxious to meet her. Anybody that has got you so inside out, I want to see."

"What's today, Wednesday? Why don't you and dad and Deena and I go out to eat Friday night? Would you all like to do that?"

"I would, but you need to ask your daddy."

He said, "Dad, I want you and Mom to go to eat Friday night with me and my girl. Mom said she wanted to go, but I had to ask you. Will you go?"

"Where are we going?"

"I don't know. Some nice place where the food is good. I want you to meet my girl. Will you go?"

"I guess so. Now, I don't want to go to one of those places where you have to wear a tie."

"I don't either. I'll let you pick the place if you want to."

"Naw, I don't need to pick it. Anywhere you say will be fine."

"Does that mean you'll go?"

"Yeah, I'll go."

"Good. Look, I've got to go get ready. I'm supposed to pick Deena up at seven o'clock."

He was at the Kunkles almost exactly at seven, and as soon as he raised his hand to ring the doorbell, the door opened. He didn't even have to ring the bell. Bobby was the one to greet him that night, and he invited him to come in, which he did.

Bobby said, "Deena will be ready in a minute. Did you have a good day today?"

"Yeah, we started on four buildings in the apartment complex this morning."

"Who are you working with, Bill?"

"Yeah."

"Well, he's a good one. Pay attention to him, and you can learn an awful lot."

"I've already found that out."

Deena walked in and said, "Hi Stony."

"Hi Deena. Ready to go?"

"I am."

She took his hand, and they walked out the door. On the way to Oliver's, Stony said, "Before I get started talking and forget it, would you like to go out to eat with my parents Friday night?"

She looked at him with a huge smile and said, "You want me to meet your parents?"

He said, "Yeah, unless you'd rather not."

"Oh no, I'd love to meet them, and Friday night is perfect," and she thought, *it doesn't get any better than this. Stony wants me to meet his parents.*

They were shown to a table at Oliver's and immediately looked over the menu. They decided what they wanted and ordered their dinner. While they waited, they talked.

Stony asked, "Did you have a good day?"

"Yeah, it was really good. Did you?"

"Yeah, it was very busy, and I was thinking so much about going out with you again tonight, that the time flew by."

"That's so sweet."

"I didn't say it to be sweet. I meant it."

"It's still sweet."

"Deena, promise me that you won't get up and leave when I tell you what I'm going to tell you. Will you promise me?"

"For Heaven's sake, what could you say that would make me get up and leave?"

"Do you know what I told my mother before I left to pick you up tonight?"

"No, what?"

"I told her that I think I'm going to marry you."

Her mouth flew open, and for several seconds, she was speechless. "You told your Mom that?"

"I did. What do you think about that?"

"Well, before I answer you, let me tell you what I told my Mama last night."

He laughed and said, "You mean Kitty Kunkle?"

"Yeah, Kitty Kunkle. When you and I got home last night, she and daddy were in bed, and I woke her up and got her out of bed. We walked into the kitchen, and I told her that I know I haven't seen you but two times, but if you asked me to marry you, I would say yes. What do you think about that?"

He said, "I think we've got a situation here. A Good situation, but what do we do now?"

"Stony, do you think you love me?"

"I know I love you. I've never loved anybody before, but I love you after one date. What about you?"

"I love you, too. That's why I told that to Mama last night."

"Well, what are we going to do about it? I think we need to discuss our options before we make any rash decisions, don't you?"

"What do you mean?"

"Well, let's think for a minute. We both live with our parents, meaning neither one of us has a place of our own. You're still in school and without a job and knowing my parents the way I do and knowing your daddy the way I do, I don't think any of the four would be very happy if we got married right now."

"What do you suggest?"

"Here's what I suggest, but first, Deena, I love you and want to spend the rest of my life with you. Will you marry me?"

"I love you, too. Yes, I'll marry you."

"Good, now here's my suggestion. I've been talking about getting a place of my own for a good while, so why don't we look for a place for us and let our parents think it's my place. Secondly, I've got a fairly good job, and it's getting better, but I don't know if I make enough to support us the way we want to live, but you'll be graduating in six months, and the way the demand is for nurses, you'll be sure to get a job, and as you know, nurses make good money.

"Now, we want to get married, and I suggest we agree to marry, but I suggest we keep it quiet for a few months, maybe even until you graduate. Then we can announce it, and you and Kitty Kunkle can plan whatever kind of wedding you want. What do you think about that?"

"I think those are good ideas. Let's do it."

At that point, each one of them leaned across the table and kissed.

When they sat back down, she said, "Can I ask you something?"

"You know you can. What is it?"

"When we're married, are you still going to call my mother Kitty Kunkle?"

They both laughed, and he said, I don't know; I might. I love that name."

Their food finally came, and they quit talking and ate. Stony asked Deena, "Is your mother a nurse?"

"Yes, she is."

"I guess that's why you decided to become one isn't it?"

"Maybe it is. All I know is I've wanted to be one ever since I was a little girl."

They finished the delicious meal, but it was doubtful that either one even knew they had eaten. The waitress came and cleared their table and said the band would begin playing at nine o'clock, and it was only eight twenty.

Stony said, "Do you want to stay and wait for the band, or do you want to do something else?"

"Let's wait for the band. I want to dance with you so I can put my arms around you."

While they were waiting for the band, Stony asked, "Do you have any idea where you'd like to live when we look for a place?"

"Not really. I think we'll just have to look and find what we want in some nice section. I don't care where it is, if it's nice, and I'm with you. Do you have any particular area in mind?"

"No, anywhere is fine with me as long as the house or apartment is nice. Would you rather get a house or an apartment?"

"I think to start out, we should get an apartment, don't you?"

"Yeah, I do."

As they were talking about where they would like to live, the band cranked up with Elvira. Stony couldn't sit still, and he told Deena, "Let's dance, do you want to?"

"You know I'm not a very good dancer. Why don't we wait on a slow one?"

"Nonsense. You're a good dancer. Come on. Let's dance to this one, and maybe the next one will be slow."

"Okay, but just remember I told you so," and they walked out to the dance floor.

Stony had unbelievable moves and they were all over that dance floor. Deena thought back to when they were at Jerry's pig pickin, and sure enough, the next tune was a slow one, and they stayed out and danced to it. They really enjoyed the dance, and it seemed that they couldn't get close enough to each other. They danced a couple more and then returned to their table.

They talked and danced and danced and talked 'til about ten thirty, and then Deena asked, "Are you tired?"

"A little. It's been a hard day. Are you tired?"

"I really am. Would you mind if we left?"

"Honey, I want to do whatever you want to do. No, I don't mind if we leave."

They got up and left. Stony asked, "Do you want to do something else?"

"Not really. If you don't mind, I'd just like to go home."

"Then home it is." He thought for several seconds and then asked, "Are you all right?"

"Yeah. I'm just tired. I really had a good time tonight, and I didn't know I was going to get engaged. I love you, Stony."

"It was a new experience for both of us. I love you, too."

When they pulled up at her house, before they got out, Deena asked Stony, "Stony, you were serious about tonight weren't you? You're not going to go out with me for a while and then leave, are you?"

"I can't believe you asked me that. I absolutely am serious, but I think that what we said about waiting is the best thing. I love you so much. I wish we didn't have to wait, but I know it's the best thing. I wish I could get you a ring, but if I do, everybody will know what we're going to do."

"I don't need a ring. All I need is you and your word."

"Honey, you've got both. Listen, I want to say something, and I don't know how to say it."

"What is it? You're scaring me."

"It's nothing to be scared about, but it's something I feel strongly about, and that is I don't want us to be intimate until we're married. Does that bother you?"

"No, because that's the way I want it too. You're unusual because most guys would want to go to bed as soon as possible. I'm surprised at you. Where did you get your morals?"

"Well, first of all, that's what I was taught in Church, and then, I got pretty close to Jerry Martin, and we had a lot of serious talks. Of course, he doesn't know about you and me, but he taught me that a person should practice good morals, and it will pay off in the long run."

"Remind me to thank Jerry sometime will you?"

"I will after we're married."

"Deena, do you all go to Church?"

"Yeah, I was raised in Church, and Daddy is a deacon in ours."

143

"Good. Are you a Christian?"

"I have been since I was thirteen."

"Are you?"

"I am now. I wasn't until I started working for Jerry, and he introduced me to Jesus. Now, do you see why I think so much of him?"

"Yeah. Boy, that's something."

As they were getting out of the car, Stony asked, "What do you want to do tomorrow night?"

"Why don't you just come over here, and we'll stay home. You don't have to take me somewhere every night. Would that suit you?"

"It absolutely would, but what will your Mom and Dad say about having someone in the house for two or three hours?"

"They won't say anything. They'll be in the den, and you and I can stay in the living room. If you don't mind, let's do that."

"Okay, we'll do it."

They kissed and Stony said, I'll see you the future Mrs. Gray, and he left to go home. As he was walking to his car, he turned around and said, "You know, Deena Gray has a nice ring to it."

She said, "I can't wait. Good night."

The next morning, Stony was just as happy as he was the morning before, and Bill said, "Well, it looks as if you had another encounter with Miss Deena again last night."

"Yeah, I did."

Bill began to kid him when Jerry drove up. "Hi guys, what's happening?"

"Well, it looks like our friend here is in love."

Jerry said, "You don't mean it."

"Yep. He has flown into work the past two mornings. I don't think his feet have touched the ground."

Jerry asked, "Who's the lucky lady?"

Bill said, "Bobby Kunkle's daughter."

"Deena? Sure enough? Boy, she's a looker, and I understand she's a really good girl. How did you luck into that, Stony?"

Stony grinned and said, "I guess when you've got it, you've got it."

Jerry laughed and said, "I guess. Are you going to see her again?"

"I'm going over to her house tonight."

"Stony, I'm happy for you. You're what now, twenty two, twenty three? It's time you found yourself a nice girl. I hope you all continue to see each other. You all are a good match."

"I think so, too. I'm going to keep seeing her as long as she can stand me."

"Atta boy.

Just then, one of the workers called Stony, and he said, "Excuse me, Jerry. I'll be right back."

"You go ahead. Don't let me hold up production."

When he went to see what the worker wanted, Bill said, "Did you notice that, Jerry?"

"Notice what?"

"Jack called for Stony instead of me."

"He did, didn't he? I guess I didn't notice it. That's good, isn't it Bill?"

"I'd say it's very good. Stony's only been out here a few days, and the employees are already calling for him. To me, that shows they respect him. I'll tell you something, Jerry. You've got a winner in him."

"Do you remember when we first met Stony?"

"Yeah, I do, but you know what? He wasn't any worse than most of the other kids his age. He just got caught, and he acted like a man and worked to pay off his sentence. I'll tell you something else, Jerry. I hope Bobby Kunkle doesn't hold that against him, with his dating his daughter and everything."

"I don't think he will. Bobby and I have talked about Stony before, and he doesn't seem to hold anything in his past against him."

"Yeah, but when he's dating his daughter, it might be different."

"I hope not. Listen, the reason I came out here instead to going to the Chrisman House is to tell you that it looks as if we're going to be able to start on the new neighborhood project earlier than expected, and I might have to pull you off this job to go out there and lay out the houses."

"Of course, I'll do whatever you say, Jerry, but the way Stony handled the Lay Out Pro on this project, he might be the best one to lay those houses out."

"Do you really think so?"

"I definitely do. He'll have those houses laid out before you can turn around."

"I'll think about it. I don't have the surveyor's stuff back yet, so we don't know where the roads will be or anything else for that matter, but this will be a big deal, and the minute we get some of these details, we want to start laying out houses. It looks as though there's going to be about eighty."

Bill asked, "How are you coming on the Chrisman House?"

"I think we'll be finished sometime next week. You should drive out and see it when you can. It's beautiful."

"Has Mr. Thomas decided yet what he's going to do with it?"

"I don't think he knows. Until he decides for sure, he'll probably just rent it out for conventions and weddings and things like that. He would like to move in it, but he's having a hard time getting his wife to agree to it, so it'll probably just sit there most of the time."

"That's a shame to have something like that and not know what you want to do with it."

"I know, but maybe when you have so much, nothing is really a treasure to you. I don't know how well you know Frank, but he's one of the most down to earth people I know. If you didn't know him, you'd never know that he's so wealthy. He would be at home with any one of these guys working out here, and he would be equally at home with the President of the United States or the Pope. You just don't find many people like that."

As they were talking, Stony interrupted them with a question for Bill. It was a pretty technical question, and Bill explained the answer. "Thanks, Bill."

He left them and went back to what he was doing, and Bill told Jerry, "You saw how technical that was, Jerry. Well, I guarantee you he will remember it and not have to ask again."

Jerry didn't comment on Bill's statement, but he stored it in his mind and asked Bill, "Do you really think he should lay out the houses in the new development?"

"Yeah, I do. You won't find anybody that will be as efficient as he."

"Except you," Jerry said.

"No, including me. He's what some would call a whiz."

"That's good to know. I'll keep it in mind, except I hate to move him off these apartments because he was so excited about being the assistant foreman."

"Maybe you can make him assistant foreman on the development. Who's going to be your foreman over there?"

"I've thought about Bobby when he finishes White Rock. I guess I'll be the foreman until then."

Bill asked, "Where are you going to put me when we finish these apartments?"

"I don't know for sure. I feel like Frank will want to go right into building another complex when this one is finished, and I'd like to keep you on them. If he doesn't want to start another one, then you might have to go to the development."

"Can I make a suggestion, Jerry?"

"Of course, what is it?"

"I know he's young and relatively inexperienced, but if you count all the time he's worked for you, he has gained experience, and I wouldn't be afraid to make Stony foreman.

147

He's smart, he gets along well with people, and he's a really hard worker. If he worked for me, that's what I'd do. You've heard of child prodigies? Well he's not a child, but I think he's a prodigy. I heard that you're going to build eight or ten houses at one time over there, and in my opinion, that's a lot for one man to oversee, so I suggest you think about it."

"I will. Thanks Bill. I need to get out to the Chrisman House. I'll think about what you said, and I'll talk you more about it later."

"Okay, have a good day, Boss."

Before he left he went down to see Stony. He asked, "Are you catching on to this job pretty well, Stony?"

"I think I am, but I'm not the one to ask. You need to ask Bill."

"I did, and he says you're doing a good job. Keep it up. I'll see you later."

"See you, Mr. Mar..,uh Jerry."

Jerry smiled and said, "You almost forgot, didn't you?"

"Yes sir, I did."

"Okay, I'll see you," and he left for the Chrisman House.

Every time he went there he was bowled over by the beauty of the place. Just about everything had been done in the renovation except for the landscaping and some minor tweaking inside. They might even finish it that week instead of the following one.

He stayed at the Chrisman until a little after lunch, and then he went out to the Cummings place to drive over his land and visualize what was going to happen out there. He tried to visualize the streets and fences and the swimming pool and tennis courts. He thought about the lake he was going to build and all the other things he wanted to do. He even dared to think about something that might not ever happen. He thought that if Clarence liked the way the development turned out, he might even sell him some additional land.

Chapter Thirteen

He got so excited driving and visualizing that he thought he would call the surveyors when he got back to the office to see if he could jack them up a little. He had asked Tracy to try to come up with a name for the development, but she hadn't said anything since he asked her to do it, so he made up his mind that if she hadn't come up with a name when he got home, he would name it himself. He had been thinking that 'CUMMINGS ACRES' would be a good name, and if Tracy didn't have something better, he would use that. It was time to have a sign made to post at the entrance, and the name of the development would need to be on it.

Jerry always prayed each morning and night and at other times as well, and that particular day, he was so thankful that everything was going so well, he pulled off the road on his way back to thank God for all His blessings. He then pulled back onto the road and headed to his office.

The men at the apartment complex all knocked off at five o'clock, and before he left the site, Stony called Deena. She answered, "Hi, I was wondering when you were going to call. You must have been busy."

"I have been. This is the first chance I've had to use the phone. How are you?"

"I'm fine. Are you coming over tonight?"

"Are you sure it's alright with your parents? I don't want to get on Bobby's bad side."

"No. It's fine. I told them you were coming over and they both said it's fine. What time can you get here?"

"I'm not sure. I know my mother is cooking, so I probably should eat before I leave. Is that alright?"

"Of course it is. I'm just anxious to see you. Hurry all you can. I love you."

"Love you, too. Let me go so I can get started home. I'm still at the building site."

"Okay, I can't wait to see you."

Jerry left his office at five, as well. Beverly and her two office girls were running behind on something, so he left before they did.

He went home, and Tracy met him at the door with B.J. right at her side. He hugged B.J. first and then Tracy. He asked, "How about a Margarita?"

"Sounds good. Let's have one," so he fixed a pitcher full, so they could have two if they wanted 'em.

"How was your day," he asked?"

"Fine, guess who came out here today?"

"I don't know; who?"

"Wendy. She hasn't been out here in forever. It sure was good to have her. We went to the 129 Café for lunch."

"Did she like it?"

"She loved it."

"Honey, I went out to the land where we're going to build the new development this afternoon, and I was wondering if you've come up with a name yet. Have you?"

"No, I've racked my brain trying to think of a neat name, but every time I think I've got one, I decide I don't like it."

"What do you think about this? Since I bought the land from Mr. and Mrs. Cummings, what do think of the name 'Cummings Acres'?

"I like it. Why didn't I think of that? It's simple and not flashy. For a development with that much class, it doesn't need a flashy name."

While they were on their second Margarita, Tracy put dinner on the table and they sat down to eat. She had fixed a wonderful dinner, but all B.J. wanted was macaroni and cheese.

About the same time they were eating, Stony was eating with his parents and anxious to get over to Deena's. He told them that he was going to begin looking for an apartment on the weekend, since he was twenty three years old. He thought it was high time that he got out on his own.

As he finished and got up to leave, he told his mother that dinner was delicious and for them not to forget that they were going out with him and his girl the next night. He kissed his mother on the cheek and said, "Bye, I love you. Bye Dad, I love you."

He timed himself from the minute he left his parent's driveway to the minute he pulled into Bobby Kunkle's, and it was thirty-eight minutes. He thought, *one day I won't have to miss thirty-eight minutes seeing Deena. I need to find someplace closer."*

He got out of the car and went up to the door, and that time, Deena answered it. He looked around and didn't see anybody, so he gave her a quick kiss on the lips. She said, "Come in. Have you eaten?"

"Yeah, I ate at home."

"Well, come in and speak to Mama and Daddy," and they went into the den where Kitty and Bobby were sitting in front of the TV.

"Hi folks," he said, and they both acknowledge him and spoke. Bobby said, "Did you keep Bill straight today?"

Joking, Stony said, "Yeah, I had to get after him a couple of times for not working, but overall, he did pretty good. I think I'm going to keep him."

Deena said, "Come on Stony. There's a TV in the living room. Let's go in there and watch that one and leave the elderly in here."

Kitty said, "I heard that."

Stony said, "I didn't say it, Kitty Kunkle," and she burst out laughing.

Every time Stony was around her, he kept her smiling or laughing, and she smiled and said, "I know you wouldn't say anything like that, Stony. You're too much of a gentleman."

He smiled back and said, "I know I am. You're right about that."

They went into the living room and Deena turned on the TV, then she sat down next to Stony on the sofa across from it. They held hands while sitting there, and they talked about different things. At one point, Stony said, I think I'm going to look for an apartment Saturday. Do you want to go?"

"Yeah, I do. Is this going to be for you or for us?"

"I hope it will be for us. Do you have any furniture?"

"Not a stick. Do you?"

"No. I guess that will be the next thing to look for."

Deena asked, "Do you have any money saved?"

"A little. I've been trying to save some out of each paycheck, but I haven't worked enough to save a whole lot. I'm doing pretty good now, and I should be able to save a good bit."

"I wonder what we'll have to pay for rent?" she asked.

"I don't know. I wish we could get one of the apartments that I'm working on, but I'm sure they're too high."

"Why don't you just casually ask how much they are?"

"I don't know if anybody at our company would know. They belong to Mr. Frank Thomas or as I call him, Uncle Frank."

"What do you mean, Uncle Frank? You call him Uncle Frank? Why?"

"Because his son, Reed, is like my brother. When I was in school, I spent as much time at their house as I did mine. I was just like his other son."

"Every time I'm with you, I learn something different about you. I bet Jerry would know how much the apartments rent for. Why don't you ask him?"

"Okay, I will, but you know something, Honey? With just my income, I don't know how much I can afford. When you start working, we can get a whole lot nicer place. Maybe, I ought not to look for one yet because I want us to have a nice one. You know, the ones I'm working on are supposed to be extra nice and they won't be finished until after you get out of school, so maybe we can get one. When do you want to get married? Pretty soon after you graduate or are you going to take a long time to plan?"

"You know what, Stony? We said we would keep it a secret until I graduated, but I don't think we'll have to do that. We can tell people that we're going to get married in two or three months. We can still wait until after I graduate to marry, but I don't think we should have to wait that long just to tell it, do you?"

"That's a great idea. No, I don't think we have to. Three months is a whole lot better than six months, and that will let us start looking for deals on furniture and other things that we're going to have to have. Do you have any idea what you'll be making when you get a job?"

"According to the latest information I heard at school is that the current salary for a registered nurse is sixty-eight thousand dollars a year. That's more than five thousand dollars a month."

"Wow! That's great. That, with what I make will make it possible to live in a real nice place. Have you seen any of the apartments that Martin Builders has built for Uncle Frank?"

"I think Daddy worked on some of them. I don't know if I have seen any of them after they were finished."

"Why don't I find out where some of them are, and lets you and I go see some of them Saturday. Do you want to?"

"Yeah, I'd like that."

Stony heard something and turned around, but it was nothing. He asked Deena, "Do you think your Mom and Dad can hear us?"

"I don't think so, but maybe we had better talk a little lower."

Every time a commercial came on they would kiss, and it got to be funny. They didn't realize it until one time when one came on, Stony said, "Well, here's a commercial. Give me a kiss. They laughed about that and decided that that would be when they would kiss every time. They had a good time that night, and about ten or ten thirty, Stony said, "I guess I had better go. It's getting late. He kissed her one more time and got up to leave. He told Deena that he wanted to tell her parents goodnight, but when they got into the den, they had both gone to bed.

As he was leaving he said, "Don't forget that we're taking my parents out to eat tomorrow night. I'll have to call you tomorrow afternoon with all the particulars."

"Okay. I had a good time tonight. I love you."

"I love you more. I'll see you tomorrow night."

"There's no way you love me more. Give me one more kiss."

He kissed her, and she responded with an extra amount of passion. When they broke away she said, "See?"

Everyone was always glad to see Friday come. It was payday, the end of the work-week, and the beginning of the weekend, but that Friday had even more meaning to Stony. He was going to introduce his girlfriend to his parents that night, and he could hardly wait.

He always seemed happy, and that day he was overly so. When Bill arrived, he said, "Hi Stony," and Stony replied, "Good morning Bill."

"Did you have a date with Deena last night?"

"If you want to call it a date. I went over to her house and we stayed there the whole night."

"Are you going back tonight?"

"Tonight, I'm going to introduce her to my parents, and we're going to take them out to eat. Have you got any suggestions where we could take them?"

"What kind of food does your parent's like?"

"They like Mexican a lot."

"Then I suggest you take them to Tlaquepaque's. The food

is good, and it's very reasonable."

"That's where we'll go then. Thanks."

Friday morning was very productive, but it began to rain about eleven o'clock and turned into a downpour a little later. It settled in to a steady rain, and all the guys ran for their cars and sat, waiting for the rain let up, but it didn't let up. Stony got into Bill's car with him, and after several minutes, Bill saw that they wouldn't be able to work, so he gave them their checks and let everybody go home.

That suited Stony just fine because he would have the afternoon to plan out the evening with Deena and his parents. He didn't know what time she would get out of school, but he thought that surely, she would be out by three o'clock, so he waited until then and called.

She answered, "Hi."

"Hi. Did you have a good day?

"Yeah, did you?"

"Yeah, except it rained, and we only got to work until a little after eleven. Are we still taking my parents out tonight?"

"I guess so, but I'm a little nervous."

"You certainly don't have to be nervous around my parents. They're just plain folks, and you'll feel perfectly at ease around them. Do you like Mexican food?"

"I love it. It's about my favorite."

"Have you ever been to Tlaquepaque's?"

"Yeah. It's good."

"That's where Bill suggested we go, so if it's alright with you, that's where we'll go. I'm going to see if Mom and Dad will meet us there, and that will save us a lot of driving."

"Okay, whatever you say. What time are you going to pick me up?"

"How far is the restaurant from your house?"

"About fifteen minutes. It's not far at all."

"I'm going to tell Mom and Dad to meet us at seven o'clock, so I'll get you about a quarter 'til."

155

"Okay, I'll see you then. Love you."

"Love you."

Everything went smoothly that evening. Stony's parents, Nancy and Harold liked Deena a lot, and she really was glad to meet them. She thought that she and Nancy would become good friends as time went on.

They stayed at the restaurant and talked for a long time after they ate, and after they pretty much ran out of things to talk about, Harold said, "Nancy, I think we need to go."

"Okay. Deena it was really nice meeting you, and I hope we'll see each other again." She looked at Stony and said, "Son, bring her out to the house sometime," and he said, "I will."

Deena said, "It was nice meeting you, too."

Stony picked up the check and said, "My treat," and Harold said, "Thank you, Son."

They all walked to the parking lot together and got into their cars. As Nancy and Harold were pulling out, Stony said to Deena, "There go your future in-laws."

"I really do like 'em, Stony."

"I could tell my mom likes you or she never would have told me to bring you out to the house, so I think the night was a success."

He took her home, and they sat in the car for a few minutes before they got out. Stony walked her to the door and said, "Do you still want to go look at some of Uncle Frank's apartments tomorrow/"

"Yeah. I'm excited about maybe getting one."

"How about I pick you up around eleven, in the morning?"

"That will be fine. Give me a kiss and I'll let you go home."

He kissed her and said, "I'll see you in the morning. Love you."

Chapter Fourteen

Tracy usually had a hard time getting B.J. up to go to kindergarten in the mornings, and so she and Jerry thought they would sleep in Saturday, but as luck would have it, little B.J. was up at six-thirty and in their bed, right in the middle of them.

They soon got up and Jerry fixed a pot of coffee, and Tracy fixed some cereal for B.J.. They just lounged around for a good while, and about ten o'clock the phone rang. Jerry answered it, and it was Frank. "Good morning, Jer, how're you this fine morning?"

"I'm good, Frank. I hope you are."

"I'm great this morning. Look, I just called to see if we're still on for the Atlanta Athletic Club tonight."

"Yeah boy. I'm looking forward to it. What time?"

"Is seven-thirty alright?"

"It's perfect. We'll see you there."

"Okay Pal. I'll see you. You have a good day."

Jerry reminded Tracy that they were supposed to meet Frank and Marilyn for dinner, and she said she would have to call the baby sitter and tell her what time. They had a sixteen year old girl baby sit for them, and she drove her own car, which helped a lot."

The Atlanta Athletic Club was a very exclusive place and most people dressed up when they went there. Jerry put on a pretty pair of slacks and a very nice sport coat with a nice shirt and pretty tie. Tracy looked amazing. Jerry even washed Tracy's car, which is what they drove.

Frank and Marilyn were there, waiting, when they got there. Frank told the Maitre d' they were ready, and he showed them to their table. A waiter came for their drink order, and Jerry and Tracy both ordered Margaritas, and Frank and

Bud Fussell

Marilyn ordered Vodka Gimlets.

Jerry told Frank, "I think we'll be through with the Chrisman House early next week. You should come out and see it as soon as you can. It's beautiful."

"I'll definitely do that; maybe Wednesday."

"Marilyn, you should go out, too."

Marilyn asked Tracy, "Tracy, would you go out there with me? I'm not sure I can find it."

"Yeah, I'd love to see it. Jerry has talked so much about it. I can't imagine what it looks like. Just call me."

In a little bit, they finished their drinks and the waiter asked if they wanted another, and Frank said yes. While they waited for their second round of drinks, someone brought menus to them. Frank said, "Jerry, Tracy, you can order anything you want, but I strongly recommend the filet mignon. It's outstanding."

Jerry said, "Thank you. That's what I'll have," and Tracy said, "Me too."

Soon, the drinks arrived, and the waiter wanted to know if they were ready to order. Frank said, "Yes, we're ready. I think we're going to have four filet mignons. How do you folks want yours cooked? Tracy? "Medium," Marilyn? "Rare," Jerry? "Medium Rare," and Frank said, "I'll have mine Medium Rare."

The waiter thanked them for their order and left the table.

While they were sipping on their drinks, Frank said, "Jerry, I'm so glad to have you and Tracy with us tonight. There are two reasons why I invited you this particular night. First is to thank you for what you did at the Chrisman House the other day, and especially for saving Melissa's life.

Before he could go on, Tracy interrupted and said, "You saved Melissa's life?"

Frank answered for Jerry. "Jerry, didn't you tell Tracy what happened at the Chrisman House last week?"

"I told her most of it. I must have left out part of it."

158

Frank continued, "I guess he told you about J.D. Tabor going out to the mansion and trying to kill Cliff Jackson and Melissa."

"No, I didn't hear that part, either."

"Shame on you, Jerry, for not telling that part of the story. Tracy, J.D. went out there with the intention of killing Melissa and Cliff before they could find Natalie Coleman's diary. He shot Cliff, and Melissa ran into house and down to the basement, and he followed her down there. It was dark, and Melissa found a board to use as a weapon. When J.D. got close enough to her, she hit him with the board, stunning him, and she ran up the stairs and wedged the board under the doorknob. He couldn't get the door open, so he went back down to the basement and found the dumbwaiter frame, and he was able to climb up the frame to where Melissa was. He had the gun in his hand, and he held it on her.

"Jerry had driven up the road to call the police to tell them that Melissa had found Natalie's diary, and when he got back, he saw Cliff lying on the ground with a gunshot wound. Cliff was conscience, and he told him that J.D. and Melissa were in the house, and J.D. had a gun, so he went in. When he got in the house, he heard them talking, so he knew where they were, and he slipped in to where they were. J.D. was still standing on the dumbwaiter frame, holding the gun on Melissa, and in a minute, he raised the gun to shoot her, and that's when Jerry lunged and knocked the gun out of his hand, causing him to fall back down to the basement. The police came and arrested him, and now, as Paul Harvey used to say, you know the rest of the story."

Tracy had a mixture of emotions; she was happy that Jerry was alright, happy that Melissa was okay, too, and mad at him for not telling her about it."

"Honey, why didn't you tell me all this?"

"Well, I told you most of it."

"You could have been killed. Did you think about that?"

"Not until it was all over."

"Well, I'm very proud of you for saving Melissa." She looked over at Marilyn and said, "Men."

After that, Frank took over again. "Ladies I told the police Lieutenant that God put a special man on this earth when he put Jerry here, and I meant that. I told you I invited you tonight for two reasons. We just finished the first one, and now for number two. Jerry, did you know J.C. Newcomb?

"He's your partner, isn't he? I've heard a lot about him, but I don't know him."

"Well, he passed away last month, and his wife doesn't want to continue on with the partnership. Jerry, I'd like to have you as my partner, if you're interested."

"Am I interested? Wow!! Frank, I don't know what to say. Are you sure you want me?"

"I'm sure. When J.C. was alive, I knew I could trust him with everything I had, even my life if I had to, and I feel that way about you. The first time we met, you were already trying to help my family, and I didn't have any idea who you were. You convinced the judge to assign my boy to you so you could keep him from going to jail, and you have no idea how much that has meant to Marilyn and me. You did the same for Stony, who is like our own son, and that little girl, even though she had such a bad attitude. I give you credit for making all three of them, upstanding citizens.

That day when you came to my office to try to convince me to give you the loan for your White Rock development was a turning point. I knew I wanted to repay you in some way, and when you masterfully laid out your plans and the payback, I knew that was a way to do it. Your help with Reed certainly didn't hurt your chances to get the money, but being what some people call a tough banker, I could see the possibilities, and you exceeded what you said you would do. And then, there are the apartments and the mall. If you'll think back, you were too small to do a project as large as the mall, but you proved yourself when you built my apartments, and I had faith in you, and I knew you could do it. You have been totally honest with me in everything you have done, and I hope you'll agree to become my partner."

"Frank, if you've got that much confidence in me, then I'm in. You have never steered me in the wrong direction, and I have no reason to think you will now. A partnership is new to me, so you'll have to help me get started. When will I start and what do I do"

"You'll continue doing exactly what you're doing now, except you'll have more responsibility on your plate. I would like for you to start by becoming my partner on the ninety-six units that you're building now."

"How do I do that?"

"I'll have partnership papers drawn up, and your first transaction will be to assume J.C.'s share of the loan on the apartments and the land. If you can, come by the bank Monday morning, and we'll get started."

"I'll be there.

That just about wound up the night. Jerry said, "Folks, tonight has been one of the highlights of my whole life, and I don't know what to say except thank you. It seems as if there should be a better way to say it, but I don't know what it is. Frank, please know that I won't let you down. I'm going to make you the best partner you could ever have."

Frank smiled and said, "This is going to sound funny, but I know you won't, and I know you will."

They all laughed about that. The waiter brought the check, and when Frank signed it, he asked, "Is everybody ready?"

They all got up and started out to the parking lot. Frank hugged Tracy, and she said, "Thank you and thank you for a delicious dinner."

Jerry hugged Marilyn, and said, "This has been a wonderful evening. You have a great guy there. We need to get together more often."

She said, "I know we do. We'll try to do that."

On the way home, Jerry asked, Well, what did you think of tonight?"

"It was great, and it was also a night of surprises."

"You're right about that. Man, I was bowled over when Frank asked me to be his partner. Do you realize how big that is?"

"Probably not, but I know it's big. The main surprise for me was when he said you saved Melissa's life. Why didn't you tell me about that?"

"I told you everything else, but you seem to have such a thing about her, I just figured it would be better if I skipped that part."

"Just know how proud I am of you."

"Thank you."

Jerry was so keyed up when he got home, he made a Margarita to relax. Tracy didn't want one, and she went on to bed. He sat in his recliner thinking about the partnership that Frank offered him. The more he thought about it, the more he was convinced that he would become a wealthy man because Frank didn't go into anything that didn't make a lot of money. He thought about the ninety-six unit apartment complex that he was building and would be a partner in it come Monday morning. He didn't know how much his part of the loan was, and he didn't know how much the rent would be on each unit, but he guessed that each unit would probably bring in about twelve hundred dollars a month, and if that's multiplied by ninety-six, a hundred and fifteen thousand dollars would come in each month. Multiply that by twelve, and that equals almost a million and a half per year.

He thought, *I don't know how Frank handles the money, but I know that if we split half the rental income, we'll get almost three hundred and fifty thousand each per year, and that'll still let us pay back almost three quarter of a million dollars on the loan. It's going to be interesting to see how he handles all that money. Ever how he handles it is alright with me because I know he always comes out on top when it comes to finances.*

When he ran out of things to think about, he finished his Margarita and went to bed.

Sunday was a great day. It was raining, and that made the perfect afternoon for Jerry. He loved rainy Sunday afternoons because he could just lay around and nap and watch the ball game without feeling guilty for not doing anything. He, Tracy, and B.J. went to Sunday School and Church where he told people about the good fortune he was having without going into detail, and then went home to get started on his lazy day.

A large part of his awake time that Sunday was spent thanking God for all His blessings. While he was lying on the sofa he thought, *I think I'll call Monty Shepherd tomorrow after my meeting with Frank. I've got several things to add to my story, and I'd like to tell people about them. If he wants me to go to some college with him, I might ask him if we can take Stony with us. He's about the same age as the college students, and although he may not know it, he has a story to* tell, *and he should be able to relate to the students.*

It poured rain most of the night, Sunday night, but when he woke up Monday morning, the sun was coming up, and there wasn't a cloud in the sky. He thought, *what a beautiful day. This is going to be a cracker jack week.*

Frank didn't tell him a time to be at the bank, so he got there at nine o'clock, hoping he could see him then. As luck would have it, when he got to Frank's office, Sandra sent him right in. "How about a cup of coffee?"

"I'd love one."

He yelled to Sandra in the outer office and said, "Sandra, would you take this carafe and bring it back full for Jerry and I. We may be in here for a while. You take sweetener, don't you, Jerry?"

"Yeah, but I can drink it black if you don't have any."

"We have plenty. Bring Jerry some sweetener, will you, Sandra?"

While they waited on Sandra to return with the coffee, Frank asked, "Did you think any about what we talked about Saturday night?"

"That's about all I've thought about since I left you Saturday night. I was so excited, I almost never went to sleep Saturday night. Frank, I can't tell you how much this means to Tracy and I."

"Jer, I know we're going to make a great team. With your expertise in construction and handling people and your level headed common sense, and my knowledge of finance, I don't know how anybody can beat us. I'm thrilled that you agreed to become my partner."

"Thank you, Frank."

"Now, I'm having Melissa type up some partnership papers, and she should have them in just a few minutes, and after you sign the partnership papers, I'll need you to sign notes, assuming J.C. Newcomb's part in the purchase of the apartment property and the construction costs. You and I will be equal partners in the apartments."

"Equal partners? I had no idea we'd be equal partners. I thought you would be bringing me in sort of like a junior partner."

"I don't do junior partners. If I'm going to have a partner, I want a full partner. Occasionally, in some things, I might want a larger percentage, but in something like this, I think fifty fifty is the only way to go.

They talked about some other things for a few minutes, and then Melissa brought the papers in and handed them to Frank. He looked at them and handed one copy to Jerry and said, "Look these over, Jerry, and if there's something you don't agree with, we'll take a look at it. This is a standard partnership contract, so there's nothing outside the box in it. Mostly, it has our names and the percentages of ownership for each one of us, and that's about it, but look it over, and if you agree with what's in it, sign it, and I'll sign it, and that'll do it."

When he saw the name, THOMAS-MARTIN PROPERTIES, he said, "Frank, I didn't know you were going to put my name on it."

And Frank said, "Well, you're a partner, and your name needs to be there. Is that alright?"

He read it and signed it, and Frank signed it, and then Frank asked, Do you have any questions, Jerry?"

And Jerry said, "Yeah, I have one."

Frank said, "Shoot."

"I'm going to be signing notes transferring J.C.'s debt to me, and I'm wondering how we get paid back for any of that after the apartments are finished."

"That's a good question, Jerry. You'll be signing notes in a few minutes, and you'll see that the due date is ninety days from the time you sign them. We are making changes in my notes to make them come due on the same date that yours will come due.

J. C. and I have had a gentleman's agreement that we would draw out one third of the income and pay back two thirds until the note is paid off. This withdrawal takes place on the date that the note is due. We then renew the note and start over. Understood?"

"I understand," and then Jerry, trying to be cute askes, "Are you sure your banker will renew it?"

Frank smiled and said, "Well, he has so far. Let me give you an example." He reached for his little calculator and said, "Let's say that all ninety-six apartments rent for twelve hundred dollars each. That would be almost a million four. Divide that by four, and that would give you almost three hundred and fifty thousand dollars every three months. Two thirds of three hundred and fifty thousand gives you two hundred and thirty thousand to be paid against the note. That leaves a hundred and fifteen thousand dollars for you and I to split every ninety days. No matter how you cut it, that's pretty good money. Now, these figures are just examples. They are not totally right because I left out the expenses for maintenance and vacancies, which amount to eleven percent, but after the notes are paid off, we make some good money, don't you think?"

"I'd say. Man!"

Frank continued. "Now, when we find a piece of land that is suitable for an apartment complex, we know what it costs, and that's what one of the notes you'll be signing covers. The other note is dedicated to Martin Builders' costs. As you know, when I tell you what we want to build, you give me an estimate of the total cost of the project. I normally add ten percent to that for contingencies, and that's what the other note is for. We usually pay the same amount against each note, and then when the smallest one is paid off, the amount that has been paid on it before goes to pay against the remaining one. When they're both paid off, you and I get to keep the whole amount less the maintenance fund. Any more questions?"

"No, but I'm sure I'll have some after I leave."

"If you do, call me, but you probably understand everything. This isn't rocket science. You find some land, borrow some money, build something, and rent it out. You pay back the money and keep what's left."

"You make it sound simple."

"It is simple. You're going to have a good time."

"Oh, there is one question."

"Okay, shoot."

"When the complex we're working on now is finished, are you planning more?"

"As a matter of fact, I am, or I should say, we are. J.C. and I talked about at least three more after the ninety-six units are completed, and we'd like for all of them to be ninety six units or larger, maybe a hundred and twenty units. We don't have any land yet, so when you're out and around, if you see any that you think would be suitable, let me know, and we'll take a look at it."

At that point, Melissa came in with the notes, and when he saw the amounts on them, he whistled, and he said, "Frank, one time a man came into my office and said Jerry, I've got it made. I asked him how did he have it made, and he said, I owe a million dollars. You know, last week I borrowed a million dollars to buy the Cummings land, and right now, I'm borrowing a lot more than that, so if he was right, I've must really have it made."

Frank said, "I'd say you've got it made."

They talked for a few more minutes, and Jerry said, "Well, folks, I need to run. I've got an antebellum mansion to finish and some houses and apartments to build. I'll see you later, and Frank, thank you again."

When he got to his truck, he got in and bowed his head. He said, *"Father, thank you so much for all your blessings. You're such a good God. I know I don't deserve any of these things, but through Your grace, You give them to me anyway. Thank you so much Father. I'll be sure You get the praise. I make this prayer in Jesus' name. Amen."*

He left the bank and went to his office. When he got inside his office, he called Beverly to come in there. When she got in there, he smiled and said, "Well, you will probably want to treat me with more reverence now."

"Why?"

"Because I am now an equal partner with Frank Thomas."

"Really? Well congratulations. What are you his partner in?"

"Right now, in the apartments we're building and in future apartments, and who knows what else."

"Should I ask you for your autograph?"

"You'll probably want one before we're through."

They both laughed and kidded around some, and then she

167

said, "Seriously, Jerry, congratulations. You deserve it."

"Thank you, Bev."

After Beverly went back to her desk, Jerry called Tracy, and when she answered he said, "Well, you're now talking to the Martin in Thomas – Martin Properties. What do you think about that?"

"I think it's wonderful. You all got everything done, did you?"

"Yeah, and now we owe a whole lot more money than we did when we got up this morning."

"Well, it's only money."

"I know. That's something, isn't it?"

"Are you happy about being a partner with Frank?"

"Yeah, I am. I don't think I would have agreed to partner up with anybody else, but we will make some good money with him."

"I'm glad you're happy. Maybe we need to go somewhere and celebrate."

"Maybe so. You think about it and we'll go wherever you say."

"Okay, Honey. I'll see you tonight. Love you."

"Love you, too. Bye."

Chapter Fifteen

He was so fired up, he wanted to tell people about it, and he looked in his directory and found Monty Shepherd's number. Before he dialed it, he sat and debated with himself about whether or not to call him, and finally, he picked up the phone.

When they answered he said, "This is Jerry Martin. May I speak to Monty, please?"

"One moment, please."

"Jerry, whatta ya say, Buddy?"

"Everything's lovely. How are you?"

"Did you get that mall finished?"

"Yeah, and it's doing an unbelievable amount of business. You need to come down here and see it."

"I'd like to. Maybe I can before long. What are you doing?"

"Well, I'm finishing the renovations on an antebellum mansion, White Rock is about two thirds finished, and I'm building a ninety-six unit high end apartment complex. Other than that, I'm not doing much. What are you doing?"

"Same old, same old. I don't remember how many countries we were in the last time I saw you, but we've just added the Scandinavian countries to our list, and they're doing very well."

"Are you still speaking at colleges and universities?"

"Yeah, some, but I've slowed down a little for the last year or so because of our expansion into so many different places around the world. Funny you would mention that because I'm scheduled to go to the University of Florida the last weekend in this month. Do you wanna go with me?"

"I don't know; maybe. Let me tell you some of the things that have happened to me since I last saw you. How long has it been since we were together; five or six years?"

"I guess it has. You were in the process of laying out the mall when I was down there, and you were planning your neighborhood development, but had put it on hold until you finished the mall."

"Gosh, has it been that long?"

"I guess it has. We've talked a few times, but that's the last time we saw each other."

"Did we have our little boy then?"

"No, I don't think so."

"Monty, I've got a lot to tell you. You might not have the time. Should I call back later?"

"No, no. I have time. Let me hear what's on your mind."

"Okay, if you're sure. Let me start with B.J.. Do you remember me telling you about the three teenagers that damaged one of my houses?"

"Yeah, I remember."

"Well, there were two boys and a girl, and they were turned over to me to work out their sentences. On the very last day of their work, Tammy, the girl, was kidnapped and raped several times, and it resulted in her becoming pregnant. Since Tracy and I couldn't have children, things worked out to where we were able to adopt Tammy's baby, and we named him B.J.. If I had time to tell you the whole story about that, you'd know that it was God that worked things out to let us adopt him."

"Halleluiah."

"You may remember me telling you about Frank Thomas, the Chairman of the bank."

"Yeah, I remember hearing about him."

"Monty, Frank is the one I built the mall for, and I've been building apartment complexes for him ever since I started on the mall, and right now, I'm building a ninety-six unit complex. Well, last week he called me and asked if he and his wife could take Tracy and I out Saturday night, and of course we went. He took us to the Atlanta Athletic Club, and while we were there, he told me that his partner in the apartments died a month or so ago, and he asked me to be his partner, beginning with the complex I'm building now. Monty, if that isn't God working, I don't know what is."

"You should add these two things that you just told me to your story."

"There's more. Going back to the teenagers, I told you about Tammy and the baby, but there's something else that, to me is even better than that."

"How could it get any better?"

"One of the boys named Stony asked me to hire him, since his parents weren't able to send him to college, and I did. Monty, he has turned into one smart kid, in fact; he's so smart and such a good worker, I sent him to college, myself, and he graduated with a degree in Building Sciences, and I firmly believe he's going to climb to the top in my organization. Now here's the good part. I've been talking to him about Jesus, and a while back, he accepted Christ as his Savior. In the words of Jerry Clower, Ain't God Good."

"That's amazing. Jerry, you've got to go to U.F. with me and tell these things."

"Okay, I'll go, and Monty, I sure would like to take Stony with us. Would that be possible?"

"Yeah, we can work him into the program."

"I was hoping you would say that. You know, he's about the same age as a lot of the college students. He's only twenty-three. He graduated last year. If you're short on time, he can take my place. I think his story is better than mine."

"If anybody has to give up time, it'll be me, but we'll see. The way you spellbound the audience last time, I want you to talk as long as you can."

"I'll have to ask Stony if he'll go. He might not want to."

"Well, you ask him, and I'll be back in touch with you one day next week. Twist his arm, if you have to. Jerry, it's great to hear from you, and I'm so glad things are going so well for you. When you put God in charge, things seem to work out, don't they?"

"They absolutely do. Monty, it sure is good talking to you. We need to stay in touch more often. I believe we said we would five years ago, didn't we? Let's try to do that now."

"I'm all for that. I think the last time, you were trying to get ready to build that mall, and it kept you tied up, but now that you're not tied up with that any more, maybe we can do better. Jerry, I appreciate you calling. I'll talk to you next week. Give Tracy a hug for me, will you?"

"I sure will. Bye, Monty."

When he hung up from Monty, he called Stony. When Stony answered, Jerry said, "Hi Stony. How's it going today?"

"Fine, Mr. M… uh, Jerry. How are you."

"Look, I need to talk to you about something. Could you come by my office this afternoon, or do you have plans for when you get off?"

"I'm going over to Deena's, but I don't have to be there at any certain time. I can come."

"Tell Bill I said to let you off a few minutes early. Come on by, and I won't keep you but a few minutes."

"Okay, I'll see you this afternoon."

As soon as he hung up from Jerry, he went back to what he was doing, but before he got into the job, he found Bill and told him, "That was Jerry. He wants me to come to his office this afternoon, and he told me to tell you to let me off a few minutes early."

"Okay. What time do you need to leave?"

"I don't know; maybe around four thirty. Is that alright with you?"

"Yeah, that'll be alright. When Jerry calls, you'd better go. Do you know what he wants?"

"No. Maybe he's going to fire me. I'm kinda nervous about it."

"Relax. If he wanted to fire you, he'd have me do it. He's impressed with your performance, so it's certainly not that."

At four thirty he left the job and headed to Jerry's office. On the way, he called Deena. "Hi Pretty Lady."

"Hi."

"Look, Jerry Martin called me and told me to come to his office when I got off, so I'm on my way over there now."

"What does he want?"

"I have no idea."

"Maybe he's going to give you a promotion."

"I doubt that, but we'll know soon enough. The reason I called was to tell you about my meeting with him and to tell you I don't know what time I'll be at your house. It depends on what time I leave him. Wish me luck, and I'll see you tonight. Love ya."

"Love you."

He pulled into the Martin Builders parking lot and got out to go in. He was truly nervous, not knowing what Jerry wanted, but when he opened the door, Jerry saw him, and with a big smile said, "Hi Stony. Come on back," and he went straight into his office.

"Sit down, Stony. Did you have a good day?"

"Yes sir. Every day is a good day."

"Atta Boy. Stony, the reason I asked you to come in is to ask a favor."

"You're asking me for a favor?"

"Yeah. Have you ever heard of Shepherd Apparel?"

"Are they the ones who make shirts and things?"

"They're the ones. Monty Shepherd is a friend of mine. Although he is a billionaire, with a 'b', he is a very dedicated Christian, and he travels around speaking to Fellowship of Christian Athletes clubs at different colleges and universities. I've been with him a couple of times, and it's a great experience. I talked to Monty earlier today, and he told me he is going down to the University of Florida later this month and he invited me to go with him. I told him I would, and then when I told him about you, he wanted me to invite you to go with us, and I told him I'd ask you. Do you think you would want to go with us?"

"I don't know. If you don't mind me asking, what did you tell him about me?"

"I told him about your life, beginning when you and Reed broke into my houses and nearly destroyed them. Then I told him how you manned up and paid your penalty, and then I told him how you accepted Christ and how well you do your work. He was impressed and wants to meet you, and he really wants you to go with us to Florida to share your story. He'll pick us up on the day of the meeting and bring us back that night."

"You mean we'll fly?"

"Yeah, Monty' company has two or three airplanes that are state of the art, and he will pick us up in one of them."

"I don't know. I've never flown before."

"Stony, you don't have to give me an answer right now, but Monty's going to call me next week to find out what we're going to do. You certainly don't have to go, but think about this. If you go, you'll be speaking to guys and maybe a few gals around your age, and if there happens to be some that are not yet believers, if just one of them would accept Jesus as a result of your talk, can you imagine what a blessing that would be?"

"That would be something, wouldn't it?"

"It sure would, and it could happen. Think about it, Stony, and let me know as soon as you can, so I'll know what to tell Monty when he calls."

"Okay, Jerry. I'll think about it and thank you for your confidence in me. It means a lot."

It was after five when they got through, and everybody was leaving at once; Beverly, the other two girls, and Jerry and Stony. The girls said goodbye to Jerry and Stony, and Jerry asked Stony, "Did you say you were going over to Deena's tonight?"

174

"Yes sir. We've been seeing each other every night, but we haven't gone out every night. Most of the time I just go over to her house and we stay in the living room while her parents stay in the den."

"Is Bobby okay with that?"

"He acts like he is, and Deena said that he said it is fine for me to come over. Her mother and I are big buddies. I call her Kitty Kunkle every chance I get, and she seems to like it. We go out some, but it gets really expensive if you go out every night."

"Well, you have a good time and think about what we talked about. Monty and I want you to go, and I feel that whenever you have a chance to tell people about Jesus, He expects you to do it and make no mistake about it; you will be rewarded in some way."

"Jerry, it scares me to speak in front of people. I had a hard time giving book reports in school because I was afraid to stand up in front of the class."

"You know what, Stony? I'll be telling my story after Monty and before you, and I'll be telling a little about you. I won't mention your name, but I'll be talking about the three teenagers that broke into and wrecked my houses. I'll be telling about how my willingness to let them work out their sentences for me instead of going to jail led to so many good things for me, and I give God all the credit for that. If I hadn't done that, I would never have met Frank Thomas, who has been my angel for the last few years.

"You don't know this, but this morning, I signed partnership papers making me an equal partner with Frank in the apartments we're building and in future building projects. God has taken care of me ever since that act of kindness toward you three kids, and I'm going to always do whatever I can to tell people about it. Think about it, and I'm sure God will help you with your butterflies. Think what an impact it will have if you get up to tell your story, and you say I was one of those teenagers. They'll be hungry to hear everything you say after that. You won't have to speak for more than five or ten minutes; whatever you want."

"Jerry, I'm afraid to get up in front of those people, but after what you've said about Jesus expecting me to tell people about him, I'm afraid not to, so I guess I'll go with you. I'm not sure what I'll say, but maybe I can come up with something."

"I'll tell you what. Whenever you get ready, you come by my office and I'll help you put some thoughts together. You won't have to say much; just tell them what Jesus means to you, and how you got to where you are now."

"Okay. I'll call you in the next day or two."

"Good boy. Have a good time tonight with Deena."

"Okay, thank you." As soon as Jerry left, he dialed DKUNKLE, and she must have had the phone in her hand because she answered instantly. "Hey Stony."

"I can't wait to see you. Have you eaten yet?"

"No, Mama's running late, and dinner is going to be late; why?"

"Well, I just have left Jerry, and I thought if you'd like to, we'd go to the Steak and Shake."

"That sounds really good. Let's do it."

"Okay, I'm leaving Martin Builders right now, and I'll see you in a few minutes."

By the time he got to Deena's and then back to the Steak and Shake, it was after six thirty, and there was a crowd waiting for a table, but since they didn't have anything else to do, they waited. It didn't matter where they were as long as they were together.

Deena asked. "What was your meeting about?"

"Let's wait 'til we sit down, and then I'll tell you. Have you had a good day?"

"Yeah, we had a test this morning, and I made a ninety-two on it. Pretty good, hunh?"

"I'll say. You might be too smart of a chick for somebody like me."

In a minute or two they got a table and sat down. They already knew what they wanted so they went ahead and ordered. While they were eating, Deena asked once again, "Are you ready to tell me about your meeting?"

He looked her in the eyes and asked, "Deena, do you know how I came to be employed by Martin Builders?"

"No, I guess you just asked for a job. How else?"

"Did Bobby not ever tell you about me going to work for them and him being my boss?"

"No. You're sure sounding mysterious. How did you start?"

"Okay. Now brace yourself. Deena, when I was sixteen years old, my best friend Reed Thomas, Frank Thomas's son, and me and a girl named Tammy Mills were out one night and we saw some houses that Martin Builders were building. We thought it would be neat if we broke into them and tore up the walls and ceilings by putting our feet through the sheetrock. We did a lot of damage, and later that night, the police caught us and took us in. We went before the Magistrate and Jerry Martin was called. He went down to the Magistrate's office to face us and our parents face to face.

"They set our bail at twenty-five hundred dollars each, and our parents had to come up with ten percent of that to keep us from going to jail. Tammy's mother didn't have the money, and would you believe Jerry loaned her the money to pay Tammy's bail? Then, when we went to trial, Jerry convinced the judge to let us work out our sentences at his construction jobs rather than send us to prison. You see, these were felonies, and we would have had to go to prison; not jail, and these records would stand the rest of our lives. Jerry talked the judge into not only letting us work out our sentences, but to erase the felonies from our records if we completed the job, and that's how I started working for Martin Builders. When we finished our sentences, I knew Mom and Dad wouldn't be able to send me to college, so I asked Jerry if I could work for him, full time, and he gave me a job.

"I worked really hard to show Jerry how much I appreciated him and what he did for me, and apparently it paid off because he's the one who sent me to college and I graduated with a degree in Building Sciences. I still work hard, and Jerry seems to appreciate it. We talk, occasionally, and in some of our talks he would tell me about Jesus, and what He did for him, and one day I invited Jesus into my heart and became a Christian.

"Now, to answer your question about what was our meeting about; Jerry has a good friend named Monty Shepherd, who goes around speaking to the Fellowship of Christian Athletes at different colleges and universities, and sometimes Jerry goes with him. Well, here's the kicker. Monty is going to the University of Florida later this month to speak and he invited Jerry to go with him. For some reason, Jerry told Monty about me, and Monty wants me to go with them. That's why I went to Jerry's office this afternoon."

"Are you going?"

"I guess I will. Jerry said he would help me with my talk. I'm scared to death."

"How long will you be gone?"

"Jerry said that Monty would pick us up in his plane the afternoon of the meeting and bring us back home that same night. I never have been on an airplane, have you?"

"No. You mean he has his own airplane?"

"Yeah, Jerry said he has two or three of them. Now that you know my story, are you going to break up with me?"

"Break up with you? Heavens no. I'm prouder than ever of you. I wouldn't let you go for a hundred dollars."

"That much, hunh?"

"Yep, that much. Honey, our children are going to have a great daddy. Did you know that?"

"I hope so. Are you through?"

"Yeah. Are you ready to go?"

They went back to her house, and before they went in the living room to stay, they went into the den to speak to her parents. Bobby was there, but Kitty had gone next door for something, and that gave Stony a chance to say something to Bobby that he felt he should say.

"Bobby, can I talk to you for a minute?"

"Sure. What's on your mind?"

"Well, I met with Jerry Martin this afternoon, and he invited me to go with him and Monty Shepherd to speak at the University of Florida's FCA group. My meeting with him made me be late seeing Deena, and I had to explain to her where I was and why Jerry wanted me to go with them. When I told her about why I first went to work for Martin Builders, she said you had not told her anything about what I did to cause me to have to go to work for them, and I just want to thank you for not telling that to anybody."

"I didn't think it was anybody's business, and besides, you stood up like a man and worked things out. That makes you a man in my eyes, and anything you did in your past has no bearing on what you are now. And for what it's worth, I'm glad you're seeing Deena. I feel she's safe with you."

As he and Deena were leaving the den to go to the living room, Bobby called out to him and said, "Stony, congratulations for being invited to go with Jerry and Monty. It should be a great experience for you."

"Thank you Bobby."

They went into the living room and turned on the TV and stayed in there until about ten or ten thirty when Stony said, "I guess I had better go. I've got to try to build up some courage for my speech. Tonight will probably be a sleepless night."

When he went to bed, the thought of speaking at the FCA meeting consumed him. Instead of thinking about a small audience of a hundred and fifty to two hundred people, his imagination ran away with him, and he visualized a full football stadium full of thousands waiting for him to speak. He broke into a sweat, his eyes were wide open, and his stomach was in a knot. He thought, *I can't do it. I'm going to call Jerry in the morning and tell him not to count on me.* He finally went to sleep, but tossed and turned most of the night, and when he got up, he was tired.

Bill noticed a difference in him when he arrived at work, and he asked, "Did you and Deena have a fight last night?"

"No. Why?"

"Because you look like you lost your best friend."

"No. that's not it."

"Son, can I help you? If you want to talk, I'm a good listener. Tell me what's wrong."

"Do you remember I had to go to Jerry's office yesterday?"

"I remember. What happened?"

"Do you know who Monty Shepherd is?"

"Yeah, he's that wealthy friend of Jerry's from Chattanooga."

"Well, he and Jerry are going down to the University of Florida to speak at a Fellowship of Christian Athletes meeting, and they want me to go with them, and I'm scared to death to get up in front of a lot of people. I told Jerry that I'd go, but last night I decided I wasn't going to, and I've got to call and tell him."

"Are you sure that's what you want to do?"

"Bill, I can't get up in front of all those people."

"How many will there be?"

"Jerry said he thought there would be around a hundred and fifty, more or less."

"Stony, let me tell you a couple of things. First, Jerry must want you to go with him or else he wouldn't have called you to come to his office just to ask you that, and second, that's not very many people, and you shouldn't be afraid of speaking to them."

"A hundred and fifty people sound like a lot to me."

"What does Jerry want you to talk about?"

"He wants me to tell how I got started with this company, and how things are going so well since I found Jesus."

"Let me ask you something."

"What?"

"If that's what you're going to talk about, don't you think Jesus will help you?

"That's what Jerry said, but I'm just not sure he will."

"I can promise you he will. He's not going to keep you from having butterflies, but when you get up there to speak, He'll be right there to help you know what to say and make you strong. I can't make you go, but I hope you won't disappoint Jerry, and Jesus for that matter. Did you tell Deena?"

"Yeah."

"What did she say?"

"She wants me to do it."

"Did you tell her that you're going to chicken out?"

"Not yet."

"What will she think?"

"I don't know."

"Well, you think about that. I bet she'd be disappointed if you backed out. I'm going to say one more thing, and then I won't say anything else about it. Stony, when you came to us, you came to pay off a serious debt, and you stood up like a man and worked hard to settle the debt. I think that experience made you a man, and I'd hate to see you jeopardize that position."

"You're a convincing man, Bill. Okay, I'll do it. I guess we had better get back to work, hadn't we?"

"Yeah, I guess we had."

Chapter Sixteen

The surveyors called and told Jerry that the Cummings Acres surveys were completed, and he could get them whenever he wanted them, so he sent one of his office girls to pick them up. He told her to have them send him six copies.

Since the surveys were done, he wanted to get the Douglasville – Douglas County Water and Sewer Authority to run the lines to the development, so he called them. He asked for the man he had talked to earlier, and when he told him the surveys were done, the man told him that his request had been discussed, and he thought they were going to approve running the lines. However, his request had to be finalized by the board, and they wouldn't meet until the following Wednesday, so he would have to call back. Jerry thanked him and said he would. He felt good when he hung up, since the man said he thought they were going to run the lines.

Next, he called Georgia Power Co. to tell them he was ready for them to run their lines, and that he would bring the surveys to them whenever they were ready for them, and they said they would be ready whenever he could get them to their office.

In a few minutes, Laura got back with the surveys and took them into his office. He took out one set and went over it from top to bottom, and then he called Tracy.

When she answered he said, "Hi Honey. What are you doing?" When she told him he asked, "Are you absolutely sure you're going to sell the Cummings Acres houses?"

"Yeah, if you still want me to. Why?"

"Because I'm going to have a sign painted to put up at the entrance, and I'm going to have your name and number put on the sign."

"Go ahead because I'm planning to sell them."

"Okay. I'll see you tonight. Love you." As soon as he could get away, he left the office and went to a sign painter and ordered a large sign to put up at the entrance to the development.

From there, he went out to Cummings Acres with the surveys and carefully drove over the entire piece of land. His pickup was four-wheel drive, so about half of where he went wasn't on the original road. He planned to have two main streets in the development, with either two or three connector streets, and he wanted to drive where the streets would be. At the top of the large drawing was the lake that he was going to build, and he was very pleased with the way things were laid out.

After he was satisfied that everything was the way he wanted it, he left and headed back to his office, but on his way back, he went by the Georgia Grading and Excavating Company to talk to them about grading the streets and excavating the dirt for the lake. He had used them before, so he knew what kind of work they did. Hopefully, the county was going to do the paving, and hopefully the sidewalks and curbs, but just in case they wouldn't do it, Georgia Grading would be hired to do the job. If the county refused to put in sidewalks and curbs, he might just not have them because of the costs. He left his set of the surveys with them to use so they could figure the costs of doing the grading and excavating, and he left to go back to his office.

It was approaching five o'clock when his phone rang. It was Stony. "Jerry, you said you would help me put some things together to talk about when we go to Florida. Would this afternoon be a good time for you?"

"Yeah. This afternoon is good. Are you coming right now?"

"If it's alright."

"Yeah. I'll be looking for you." He called Tracy and told her, "I told Stony if he would come by that I would help him put together some thoughts for his talk when we go to Florida, and he wants to come this afternoon. I don't know how long we'll be. Will this mess you up about supper?"

"No, it'll be alright. You help Stony. Why don't you all go out and get something?"

"I don't know. It'll depend on him. He probably has a date and won't want to be too late, but we'll see. If he would like to, we'll go somewhere. I'll let you know."

"Okay. See ya."

Stony got to Jerry's office about five fifteen, and they began talking about the Florida trip immediately. Stony told him that he almost called him to back out, but Bill convinced him not to, and Jerry said, "I'm glad he did."

Of course, Jerry knew Stony's complete story, so it made it easier for him to suggest things to him. Jerry did most of the talking, and Stony took notes. They talked for thirty to forty-five minutes and when they were winding it up, Jerry asked, "Do you have a date tonight?"

"Yes sir, but I don't have to be in any hurry."

"Would you like to go grab a bite with me? My wife suggested we go out."

"Yes sir. I'd like that."

"Do you like Gabes Downtown?"

"I never have been there."

"Well, the food is good. Why don't we go there?"

"Great."

While they were at the restaurant, they didn't talk about the Florida trip, rather Jerry began talking about Stony and Deena dating. He asked Stony, "I know you've been seeing Deena just about every night. Does Bobby have any problem with that?"

"No, in fact; he told me the other night that he was glad I was seeing her because he felt she was safe with me."

"Well, that's great. Stony, I got the surveys for Cummings Acres this morning, so it looks as if we'll start moving on that pretty soon."

"So, you've decided on a name. I like it."

"Stony, we're getting so much business that I've got a problem. You know, we've always been a small contractor, and then the mall happened. I put everything else aside except for Frank Thomas's apartments in order to concentrate on that. As you know, Bobby Kunkle and Bill Case are my two main supervisors, and I'm really having to spread them thin. Right now, Bill is working on the apartments with you, and Bobby is splitting his time between the Chrisman mansion and White Rock. The mansion will be finished next week, so that'll let him devote all his time to White Rock, and that will go on for several more months.

"And that brings me to Cummings Acres. We're going to be ready to lay out some of the homes pretty soon, and I told Bill to be ready; that he would more than likely have to lay them out, and do you know what he suggested?"

"No sir. I don't have any idea."

"He told me that you should be the one to lay them out because of the way you know how to use that Layout Pro program. I told him that since we're going to be building eight to ten homes at a time, that I would probably have to move him out there, and do you know what he told me then?"

Stony smiled and said, "No sir, I don't."

"He said that eight to ten homes at one time would require more than one foreman, and that I should make you one. Would you want to be a foreman, Stony?"

"I'd give my eye teeth to be one."

"Well, you won't have to give your eye teeth, but we'll promote you to foreman when we get ready to lay out the homes. You will lay out all the homes in the development, and oversee the building of several of them, probably four or five at a time. I've got to work between the plans and the surveys to decide where each house is going to be, but I've got time for that. There's a tremendous amount of work to be done before we lay out the first house, but that's what I have in mind for you."

Stony said, "Jerry, I don't know what to say except thank you so much. Not many people would take a chance on a juvenile delinquent the way you have, and I promise that I won't let you down."

"I know you won't. Now, if your through, let's get out of here. I want to go home to see my honey, and I know you want to do the same thing. Tell Deena I said hi." He picked up the check and paid it as they left. When they got outside, Stony said, "Jerry, I want to ask you something. I've been thinking for a while about getting my own place and moving out of my parents' house, and I've been wondering what Mr. Thomas's apartments rent for. They may be too expensive for me, but they sure are nice."

"I'm not sure, Stony. I think the two-bedroom ones go for about twelve hundred a month. With your new promotion, you might be able to get one if you don't owe too much on other things."

"I don't owe for anything."

"That's unusual for a young person these days. When you get ready, let me know."

"Okay. Thank you."

"I've held you up long enough. You go out there and see that pretty girl, and I'll see you later."

He called Deena the minute he left Jerry. "Hey, would you like to have company tonight?"

"I sure would. Do you think you might be interested in filling the bill?"

"Well, I've been thinking about it. Have you eaten?"

"Yeah, Mama cooked. Have you?"

"Yeah, Jerry took me out."

"Really? Why?"

"I'll tell you when I get there. I've got some exciting news."

"Hurry up and get here. I want to hear it."

"I'll see you in a few minutes."

186

She met him at the door when he got there, and as usual, he went in to speak to her parents, and then they went into the living room to talk and to hold hands.

They hadn't been in there but a few minutes until Deena said, "Well, are you going to keep me in suspense? I want to hear the exciting news. Why were you with Jerry again today?"

"After yesterday, I didn't sleep much last night, and I decided to chicken out of going to Florida with Jerry and Monty Shepherd, and when I got to work this morning, Bill noticed there was something wrong, and I told him about Jerry inviting me to go with him, and how scared I was, and I thought I would call Jerry and tell him I wasn't going. He talked pretty straight to me and convinced me that I should go, so since Jerry had offered to help me come up with some thoughts for my talk, I called him and asked if I could go to his office after work. He told me to come on, and I did. He helped me a lot and made me not quite so scared.

"When we got through, he asked me if I would like to go get something to eat with him, and I said I would, so we went to Gabes Downtown. You and I need to go there sometime; it's really good."

"Finish telling me about you and Jerry."

"Okay. We went to eat, and while we were at the restaurant, Jerry talked a lot about how much business he had, and that he had a problem because he didn't have enough supervisors to oversee everything. He told me that Bill had talked to him and told him that he should promote me, and he asked me if I would like to be a foreman. Of course, I told him I would, and he said that when they start on the Cummings Acres development, I will be one of the foremen. I think when your daddy gets through at White Rock, Jerry's going to have him work on the Cummings development, so we'll be working together."

"That's wonderful. I'm so proud of you. Give me a kiss."

He gave her a quick kiss, and then told her, "I told Jerry I was thinking about getting my own apartment and would love to get one of Uncle Frank's, and did he know how much they rented for. He said he thought the two bedrooms were around twelve hundred dollars, and when I got to be foreman, I should be able to get one. He said to let him know when I was ready. I'm not sure what he meant by that. You know what, Honey? God is good, isn't he?"

The next two weeks went by faster than Stony wanted them to because even though Jerry and Bill had tried to allay his fear of speaking to the crowd, he was still scared, and Friday was the big day. Jerry had told him he didn't have to wear a tie and coat, but to put on a nice pair of khakis and a nice shirt, and if he had a nice pair of shoes to wear them.

Jerry went out to the job site Thursday afternoon just to be sure Stony was still on go, and he told him that Monty had called and the plane would be there to get them at two o'clock the next day. Jerry asked him, "Are you still nervous?"

"Yeah, and I haven't told you this. I've never been on an airplane before, and I'm nervous about that, too."

Jerry laughed and said, "You're a wreck everywhere, aren't you?"

"Yeah. I'll be glad when it's over."

"I know it's easy to say relax, but if you'll pray about it, maybe God will help you to, and I think you'll enjoy the plane ride. Listen, tomorrow come to my office, and we'll go to the airport together. Be there at one o'clock, and that should give us plenty of time to meet the plane at two."

Bill overheard the conversation, and when Jerry left, he called Stony over to him. "I heard Jerry tell you to be at his office at one tomorrow. It will be hard for you to work in good clothes, and to get there in time, so if you want to, just take off tomorrow, and that way, you can go to Jerry's office from home."

"Thank you, Bill. I appreciate it."

"I want you to wow 'em tomorrow night, and I know you will. Turn on your personality the way you did at Jerry's pig pickin, and they'll love you."

"Thanks, Bill. Would you mind if I use the phone for just a minute?"

"No. Go ahead."

He dialed DKUNKLE, and Deena answered after one ring. "Hi, Lady."

"Hi. What are you doing calling me at this time of the day? Is something wrong?"

"No. I just wanted to see if we might could go to the mall tonight. I need to pick up some things to wear tomorrow."

"Sure, we can. I want to look for some things, too. Would you like for me to meet you to keep you from having to drive all the way out here?"

"That would be good. Do you want to eat at one of the restaurants at the mall?"

"Yeah, how about Gondolas?"

"Gondolas sounds fine. Why don't we meet at a quarter to six?"

"Okay, I'll see you then. I love you."

"Love you more. See ya," and he hung up before she could respond to that.

After dinner at Gondolas, which was part of the Skint Chesnut Mall complex, Stony and Deena went to the mall itself to look for some clothes for him to wear to Florida. They found a beautiful Polo shirt and some classy looking khakis, but they had to go to a shoe store to find some shoes. They found some pretty loafers and bought them. He was now fixed. From the mall, they went to Deena's house, and Stony stayed until around ten thirty.

He slept in the next morning, and when he got up, he studied his notes for the speech he was going to give. He hoped he wouldn't have to use them during his talk, but he would have them handy, just in case he did.

189

Finally, around eleven o'clock, he showered, shaved, and got dressed. Every time he had a break, he read his notes, and he left home at twelve fifteen for Jerry's office. He prayed all the way over that God would calm him down, and when he got to Martin Builders, he sat in his car, praying, before he went in.

When he got inside the office, he spoke to Beverly and then went to Jerry's office. Jerry looked up and saw him and said, "Hi Stony. You look nice. Give me just a minute, and we'll go."

In just a little bit, Jerry closed a folder and put it in his desk drawer and asked, "Ready to go?"

"I'm ready," Stony said. They went outside and got into Jerry's pickup and headed for the airport. Stony noticed that Jerry didn't park in one of the large lots, but went to another one, which was large, but he could tell it wasn't for people catching commercial flights. Jerry found a place and parked, and they got out and went into a nice building that was dedicated to business and private planes. It wasn't two o'clock yet, so they stood at the huge picture window wall and watched the planes come in and leave.

At one fifty-seven a beautiful Gulfstream, with the words Shepherd Apparel painted over the windows and a large shepherd's staff painted on the tail, landed and taxied up to the building. Jerry said, "Well, there's our chariot," and they walked to the door leading out to the tarmac. Stony couldn't take his eyes off the beautiful plane, and while he was looking at it, the door opened, and a man got out. He thought, *that must be Monty.*

Before they could get to the plane, the man met them and said, "Jerry, hi," and then he looked at Stony and said, "You must be Stony. After what Jerry told me about you, I've been anxious to meet you."

"Thank you. It's nice to meet you."

Monty said, "Well, are you fellows ready to go?"

Jerry said, "We're ready," and they walked out to the plane. Monty climbed the steps first, then Stony, and then Jerry.

When they got inside, Monty said, "Sit where you want to. We'll be taking off in just a minute. It should take us about an hour and fifteen minutes to get to Gainesville."

Stony was blown away by the interior and had a hard time believing it could fly. It wasn't but a couple of minutes 'til the pilot said, "Fasten your belts. We're getting ready to take off." Monty asked Stony if he was buckled up, and he said he was. He grabbed the front of both armrests and held on. They taxied out to where they would take off, and the pilot revved the engines prior to releasing the brakes, and in a matter of just a few seconds, they were airborne. He looked out the window and saw the earth quickly moving away, and he didn't relax his grip on the armrests until they leveled off high in the sky.

"What do you think," Jerry asked?

"I don't know. This thing really moves, doesn't it?"

Monty spoke up and said, "This plane cruises at five hundred and fifty miles per hour."

"Wow!"

Then Monty said, "Jerry, Stony, why don't we use some of this time to plan our times on stage tonight?"

Jerry said. "That's a good idea. You're the captain of the team, so you tell us how you want to do things."

"Okay. I'll go first, and I'll probably talk for fifteen or twenty minutes. Then, I'll introduce you, and you can talk for as long as you want to. Do you know how long that will be?"

Jerry said, "I think fifteen or twenty minutes will be enough for me."

Monty said, "Jerry, take as long as you want. I know you have a tremendous story to tell, and when you get through, you can either introduce Stony or I will, whichever you want to do. Stony, who would you rather have introduce you?"

"If you don't mind, I think I would like for Jerry to."

191

Monty then asked him, "How long do you want to talk?"

By then, Stony was getting pretty relaxed, and his personality started to show, and when Monty asked him how long he wanted to talk, he smiled and said, "Is thirty seconds long enough?" When he saw that Jerry and Monty were smiling but not laughing, he said, "I really don't know. I think ten minutes will probably be enough."

Monty said, "Okay, but if you're not through in ten minutes, don't worry about it. Take as much time as you want. I'm just trying to get an idea of how much time the three of us will take."

It didn't seem as if they had been in the air long at all until Stony could feel the nose of the plane gradually point downward, and he guessed they were getting ready to land.

They were picked up in a van that had University of Florida painted on both sides, and they were taken to the place where the FCA meeting would be held that night. It was only four o'clock and the meeting wasn't until seven, so they had a lot of time to kill. There was a steady stream of people coming through the area where they were just to speak and meet them. Some wanted to talk and tell the three about some of their experiences, and some only wanted to meet them.

At about five o'clock the leader of the FCA wanted to show them where they would be speaking, so they went into a very nice auditorium, and Stony could only describe it as cozy. It had carpet and low ceilings, and a warm, intimate feel to it. When talking, there was no echo. and that was just another thing to help him feel at ease.

They spent quite a bit of time in the auditorium, and it was finally time to start thinking about the program. The FCA leader took them back to where they had been earlier and told them he would come get them at fifteen 'til seven.

At about six forty, Monty said to Jerry and Stony, "Why don't we have a prayer before we go in? They took each other's hands and Monty prayed that God would be with them and help them say something that would benefit each person in the audience. No sooner had he finished the prayer until the FCA leader came to get them. He took them back into the auditorium where they sat down.

The meeting was called to order and the leader said a prayer. There were two or three other things that they did, and then he began his introduction of Monty. Stony didn't know about all the things they said about him, and he was really impressed. After the lengthy introduction, Monty got up and absolutely electrified the audience with his stories about his athletics, his son's athletic careers, how one of his sons died in Iraq, and how God saw him through everything.

He had said he would need about fifteen minutes and it was almost exactly fifteen minutes when he began his introduction of Jerry.

Jerry got up and held the audience in his hand for a full twenty minutes. He began by telling how three teenagers broke into his houses and how his kindness toward them led to his meeting Frank and everything that has happened since then, and when he got through, he introduced Stony.

Stony, being the cut-up that he was, began by saying, "I understand you all are called Gators. Well, I went to Georgia State, and we are called Blue Panthers. Another name is Pounce, such as Pounce on the Gator," and that drew some boos. Then he said, "I'm responsible for Jerry being the success that he is. Do you believe that?" There was some mumbling, and some shook their heads no. Then he got serious.

"You heard Jerry say that his story actually begins when three teenagers broke into some of the houses he was building. I'm embarrassed to tell you, but I want you to know tonight that I was one of those teenagers, and if it hadn't been for that man, I'd be in prison right now. We did so much damage that it was classified as a felony instead of a misdemeanor, and a felony carries a lengthy prison sentence. I'm talking about prison; not the city or county jail. Jerry convinced the judge to turn us over to him to work out our sentences by working for him and to wipe the felony off our records if we completed it. I'm happy to say that we did complete our sentences and we are no longer considered felons. That's the kind of man Jerry Martin is, but that's not all Jerry did for me.

"He hired me fulltime after I got out of high school, and I worked myself to death, trying to do good and to impress him. I'm fortunate to be able to catch onto things pretty fast, and one day he told me he was going to send me to college. You see, my parents couldn't afford to send me, and I jumped at Jerry's offer. I graduated with a degree in Building Sciences.

"From time to time we would talk. He would tell me how God loves me and how Jesus died and rose to save me, and one day, when we were talking, I invited Jesus into my heart, and I've never been sorry. If you don't have Him in your heart, I urge you to invite Him in tonight.

"I'm not going to talk any longer, but I want to tell you this. Jerry has taken this juvenile delinquent and made somebody out of him. I found out just yesterday that he is promoting me to the position of foreman, and that's a big deal at our company, and while I'm very grateful to Jerry, I'm very, very grateful to God for bringing me through all that He has. I'm not a delinquent any longer."

There was a roar of applause when Monty and Jerry finished their talks, but it seemed as if the applause for Stony reached a new level. After he sat down, the applause continued, and he stood up and waved in appreciation.

When the leader thanked them and said a prayer, he dismissed the group, and at that time Jerry put his arm around Stony's shoulder and said, "I'm very proud of you. Thanks for the nice things you said about me."

Then, Monty went over to him and said, "Stony, you did great. These people would elect you to office right now. Congratulations, Son."

"Thank you, Mr. Shepherd."

Before they could leave the stage, many of the attendees came up and thanked them and told them how much they enjoyed it and how much each talk meant to them. Since Stony was close to their ages, his talk had particular meaning for several of them.

The same van that picked them up at the airport took them back and drove right up to the steps of the plane. The two pilots were in the terminal, and when they saw them, they came out and opened the plane's door.

The plane lifted off and, on its way back to Atlanta, Monty had high praise for both Jerry and Stony. Jerry had high praise for Stony and Monty, and Stony had high praise for Jerry and Monty. They were all happy about the way things went, and Monty said, "Fellas, I do this every now and then, as you well know, Jerry, and I'm giving both of you a standing invitation to go with me again, whenever you would like to. Stony, you were amazing, and I'm sure glad that I got to know you, and Jerry, thank you for bringing him with us."

The plane landed in Atlanta at eleven twenty, and by the time they got to Jerry's office to pick up Stony's car, it was almost midnight. On the way, Jerry asked, "Well, what did you think, Stony? Was it as fearful as you thought it was going to be?"

"No sir. I was really scared until they took us into the auditorium this afternoon. When I saw how cozy it was in there, I relaxed, and when it came time for me to get up and talk, I wasn't scared at all. I don't know if I said anything important or not, but I hope that maybe somebody there could relate to what I said."

"You may never know, but I think I can almost guarantee that more than one person was touched by what you said. I know I was and Monty was, and I'm very proud of you."

"Thank you, sir. You know, I'm really glad tomorrow's Saturday."

"I am, too."

They said bye to each other, and as soon as Stony got into his car, he called Deena. She was still up, waiting for him to call, and she answered on the first ring. "Hi."

"Hi. Are you still up?"

"Yeah, I didn't want to go to bed until I heard from you. How did it go?"

"Good. I got a big round of applause, and Jerry and Mr. Shepherd said I did good. Mr. Shepherd said I was amazing, whatever that means."

"I'm so proud of you."

"Actually, I'm sort of proud of me, too. I never thought I could do something like that. Look, you get to bed, and I'll talk to you in the morning. I love you."

"I love you, too. Good night."

Chapter Seventeen

Saturday was a beautiful day, and since Stony was so used to getting up early on work days, he woke up early that day as well. He went into the kitchen and had some coffee and his Mom fixed him a big breakfast.

He had told her and his Dad about his trip to Florida, and she wanted to know about it. He was excited to tell her because she had never been on an airplane, either, and he wanted to share the good stuff with her.

He said, "Mom, you wouldn't believe how comfortable the seats were on the airplane. Mr. Shepherd had had the interior custom made for him. It even had an office, where he could work while flying to no telling where at over five hundred miles an hour, eight and a half miles high. He had two pilots, and they were both good guys. It only took us a little over an hour to fly from Atlanta to Gainesville, and when we got there, a van picked us up and took us to the University of Florida.

"I was still scared, but after I got down there and saw where we would be speaking, and after meeting a lot of people, I relaxed some. Mr. Shepherd spoke first, and then Jerry talked. When he finished, he introduced me and I talked for about ten minutes. All three of us got a big hand, and Jerry and Mr. Shepherd both said I did real good.

"I don't think I saw you the day before yesterday. I got home late Thursday night, and you had already gone to work when I got up yesterday, but I want to tell you that Jerry is promoting me to foreman."

Nancy said, "Stony, that's wonderful. I guess you'll get a nice raise with that, won't you?"

"I don't know, Mom. Money wasn't mentioned, but Jerry has always taken care of me, and I don't have any reason to think he won't with this."

She said, "I hope so. You've worked hard."

"I know I have, but you've got to remember, if it wasn't for him, I'd be in jail right now, so even if I don't get a raise, it's alright because of everything else he's done for me."

He got up to leave the kitchen and thought, *Deena doesn't usually sleep late and she's probably up. I think I'll call her*. He dialed her number, and after two rings, she answered, "Good morning."

"Good morning to you. Are you up?"

"Yeah, I've been up. I'm cleaning my room and changing my sheets. What are you doing?"

"It just dawned on me that there is a set of blueprints and an artist drawing of the apartments that I'm working on in the construction office at the job site, and I have a key. Would you like to go out there and see what the apartments are going to look like when they're finished, just in case we want to get one?"

"Yeah, I'd love to."

"About eleven o'clock?"

"Sounds good. I'll see you then."

He unrolled the blue prints and laid out the front sheet showing the drawing of the apartments, and Deena said, "Honey, these are the most beautiful apartments I have ever seen. I know this is where I want us to have our first home. Do you think some of them will be ready when we get married?"

"I think so. Eight and possibly sixteen. I feel like eight will definitely be finished by then. Do you think you're sure about wanting one? If you are, I'll try to make sure we get one."

"Yes, I'm sure. Where will the pool be, and will it be ready by the time the first ones are ready?"

He showed her on the blueprints where it would be, and it looked to be pretty close to the first building.

"Okay. If you're sure, I'll try to be sure they don't all get gone. Sometimes, they rent before they are finished."

They looked at various floor plans and then she wanted to see the artist drawing again, and then he put them up, and they left.

They spent most of the weekend together and then it was over; time to go back to school and work.

Jerry's first stop Monday morning was at the apartment complex. Bill and Stony were talking when he got there. When he got up to them, Bill said, "Good morning. Stony was just telling me about your all's trip to Gainesville."

Jerry replied, "Yeah, our boy here was a hit. He did an amazing job speaking."

Stony said, "Thank you, Jerry, but you were the one who had them eating out of your hand."

"Oh no. You were the hit."

"Well, thank you, but that's not the way I saw it."

"Okay. What I came to tell you guys is we're going to finish the Chrisman House today or tomorrow, and I might send a couple of the guys that have been over there over here to help on the apartments. The others, I'll send out to White Rock. I'm anxious to complete that because it won't be long 'til we start on Cummings Acres, and we'll need everybody we can get on that."

He went from the apartments to the Chrisman House and when he got there, he found that just about everything had been done, that they were going to do. Bobby put a couple of men to sweeping and picking up and three others to cleaning windows. He said they should be through by the end of the day, and that would wind up the renovation. Jerry went up to the top and called Frank. "Frank, the renovations on the Chrisman House are complete, so you and Marilyn can move in whenever you want to."

"Ha Ha. You're funny. I'm glad you're through with it. I can't come today, but I'll be out tomorrow to see it. Will you be available tomorrow?"

"I'll be available whenever you want me."

"I'm going to bring Marilyn. Why don't you bring Tracy?"

"Okay, I will. What time?"

"Why don't we have lunch and then go out there?"

"Sounds like a plan. Can we see you at the bank at twelve o'clock or would you rather meet at a restaurant?"

"Have you eaten at Burke's Grill?"

"Yeah, it's good. Is that where you want to eat."

"If that's alright with you."

"That's fine. We'll see you at Burke's at noon."

They ate and then went to the Chrisman House. Tracy and Marilyn were amazed at the Mansion. They couldn't get over the Grand Staircase and the Italian marble foyer. They loved the 'new' old windows in every room, and they agreed that neither of them had ever seen anything like it.

Tracy said to Marilyn, "I guess you've decided to move down here, haven't you?"

"No, I don't think so."

"But Marilyn, it's so beautiful. Nobody else has a house like this. If you wanted to, you could sleep in a different bedroom every night of the month."

She smiled and said, "That would be good if I wanted to get away from Frank, wouldn't it?"

"I'll say. Why don't you have an open house and show it off to your friends?"

"That's a good idea. Will you help me?"

"Of course, I will. When do you want to have it?"

"Do you think we could be ready by Saturday? I don't want a big crowd; maybe fifty or sixty."

"I think Saturday would be perfect. Are you going to mail invitations or call the people to invite them?"

"Maybe we can do both. I can call some of my best friends and we can mail the rest."

"Why don't you stop at the store on your way home and pick up the invitations, and I'll come over to your house tomorrow and help address them. I think it would probably be best if you mailed them all."

"Okay, I will. I'd better round up Frank and get him out of here if we're going to get to the card store before it closes."

On the way back to Burke's Grill to pick up Jerry's car, Marilyn and Tracy talked non-stop about the open house, and what they needed to do to get ready for it.

When Tracy got out of the car, she told Marilyn, "If we're going to get the invitations addressed and mailed tomorrow, we had better get started early. What time do you want me to come over to your house?"

"How about nine o'clock?"

"Sounds good. I'll see you then."

Marilyn had said that she was only going to invite fifty or sixty people, but she bought one hundred invitations. When Tracy got there, she poured her a cup of tea, and they discussed how they were going to do things. They decided that Tracy would begin addressing envelopes from their Christmas card list, and Marilyn would make calls to order things they would need, such as tables to use for serving, chairs, and refreshments. She didn't want to have to make anything. She wanted to have everything ready-made, so all she would have to do would be to host the get together.

They forgot that the invitation cards weren't printed, so they had to hurriedly come up with a time, location, and everything else that an invitation required. Marilyn wrote out all the information and rushed out to an instant printer to get them printed. She left Tracy there, addressing envelopes. The printer wasn't busy when she got there, and they got onto the invitations immediately. When she got back, Tracy was almost finished with the addressing, and Marilyn went over the list to see if there were any more that should be invited. She added a few, and then Tracy asked, "Does Frank have any business associates that you should invite?"

She said, "I don't know. Maybe I should call and ask him."

Frank said, "No, I don't think I want to ask any business

friends because they might think I'm trying to show off, but I'll tell you a few that you might invite. You won't have to mail them an invitation; you can just call them or have Jerry ask them, and those are some of Jerry's key people who worked on the mansion."

"Do you know who they are?"

"Not all of them, but Jerry does, and oh yeah, I don't think he worked on it, but I'd like to invite Stony. He's becoming one of Jerry's key people, and I'd like to include him, and tell him to bring his girlfriend. I think you met her at Jerry's. Her name is Deena. Anything else?"

"No, that's all. See ya tonight."

Tracy told Jerry that night about Frank wanting some of his key people to attend the open house on Saturday plus he wanted to invite Stony and Deena, even though he didn't work on the mansion.

The next morning, he either called or saw each of them and invited them to Frank's on Saturday afternoon, and of course, each one said they would be there.

Stony told Deena about the open house when he went over to her house, and she was excited about going. He asked Bobby if he and Kitty were going, and he said they were. He told Deena that since her parents were going, it would be good if she would ride down with them, and then he would bring her back.

The open house was a success. Nearly all of the people who got invitations were there, and it was interesting to see their reactions when they saw the house. Most of them were at the top of the social ladder in Atlanta and lived in mansions, themselves, but none of them had or had even seen anything like the Chrisman House. The reactions ran anywhere from joy to jealousy. The men were all happy for Frank, but some of the women resented the Thomas's having something that they didn't.

Reed Thomas was there with his girlfriend, and Jerry was

really glad to see him. Reed still felt some embarrassment around him because of the incident when he was sixteen and tried to dodge him at the gathering. Finally, Jerry caught up to him and said, "Reed, it's great to see you. It has been a long time. How have you been?"

"Hi, Mr. Martin. I've been good, thank you. Mr. Martin, this is my girlfriend, Katie Powell. Katie, this is Jerry Martin."

"Katie, it's great to meet you. You've got a fine man here."

"Thank you. It's nice to meet you, too."

"Reed, did your Dad tell you I asked about you?"

"Yes sir, he did. Thank you. You know, Mr. Martin, he talks about you all the time."

"Uh oh, I don't know if I like the sound of that."

"Don't worry. It's all good. He thinks you hung the moon."

"That's good to know. Have you seen Stony? He's here somewhere. Have you met his girlfriend? She's here, too."

"No sir, I haven't seen him. You say he's here? I'll look for him. It's good to see you, Mr. Martin. I'll see you a little later."

"It's good to see you, too, Reed. Katie, it was nice meeting you."

After Jerry told him that Stony was there, Reed went everywhere looking for him, and finally spotted him in one of the bedroom on the second floor. He was pretty far away, so he hollered, "Stony."

Stony heard his name and looked around but didn't see who hollered. Reed hollered again, and that time, Stony saw him. They walked toward each other and when they met up, they hugged because they hadn't seen each other in quite a while. They introduced their girlfriends to each other and talked for quite a while. During the conversation, Reed asked if they would like to go to dinner that night, and they said they would like to, so they set a place and time and agreed to meet at the restaurant.

As Stony and Deena were going to her house, Stony asked her, "What did you think of Reed and Katie."

"They're okay."

"You don't sound like you care that much for them."

"They're okay. I don't know them and maybe after tonight, I'll know them much better. Katie was real nice."

"But not Reed?"

"I didn't say that. I told you I don't know him. I'm sure he's a nice guy, and I'm anxious to get to know him when we eat together tonight."

Her attitude toward Reed kind of ticked him off, and he didn't have much to say for the rest of the ride to Deena's house. There was only about an hour between the time they got to Deena's and when they had to leave to meet Reed and Katie.

Reed wanted to go to The Paddock Restaurant, and when they got there, the sign said, 'Foxcraft Resort and Sporting Club' with Paddock Restaurant beneath it. Neither Deena or Stony had been there, and the name Resort and Sporting Club made them pause. It looked as if it was a place for the high society crowd, and they certainly weren't a part of that, but they parked and went in. Reed and Katie were already there and had gotten a table and were drinking some kind of cocktail.

When Reed saw them, he held up his arm and waved them back to where they were. When they got to their table, Reed asked if they wanted a drink, and Deena said, "No, thanks."

He looked at her and asked, "What's the matter? Won't your Mommy let you drink?"

Stony looked at him, and without any hint of a smile he said, "Reed, that was uncalled for. I don't want a drink either."

"Have it your way. Sorry."

Stony debated whether to sit down or not, but he attributed Reed's remark to the drink he was drinking and sat down. Katie looked as if she could crawl under the table and Deena glared at him, but it didn't seem to bother him.

After the initial flare-up, things settled down, and they began carrying on a normal conversation. Stony asked, "Reed, are you still working at a bank?"

"Yeah, the Cornerstone Bank over in Austell. What are you doing now?"

"I'm working for Martin Builders."

"Martin Builders? Man, I didn't think you'd ever want to see them again." Being obnoxious, he asked, "What are you doing, still picking up scraps around the houses?"

"No, Reed, I'm not. Do you remember Jerry Martin giving me a job when we finished our contract with him? Remember, I had to go to work while you went to college? Well, I worked hard and learned a lot about building, and Jerry Martin actually sent me to college where I got a degree in Building Sciences. To top that off, he promoted me to building supervisor, and the best thing he did for me was to introduce me to Jesus. Do you know Jesus, Reed?"

Reed said, "Who are you? What have you done with my friend Stony?"

Stony said, "It's still me, Reed. I've just grown up, and I'm no longer a juvenile delinquent the way you and I were when we were sixteen years old." Trying to change the subject, he looked at Katie and asked, "How long have you been dating this character, Katie?"

"About two months."

"Well, you keep him straight. We go back a long way, and we've had some good and bad experiences. He's a good guy, but he needs someone like you to take care of him."

"I will."

"Reed, do you remember Bobby Kunkle when we were working for Martin Builders?"

"Yeah, he was the supervisor, wasn't he?"

"Yeah. Well, Deena is his daughter."

"Go on. You don't mean it. I can't believe he'd let her go out with you."

"I told you I've changed, and by the way, I'm working on some apartments that your Dad owns."

Reed and Katie finished their drinks, and when the waiter asked them if they wanted another, they said no, then Reed asked, "Are you all ready to order?"

Stony said, "Yeah, I'm starved."

Deena was still upset by the initial comments by Reed, and she wasn't hungry, but she thought she should order something, so she ordered a soup and salad. Everybody else ordered a full meal.

After the initial upset and after Stony talked to Reed, the rest of the evening was fairly pleasant, although Reed and Katie seemed as if they were afraid they would say something wrong, and Stony would jump on Reed again.

Deena found out that Katie graduated from college a year ago and was working as some kind of specialist in an office in Atlanta. She told Katie that she was on the verge of graduating as a registered nurse. They talked about some other things as did Stony and Reed and after a while they all decided that it was time to go. Reed insisted that he get the check, so Stony let him, and after he got his credit card back and signed it, they got up and left.

The food must have sobered Reed up some because when they got outside, he said to Deena, "I'm sorry for what I said Deena. If my man, Stony here, thinks as much of you as it looks like he does, then you're okay in my book." Then he said to Stony, "Stone, it's great to see you. It has been too long. Let's keep in better touch, okay?"

Stony replied, "Okay, I'd like to. I love you, Reed."

On the way home, Stony said, "I'm sorry about Reed."

And Deena said, "Boy, he was arrogant, wasn't he, until you calmed him down."

"He knew I'd work on him if he didn't straighten out. When we were teenagers, Reed was always the one to do the talking, and I was considered the enforcer, so he knew he was wrong when he said what he did to you. He didn't use to be that obnoxious. Maybe his drinking caused it. Sometime, if you're in a forgiving mood, maybe we can go out with him again. We were like brothers back then."

He took her home, and because it had been such a long day, he didn't stay. He walked her to the door, kissed her goodnight, and then went home. They didn't see each other Sunday, but they talked on the phone. At one point Stony asked, "How long has it been since we said we were going to get married?"

"It's only been three or four weeks. Why?"

"Because I'm anxious to tell people that you're mine."

"I am too. It will be about the same amount of time that it has been since we first got together, and then we can tell people. We said two or three months, and I'm inclined to go with the two month figure. How about you?"

"How about one month?"

"Naw, I think two months is the right time."

"You know what?"

"What?"

"I almost told Reed last night."

"You didn't."

"Yes, I did. When he was implying that I was not doing very well, and I told him about working for Martin Builders, I wanted to say and besides that, I've found a good girl that is going to marry me, but I didn't."

"I'm glad you didn't. Listen, I've got to go. We're going up to my grandmother's and Mom and Dad are ready. I'll talk to you and hopefully see you tomorrow, I love you."

"Love you more," and he hung up really quick.

When he went to work Monday morning, the first thing he did was to assign the men their jobs for the day. After he did that, he and Bill got together and talked about the open house at the Chrisman House last Saturday and how pretty it was. While they were talking, Jerry drove up and got out of his pickup. "Good morning, Guys."

In unison, they replied, "Good morning."

Jerry said, "Bill, I want you to go out to the Chrisman House and build a small guard house. Frank wants to have a guard out there all the time, and he wants a separate place from the house for them to stay in. You'll have to have someone dig and pour some footings, and then two men should be able to build it. I'm going out there now. Why don't you ride with me and help me find a place to put it?"

"Okay, let me check out with Stony, and I'll be ready."

On the way to Chrisman, Bill asked, "What's Frank going to do with the mansion. Do you know?"

"I don't know, and I don't think he knows, either. I know he would like to move in it, but he can't get his wife to. She says it's too far out."

"Wouldn't it be something to have a place like that just sitting, collecting dust, and nobody using it?"

"I know. He's paying us a pretty penny for the renovations, and if it were me, I'd figure out some way for it to bring in some money if I didn't plan on living in it. He sunk a ton in it."

They decided on a place for the guardhouse, which was out of the way, yet close enough to the house to let the guard get there in a hurry if he needed to. When they finished, they went back to the apartment site, and Bill got out. Jerry went to his office to do some paperwork, and while he was shuffling papers, Melissa came in.

She knocked on the side of the door to his office, and when he looked up and saw her, he said, "Hi. Come on in."

It was not like her to be subdued, but she absolutely was. There was no "Hey Good Looking" or "Hi Handsome" or anything else like that. She was cool, calm, and collected.

Jerry asked, "What are you doing?"

"Nothing, really. I just wanted to come see you. I told Frank I needed to get out of the office and get some air, and he told me I could have the afternoon off."

"I didn't see you at the open house Saturday. Were you sick or something?"

"No, I wasn't sick. I can't seem to get that experience with J.D. out of my head, and I'm just not ready to go back to Chrisman yet. Maybe before long, but not now."

"Well you should see it. It's beautiful."

"I know it is if you had anything to do with it."

Chapter Eighteen

Six Weeks Later

As he did every day after work, Stony called Deena. "What would you like to do tonight?"

"I don't care. Whatever you'd like to do."

"I'd like to go get some barbeque."

"Me too. I haven't had barbeque in a long time."

"I'm leaving work right now. Why don't I come by and pick you up right now, and we can go by my house and let me clean up and change clothes. Are you ready or do you have to do something to get ready?"

"I'll be ready by the time you get here."

"Okay, see ya in a few."

Just as soon as he hung up from Deena, his phone rang. There was no name on the caller ID, but he thought he recognized the number. "Hello."

"Stony, it's Uncle Frank. How're you doing?"

"Fine, Uncle Frank. What can I do for you?"

"Stony, Reed has been a wreck, and he's in the hospital in critical condition."

"When did it happen?"

"Last night. Witnesses said he ran a light and an SUV t-boned him. He's been in a coma until just a little while ago, and when he woke up, he asked for you, and I thought I would call you. Stony, you two have been like brothers, and I knew you would want to know about it."

"Did you say he was asking for me?"

"Yes, he was. That was one of the first things he said when he came to. Do you think you could come see him?"

"Absolutely. Where is he?"

"He's in the ICU at Grady Memorial."

"I'm just leaving your apartments. How long will it take

me to get there?"

"I'd say forty-five minutes to an hour."

"Okay, I'll see you as soon as I can get there."

"Thanks, Stony. We'll be looking for you."

He called Deena back. When she answered he said, "Change of plans."

"You decided you don't want barbeque?"

"No, it's not that. Frank Thomas or Uncle Frank as I call him just called and said Reed had a bad wreck last night and is in critical condition. He said Reed has been in a coma until just a little bit ago, and when he came to, he was asking for me. I told Uncle Frank I would be there as soon as I could get there, and I thought I had better call you. I'm sorry, Honey, but Reed and I have been like brothers for most of our lives, and I feel like I need to go."

"You go on. I think you need to go, too. Call me when you can."

"Okay, I love you."

And that time she said, "Love you more," and she hung up quickly.

He couldn't help but smile, and then his thoughts turned serious when he thought about Reed. He arrived at the hospital, and after what seemed like forever, he found a parking place and went it. He saw the information desk and asked where the ICU was and was given directions.

He got on the elevator and went up to the ICU and met Frank and Marilyn as soon as he got off the elevator. He hugged Marilyn and shook hands with Frank and apologized for the way he looked just coming from work. They told him it would be about twenty minutes before they could go in again, so they sat in the waiting room and talked until time to go in.

Frank told Stony, "Stony, I don't know how long it has been since you and Reed have run around together, and I understand from talking to Jerry that you've had a major life

211

change, but I don't think Reed has. I can tell you this because you're like family that Reed was drinking before he had the wreck. The police said his alcohol level was point one fifty-three, which is almost twice the level for intoxication. I hope maybe you can turn him around. By the way; I called Jerry and told him."

In twenty minutes a nurse came to the door and said they could go in, and Stony wasn't prepared for what he saw. Reed was lying there with bandages all over his head and face, a cast on his left arm, and traction on his right leg.

Always the cut-up, Stony said, "I thought I looked bad, but man, you're a mess. What are you trying to do, kill yourself?"

In a weak voice, he replied, "I wasn't trying to, but I almost did, anyway." Then he looked at his parents and asked, "Mother, Dad, would you all mind if I talked to Stony alone?"

They looked at each other and Frank said, "We don't mind. We'll be right outside."

Stony walked over to his bed and asked, "What do you need, Padna?"

"Do you remember when we ate at The Paddock Restaurant a while back?"

"Yeah, I remember."

"Well, I showed my ass that night, and when you so masterfully got me told, you asked me if I knew Jesus. Remember that?"

"I remember."

"Stony, I don't know Him, and I want to. What do I do?"

"All you have to do is believe that He died on a cross for you and rose again after three days. Tell Him that you believe and ask Him to come into your heart, and He'll come in."

"How do I ask him to come in?"

"Maybe I can help you. Let's pray, and when you pray, ask him to come into your heart. I'll start and then you can finish, okay?"

"Close your eyes, Reed." Stony bowed his head and began

with, "Thank You Lord for today and thank You for all your blessings. Thank you, Lord for bringing Reed through that terrible accident, and now he wants to ask You to save his soul, and, according to Your word, you will do it if he asks. Father, Reed and I have been like brothers for most of our lives and now that You're saving his soul, we'll be brothers in Christ. Thank you again for bringing him through this, and I make this prayer in Your name." Then he urged Reed to pray and not to worry about how he did it. He told him just to be sincere and to ask in his own words.

Reed began his prayer by asking Jesus to forgive him for the life he had been living, and he said he wanted Him to come into his heart and help him live the way he should.

Stony opened his eyes and Reed had tears in his, and because of that, Stony teared up as well. "Is that all there is to it?" Reed asked.

"If you're sincere and believe that He died for your sins, that's all there is to it."

Reed said, "Come here."

Stony got as close to him as he could, and Reed said, "Come around to this side."

When he got around to his right side, Reed raised his right arm and attempted to hug him. He tried to hug him back but had a hard time because of the cast and traction.

Stony asked him if he wanted him to get his parents, and he said he did. He went to the door and opened it and Frank and Marilyn went into the room. They were kind of at a loss for words when Stony asked Reed, "Do you want me to tell them what you just did?" and Reed shook his head yes.

"Uncle Frank, Aunt Marilyn, Reed just accepted Jesus."

Marilyn said, "He did what?" and Frank said, "Wonderful; praise the Lord."

He repeated what he said for Marilyn's benefit, and then they moved up to Reed's bed and talked about it.

Stony said, "Look, they're going to run us out of here in a

few minutes, so I'm going to leave you all to soak this in. Reed, I'll try to come by after I get off tomorrow. Do you mind if I bring Deena?"

"No, in fact; I need to see Deena about something."

"Okay, I'm really happy for you, Bro. See ya tomorrow." He went over and gave Frank and Marilyn a hug.

Frank said, "Stony, thank you so much."

As soon as he got out of the ICU, he called Deena. She answered, Hey Stony."

"Hey. I'm leaving the hospital. What should we do?"

"Well, I didn't know how long you would be, so I went ahead and ate with Mama and Daddy, but you need to eat something. Do you want to just go get you something and go on home, and we'll see each other tomorrow?"

"No, that's not a good plan. I want to see you tonight."

"Okay. If you want to come by, I'll go with you to get something."

"I'll be there in a little bit, but I haven't changed clothes."

"That's alright. Just hurry and get here."

"I'll tell you what, look for me, and I won't get out. When you see me, come on out, and we'll go to Chick-Fil-A. I'll grab a sandwich, and you can get an ice cream.

While they were at Chick-Fil-A, and he was eating, he said, "You know, we've been dating for over two months now, and we said we would tell people about our engagement after two months. Are you ready to tell it?"

She groaned, "Unh, are you ready?"

"I've been ready for a long time. What do you say?"

"Alright, I guess it's time. How do you want to do it?"

"I've been thinking about it. I think we should tell your parents first and then my parents. I want to tell Jerry after we tell them, and after we tell all of them, we can have our picture made for the paper, or ever how you want to do it."

"When do you want to do it?"

"What's today, Monday?"

214

"Yeah."

"How about this coming Saturday?"

"Stony, look at me." He looked her in the eye, and she asked, "Are you absolutely sure you want to marry me?"

"What kind of question is that? You know I want to marry you. Why are you asking me that? Are you not sure, yourself?"

"Don't be ridiculous. How can you not know that I want to marry you? I told my mother that after our first date."

"So did I."

"Alright, if you're sure. I love you,"

"Love you mo.."

She interrupted and said, "Don't say it. There's no way you can love me more."

"Well, I do."

"I thought I told you not to say that."

"Okay, I won't say it, but I do."

She laughed and said, "You're impossible."

"Before I forget it, I told Reed I would try to go by and see him when I get off tomorrow. I asked him he minded if I brought you with me, and he said no, that he had something to talk to you about. Will you go with me?"

"Of course, I will. Wonder what he wants to talk to me about?"

"I don't know unless he wants to apologize for the way he behaved the last time we were with him."

They didn't get out of the car. They just sat in front of Deena's house for about an hour, and then Stony said he should go home.

He said, "Tomorrow, let's do what we said we were going to do tonight. I'll come get you when I get off, and we'll go to my house, so I can clean up. Then we'll go by the hospital to see Reed, and then we'll go somewhere to eat. Does that sound alright?"

"That's fine."

"Oh, there's one more thing."

215

"What?"

"On Wednesday night, why don't we go look for a ring?"

"Honey, I don't need a ring. You should save your money. We can get a ring later on."

"No, I want you to have a ring. That will show all those guys trying to get to you that you're mine."

She laughed and said, Yeah, right. There are so many of them."

He said, "I'll see you tomorrow. Why don't you think about where you'd like to eat."

"Okay. I love you, and don't say it."

He smiled and said, "Love you, too."

They kissed goodnight, and he left.

The next morning, when he went to work, Stony called Jerry. When he answered, Stony said, "Good morning, Jerry, Stony. I just wanted to tell you that Reed Thomas was in a bad wreck night before last, and he's in critical condition."

"I know. I had to call Frank about something late yesterday afternoon, and he told me. He said he had just talked to you, and you were going to the hospital. Did you go?"

"Yes sir, and he's a mess, but do you want to hear something really good?"

"Yeah, I'd like to hear some."

"The day of the open house at the Chrisman House, Reed and his girl, and Deena and I went out to eat together, and Deena and I got to the restaurant after Reed did, and he was about zonkered when we got there. He said something out of the way to Deena, and I talked pretty straight to him. Among other things, I told him that I had found Jesus, and I asked him if he knew Jesus, and that was all that was said that night.

"When Uncle Frank called to tell me about the accident, he said Reed was asking for me when he came to from his coma, so I went after work. He asked his Mom and Dad to let him talk to me alone, and apparently when I had asked him if he knew Jesus, it had an impact on him because when his parents left the room, he told me he didn't know Jesus, but he wanted to, and would I tell him how. I told him as best I could and we both prayed, and he accepted Jesus into his heart. I think Uncle Frank is thrilled, but I don't know about Aunt Marilyn. I just wanted to tell you that because you're the reason I found Jesus, and I was able to pass it on."

"Stony, that's wonderful. I'm very proud of you. I plan to go see Reed when he gets into a regular room. Thanks for calling me and telling me that."

That afternoon, there was a parking place surprisingly close to the hospital entrance, and Stony grabbed it. They parked and went upstairs to the ICU, and Deena didn't know what to expect. She was kind of nervous about it. Frank and Marilyn were in the waiting room when they got there, and they were taken by Deena's beauty and her personality.

In a few minutes a nurse came to the door and said they could go in, so the four of them went into Reed's room. Marilyn went over to his bed and leaned over and kissed him on the cheek. Frank reached over and put his hand on his good arm and asked how he was feeling. His voice was stronger than it was the day before.

He spoke to both of his parents and told his Dad he was feeling better, and then he looked at Deena and Stony and said, "Hi Guys." He held up his right hand and said, "Deena, come here."

She went over to him and grabbed his hand and he said, "I'm glad to see you. I just want you to know that I'm not really the horses patoot that you saw at the Paddock a while back, and I'm sorry for the way I behaved. I hope you'll forgive me."

She said, "You're forgiven."

He looked at Stony and said, "I've been forgiven for a lot the last two days, haven't I?"

Stony said, "You sure have."

Visiting time was only fifteen to twenty minutes, and it

seemed as if it just flew until the intercom announced that it was over.

They left the same way they entered. Marilyn kissed Reed on the cheek, Frank put his hand on his arm, and Deena took his hand, and Stony said, "I love you, Bro.", and they left.

"Have you decided where you want to eat?" Stony asked.

"No. We'll go anywhere you want."

"Do you like Gabe's Downtown?"

"Yeah, it's good. Why don't we go there?"

"Gabe's it is," and that's where they headed.

After a delicious meal and like the night before, it was late when they finished, and when they got to Deena's, they sat in the car, in front of her house for a little while, and then Stony went home.

As he promised, they went shopping for an engagement ring Wednesday evening. Stony had absolutely no idea what to look for, but Deena did. They went, first, to Evans Jewelers and looked at what they had, and Stony was amazed at the prices they were asking for even a small diamond. Deena didn't see what she wanted and suggested they go to Templeton's. Templeton's had a much larger selection, and after looking at what seemed like a hundred rings, she found one that she really liked.

"Is this the one you want, Honey?"

"Yes, if it's not too expensive."

He looked at the little tag attached to it, and when he saw the price, he said to himself, *whew*, but he handed it to the man and said, "We'll take this one."

"Very well. Congratulations on your engagement. Ma'am, would you try it on, so we can be sure it's the correct size?"

She did, and it was too tight, so the man pulled out a thing that had about a hundred rings of different sizes on it, and she tried on two or three until she hit the right size.

The man said, "We can have it ready for you tomorrow afternoon, if that's alright."

"That's fine. We'll come get it tomorrow."

Stony didn't have a very large credit limit on his card, but fortunately, he had enough to pay for the ring, and he gave the card to the man.

The man swiped the card, and Stony signed the receipt, and they left. Deena said, "I'm so excited. Thank you, Honey. I love the ring."

"Now, we're officially engaged. Are you happy?"

"You can't imagine how happy I am. I can't wait to show it off."

"Well, you can start showing it Saturday. What do you think Kitty Kunkle is going to say?"

"I think she'll be thrilled for us."

"What about Bobby?"

"I think he'll be happy, too. He likes you a lot."

"I hope so because I'm going to be working with him for a long time to come."

"Don't worry. He'll be thrilled, just like Mama."

They were like two kids that had just woke up to Santa Claus, and they walked around the mall for a long time before they decided to go home. They went to Deena's and stayed for a while, and Stony said, "Do you think your Mom and Dad would go out to eat with us?"

"I'm sure they would, why?"

"Why don't you invite them to go with us to Gabe's or somewhere else Saturday night, and we'll tell them about our engagement and show them your ring."

"I'll see if they'll go. If I ask them tonight, that should be plenty of notice."

"Wait a minute. Do you think I should ask Bobby for your hand?"

"Are you serious? This is the twenty first century. People don't do that anymore, but you can if you want to. Do you want to?"

"No, because I'm afraid of what he would say."

Bud Fussell

"Look, if we can go out with your parents Saturday and tell them, when do you think we should tell my folks? We don't have to take them out; we can just go to the house and tell them. Maybe I can get Mom to cook one night and invite you to dinner, in fact; I think I'll ask her tonight, and maybe we can do it Sunday night. Would that be alright with you?"

"Sure, I'd like to come to your house."

After Stony got off work Thursday afternoon, he went by to get Deena, and they went to the mall and to pick up her ring. She tried it on, and it fit perfectly. She wore it out of the store and constantly held her hand up to look at it. They walked around the mall for a little while, and she was so happy.

Stony was extra tired after a very trying day, and he asked her, "Honey, would you mind if I take you home now. I've had a really hard day, and I'd like to go home and maybe go to bed early."

"Do you feel bad?"

"No, I'm just tired. Do you care if we go home?"

"Of course not. I just hope you're alright."

When they got to her house, Stony said, "Don't forget to take your ring off. Do you want to leave the box in my car?"

She said, "That's a good idea. I hate to take it off, but it'll only be for one full day."

"Do you have a good hiding place for it?"

"Yeah, I can put it in my dresser. Nobody ever goes through my things."

They kissed goodnight, she got out of the car, and Stony went home.

As she was walking up the sidewalk, Stony put the window down and yelled to her, "If you ask your parents about Saturday night, call and let me know what they say."

Before he even got home, his phone rang. "Hey."

"Hey, I asked Mama and Daddy about going out to eat Saturday night, and they said they would love to."

"That's great."

"Yeah, except I've got butterflies."

"Just try to relax. I'll do most of the talking."

"What will you say?"

"Well, while we're at the restaurant, at some point, I'll say, 'Can I have your all's attention?' And when I get their attention, I'll say, 'Deena has something she wants to tell you.'"

"You're awful."

"Listen, I was just thinking; when and how are we going to tell Jerry?"

"Are you wanting to take him out to eat or what?"

"No, I don't think so. I'd like to go to his office, but I would like for you to be with me. You get out of school early on Tuesday and Thursday, don't you?"

"Yeah."

"How about you coming to the apartments next Tuesday at about quitting time, and we'll go to his office together. I'll call him and tell him I need to come by and talk to him about something. I won't tell him that you're coming with me, or he'll know we're up to something. If he can't see us Tuesday, I'll ask about Thursday."

"What do think he'll say?"

"I think he'll be happy for us. He knows where I came from and what you will do for me, and I know he'll be happy."

Friday was just a normal, routine day, and the guys accomplished a lot on the apartments, and Stony was really ready for quitting time to get there. He called Deena when he got off and told her he was going to go get her before he went home. He would clean up and change clothes at home, and then they would go out, if she wanted to.

Saturday was a different animal. It was just another day for Stony, but Deena was a bundle of nerves in anticipation of telling her parents about her engagement. Her best friend was a girl named Helen, and she called to see if she would like to go to the mall, and Helen said she would, so when they got there, she seemed to forget about everything except the clothes and things they were looking at.

She kept looking at her watch, so she wouldn't be late getting home to get ready for her big night. She had already told Helen that she would have to leave for home between three and three thirty, and at three fifteen she said she had to go.

Deena, Bobby, and Kitty Kunkle were to meet Stony at Gabe's, and they arrived at the same time. Kitty and Bobby walked on ahead, and Deena waited to walk in with Stony. She whispered, "You're going to do the talking, aren't you?"

He looked at her and smiled and whispered back, "I don't know what you're talking about."

She squeezed his hand as hard as she could and said, "You're terrible."

They found a table and sat down to look at the menu. The waitress took their order after they decided what they wanted and talked. Bobby and Stony talked shop while Deena and her mother talked about other things. Sometimes, Stony would ask Kitty something, or she would ask him something, and then Bobby said, "Stony, Jerry told me about Reed Thomas being in a bad wreck. I remember him being a friend of yours. How is he, do you know?"

"He's in the ICU at Grady Memorial, and I've seen him twice. In fact; Deena went with me to see him a couple of nights ago. I think he's going to be alright, but he is sure banged up."

Deena said, Tell them what you did."

"Naw, they wouldn't be interested in that."

"Yes they would. Tell them."

"Why don't you tell them?"

"Because you're the one who did it."

Kitty said, I'd like to hear what you did."

"Okay." He looked at Deena and asked, "You want me to go back to when we ate with them?"

"Yes. That's important."

"Okay. It started the night of the open house at the Chrisman House. Reed invited Deena and I out to eat with him and his girl. When we got to the restaurant, Reed had already been drinking, and he asked us if we wanted a drink. Deena said we didn't, and he made some unnecessary remarks about it, and I proceeded to straighten him out. He had also implied that I wasn't such a hot item, so I really let him have it. Among many other things I told him how Jerry Martin had introduced me to Jesus, and I asked him if he knew Him, and that's about all that was said that night.

"Well, Uncle Frank called me the other afternoon and told me about Reed's accident and said he was asking for me. I went over there, and he asked his parents to let him talk to me alone. After they left the room, he went back to that night and said he didn't know Jesus, and would I help him get to know Him. I'm not real good with words, but I told him as best as I could how he could be saved. We prayed together, and he asked Jesus to come into his heart, and that's what Deena's talking about."

"Stony, that's a wonderful story. I'm so proud of you," Kitty said.

"Thank you." He looked at Deena and winked and said, "While we're waiting for our food, there's something else that I'd like to tell you. As you know, Deena and I have been going together for a little over two months now, and actually, after our first date, we knew we wanted to get married. I love her more than either of you can imagine, and I hope you will approve of us getting married. Bobby, I asked Deena if I should ask you for her hand, and she said people don't do that in the twenty first century, but I'm asking you for the record."

Bobby laughed and said, "Stony, I approve, and I look forward to having you as my son-in-law."

Stony asked, "How about you, Kitty Kunkle?"

She replied, "You know what? When Deena told me after

223

your first date that she wanted to marry you, I kind of scoffed at the idea, because it was just the first date, and I told her to pray about it, but over the last couple of months, I've grown to love you as my son, and I heartily approve of you marrying our daughter."

As soon as they were through with the announcement, the waitress brought their food, and before they started to eat, Stony asked Deena, "Did you bring it with you?"

She said, "Yes, I definitely did," and she reached into her purse and brought out her ring and showed it to her mother."

Bobby and Stony began to eat while Deena and Kitty ood and aahd over the ring, and talked about the wedding. He heard Kitty ask, "When are you all planning to get married?"

And Deena said, "After I graduate."

"Where will you live?"

"We're thinking that we'll get one of the apartments that Stony's working on. Some of them should be finished by the time we get ready. Stony talked to Jerry about it, and Jerry told him to let him know when we get ready, whatever that means."

Bobby said, "It looks as if you two know what you want. You must have talked about this earlier."

Deena said, "That's all we've talked about for two months. We've been wanting to tell you from the beginning, but we decided to wait until we had been going together for at least two months. We started to wait until I graduate to tell you, which is six months, and then we lowered it to three months, and then last week, we decided that two months is long enough, so here we are."

"Where do you want to have the wedding?"

Deena said, "At our church, if that's alright with Stony. We haven't talked about that. Mama. I hope you'll help me, will you?"

"I've been hoping for this ever since you were a little girl. Of course, I'll help."

Bobby and Stony finished their meal, and Kitty and Deena

had hardly touched theirs.

Bobby asked, "Are you girls going to eat your dinner?"

Kitty looked up at him and said, "Yeah," and then went right back to talking.

After a few more minutes, Stony said, "Ladies, you need to eat. I think they're wanting this table," and that time, they began to eat, but stopped after every few bites to talk some more.

Finally, they finished their dinner, and Stony picked up the check. They decided that they would all go back to Bobby and Kitty's house, and Kitty said, "Deena, why don't you ride with your Daddy, and I'll ride with Stony," so they left Gabe's and headed home.

On the way, Deena asked Bobby, "Daddy, are you really happy for me?"

Bobby replied, "Yeah, Baby. I'm really happy. Your mother and I love Stony. He's a real man, and he'll take good care of you."

In the other car, Stony asked, "Well, Kitty Kunkle, what do you think?"

"I think it's wonderful, Stony Gray. I hear people say that they're losing their little girl or boy when they get married, but I don't feel that way. I feel that I'm getting the son that we never had."

"Thank you so much. I'll try to live up to your expectations."

"I'm sure you will. Stony, that story you told about you and Reed was amazing. You said he said something uncalled for to Deena. What did he say?"

"It really wasn't much, but it flew all over me. When we got to the restaurant, he asked us if we wanted a drink, and Deena said no. Reed said, "What's the matter? Won't your Mommy let you drink?" And that's when I lit into him.

"Have you told your Mom and Dad yet?"

"Not yet. We plan to tell them tomorrow night.

225

Chapter Nineteen

On Sunday morning, Stony got up and before it got too late, he called Deena. "Hey, my hero."

"I'd say, hero. What's the hero stuff?"

"You're my hero."

"Drop that hero stuff. I'm not anybody's hero."

"Okay, but you're still mine."

"What are you doing?"

"Getting ready for Sunday School. Why don't you come and go to church with us?"

"I might just do that. Did you tell me that you go to the Douglasville Community Church?"

"That's right. Will you come?"

"I don't want to come to Sunday School, but I'll come to Church."

"Good. It starts at eleven o'clock, and I'll wait on you outside the front door."

"Okay. I'll see you there."

After church, as they were leaving, Bobby told Stony, "We're going out to lunch. You want to go with us?"

"I'd like that," so Deena rode with Stony and they met at Sam and Roscoes. The food was delicious, and Stony left them when they finished their lunch. He went home to take a nap, and he told Deena that he would pick her up around five o'clock and take her to his house for dinner.

When he picked her up, he noticed that she wasn't wearing her ring, and he asked her about it. "Well, I thought since we haven't told them yet, that your mother might see it. As soon as you tell them, I'll put it on."

His parents were altogether different than Deena's parents. Nancy and Harold were good, honest, hard-working people with very little social life. They didn't attend church, so they didn't have a life there. Harold was on a bowling team, and that was pretty much the only time he associated with people other than the ones he worked with at the mill.

Nancy, on the other hand, was much more outgoing, but she had very little social life as well. She did belong to a garden club, and that gave her a small outlet with other people. She was very nice, however, and very comical. People that knew the family said that she was where Stony got his personality.

At six thirty, she called them to dinner. Dinner was a mixture of delicious food, with the star being meat loaf, which was Stony's favorite. They all ate without too much conversation, and when they were coming to the end, Stony said, "Mom, Dad, we've got something to tell you. Deena and I have decided that we're going to get married."

Nancy said, "You told me you were going to marry her, didn't you?"

"I did, and I hope you and Dad are happy about it."

"I'm happy for you. Deena, you seem like a very nice girl, and I think you'll make Stony a good wife."

"Thank you, Mrs. Gray."

Stony's dad asked, "Can you all afford to get married? You know, it costs a lot to live nowadays."

"We know that, Dad, but I've got a good job, and in four months, Deena will be a registered nurse, and she'll be making good money, so to answer your question, yes, we can afford to get married."

He asked, "When's the big event?"

"In four or five months. We're going to wait until Deena graduates from nursing school."

"Are you going to get married in a church?"

"Yes sir. We're going to get married where Deena and her family go."

'I guess in a big wedding like that, I'll have to wear a tie."

That ran right through Stony, and his face turned red, and

he said, "No, Dad, you won't have to wear a tie. You can wear shorts and a t-shirt as far as I'm concerned, or better still, you don't even have to go because we're getting married whether you're there or not."

Harold said, "Man, you don't have to get your panties in such a knot. I didn't mean anything by that. Of course, I'll be there and I'll wear a tie. Okay? I didn't mean to make you mad."

"Okay, Dad. It's alright. Deena and I are so happy right now, we just don't need to hear something like that."

"I'm sorry."

"It's okay, Dad."

After the upset, Nancy and Deena went into the kitchen and talked. Nancy wanted to know everything, and Deena did her best to answer all the questions. Harold went to the living room and turned on the TV, and Stony went into the kitchen with the women.

Nancy said, "Son, are you alright?"

"Yeah, Mom. I'm sorry I blew up, but that just ran through me. I'm sorry."

"That's alright. Sometimes your Dad says things that come out wrong, but don't worry. We'll be there, and he'll be properly dressed."

"What do you think about us getting married?"

"I think it's wonderful. I know you all will be happy. I liked Deena the first time I met her."

"Good. Well, Miss Deena, are you ready to go?"

Nancy said, "I wish you wouldn't go. Why don't you stay for a while? I want to hear about the wedding."

Stony looked at Deena and asked, "What do you think?"

"We can stay for a little while if you want to."

They wound up staying until ten o'clock. Harold couldn't hear the TV for their talking, so after a while, he got up and went into the bedroom, where they had another TV.

On the way to Deena's, she said, "I really like your Mom.

I thought our announcement went well, didn't you?"

"Yeah, it went well except for when my Dad said what he did. He's really a good guy, but he's kind of crude, and sometimes he drives me nuts. I'm sorry I blew up in front of you. I know it was embarrassing for you."

"No it wasn't. I just hate that you got so upset."

"We've told everybody but Jerry now. I hope we can tell him Tuesday. I'm anxious to see your picture in the paper."

"Honey, I'm not sure, but don't we have to have a date before we put it in the paper?"

"I have no idea. You'll have to ask one of your married girlfriends."

When they got to Deena's, they sat in the car for a few minutes, and Stony said, "Honey, would it be alright if we don't see each other tomorrow night? I thought I would go see Reed, unless you'd like to go with me."

"I don't think I will. You go on and see him. It will do you both good to spend some time together. Mama and I can start seeing what we need to do for the wedding."

"Are you thinking about a big wedding?"

"Not too big, why? don't you want a big wedding?"

"I want what you want. It can be little or it can be big; I don't care."

A few more minutes of conversation finished off the night, and Stony went home, after telling her goodnight."

He had a renewed interest in the apartments when he went to work Monday morning. Announcing their engagement to both sets of parents brought home the realization that it was really going to happen, and he wanted to make sure they were ready when he and Deena were ready for one.

About mid-morning, Jerry went to the site, but Stony didn't say anything about wanting to come to his office the next day because he was afraid he would say to come on that night, and Deena couldn't go then.

When he broke for lunch the next day, he called Jerry and

told him he would like to come by his office after work. He told him he had something he needed to talk to him about, and Jerry told him to come on. After he hung up, he wondered why Stony would call him and what he wanted. He hoped he wasn't going to quit, but then he told himself, *I don't think he's going to quit because he was too excited about getting promoted to foreman. It must be something else.*

Tuesday morning was a crusher. It seemed as if at every turn there was a problem of some kind. They finally got them all worked out a little after lunch, and Stony asked Bill if he could leave around four thirty. That he had to go to Jerry's office, and Bill said he could. He thought about calling Deena and having her come to the site, but then he thought if she did, they would have two cars, so he decided to swing by her house and pick her up.

He fudged a little and left work at four fifteen, since he had to pick up Deena. He called ahead, and she was ready when he got there. He had timed the whole thing to where he would get to Jerry's around five o'clock, and his timing was almost perfect. They arrived at Jerry's office at five after five. Jerry was waiting when they walked in, and when he saw Deena, he said." Well, hello, Deena. I didn't know you were coming with our boy here. How are you?"

"I'm doing great, thank you. How are you?"

"Better than I deserve. What's up, Stony?"

"Well, I wanted to talk to you before I talked to anybody else about this. We want to tell you that we're getting married. We've told our parents and now you because next to our parents, you are the most important person in my world."

"Well, thank you Stony and congratulations. I'm very happy for you. When is the big event?"

"After Deena graduates. She graduates from nursing school in four more months, and sometime after that, we'll get married. We've been talking about it, and we think we would like to rent one of the new apartments we're working on, if any of them are ready by then."

"Four months, you say? There should be some ready by then. If you're serious, you all can look at the plans and pick out what you want. You all will be our first tenants."

"When you and I were talking, you said you thought the two bedrooms would be around twelve hundred dollars. Is that still the thinking?"

"Yeah. Do you all think you can handle that?"

"We think we can. I could probably handle it myself if we wanted to cut it close, but when Deena gets a job as a Registered Nurse, we know we can do it."

"That's great. Stony, why don't you take a set of plans home one night, and you all can pick out what you want and the location. Of course, you know we're just working on four building, but that will give you thirty-two apartments to choose from."

"Okay, I will. Thank you so much, Jerry.

"Thank you guys for coming by to deliver this good news. I'm very happy for you." He smiled and winked at Stony and told Deena, "I can't wait to have you as my daughter-in-law."

Smiling and without missing a beat, she went over and put her arms around him and said, "I can't wait to have you as my father-in-law either."

He stepped back and asked, "Do you all have any plans for dinner."

Stony answered, "No sir."

"Stony, I know you like barbeque. Deena, do you like barbeque?"

"I love it."

"If I can get hold of my wife, would you all like to go to Old Smokeys?"

They both said they would. Jerry dialed Tracy. And when she answered, he said, "Hi Sweetie. I've got Stony and Deena here, and we're talking about going to Old Smokies. Do you want to go?"

Bud Fussell

She must have said something about B.J., and he said, "Well, bring him. We can get him some chicken tenders or something." And then after a pause, he said, "We're leaving my office right now. If you leave now, we should get there about the same time. See ya."

Jerry, Deena, and Stony got there first and went in and got a table. It was only two or three minutes before Tracy and B.J. got there, and when B.J. saw his daddy, he ran over and jumped up in his lap.

Tracy said, "Hey, guys. What are you all doing out here?"

Jerry answered for them and said, "Look on Deena's finger," and Deena held her hand up and showed off the ring."

"It's beautiful. When did this happen?"

Deena said, "Officially, last week, but we've known we wanted to get married ever since our first date."

Tracy looked over at Jerry and said, "That's kind of like us, isn't it, Darling?"

"Yeah, I think we knew from the beginning that we wanted to get married, but we went through a whole lot of things before we actually got engaged."

Stony asked, "Such as?"

"You wouldn't believe what we went through. A couple of the more memorable things was when Tracy was almost killed in a car wreck. She hung upside down by her seatbelt for a solid week before anybody found her. And then, her jilted ex-boyfriend shot and nearly killed me, but through everything, we knew we loved each other and wanted to get married.

"As a matter of fact; Tracy was in the hospital recovering from her accident when I met you for the first time, Stony."

Stony, always the jokester, said, "Well, I'm just glad I was able to bring you two together. There are no thanks needed."

They all laughed, and Tracy asked, "Have you had your picture made for the paper yet?"

Deena answered, "No. You two are the only people

232

besides our parents that know about it. Besides our parents, you two are the most important people in Stony's world, and we wanted you to know before anybody else."

"Well, we're very flattered, aren't we, Darling?"

"Jerry said, "We definitely are. I told Deena that I'm looking forward to having her as my daughter-in-law."

"Exactly. Deena, I know your friends will want to give you some showers, but after they're all set, if there's room for one more, I'd like to give one for you."

"That's really nice, but let us make the announcement and see what happens."

Tracy asked. "Where will the wedding be?"

"I was raised in the Douglasville Community Church, and that's where it will be."

Jerry asked, "Is everybody full? If so, I guess it's time to go. Deena, Stony, we're very happy for you."

Stony said, "Thank you Jerry, and Tracy, it was great to see you. Thank you all for the delicious barbeque. Jerry, maybe I'll see you tomorrow."

"You probably will. I've got to go out to White Rock, and I'll stop by the apartments on the way. You all have a good night."

As they left Old Smokey's and started to Deena's, Stony said, "Those are good people. I thank God everyday for bringing Jerry into my life. There's no telling where I'd be if it wasn't for him."

"I know, and Tracy's really nice, too. I can't believe she offered to have a shower for me."

"Is there anything special that you want to do tonight?"

"No. I guess we can go to my house if you want to."

"That's fine with me," and he turned and headed in that direction."

Jerry had planned to go to White Rock the next morning, and he had told Stony he was going to stop by the apartments on the way, but when he went to his office, his plans got changed. The paving company called, as he was walking in the door and said they were going out to Cummings Acres to begin grading for the streets in the development and asked if he would meet them out there. They said they would also like to send equipment to start digging the lake, if he was ready.

He said, "Of course, I'm ready. I've been waiting on you guys to do your thing, so we can get started on the development. I'll see you out there."

To say he was excited when he drove out would be a gross understatement. He had been excited from the git-go when he bought the land, and now that it will be underway was beyond his belief. Jerry had taken the paving company a set of surveys, and they had apparently made another copy because the grader had a set as well as the excavator.

He spent some time at the bottom of the proposed roadway getting them started, and then he went to the site where the lake would be. They discussed the depth, the grade of the bottom, and other things necessary to construct a first class lake, and the excavator dug the first scoops. The paving company sent two large dump trucks to haul the dirt away as it was being dug, and it didn't take long before they were getting filled up. In a few minutes another big truck came in with a large bulldozer on the back.

While he was watching them dig, he looked and saw a car coming up the road. As it got closer, he recognized the driver as Stella Cummings. She pulled up next to him and rolled down her window. He walked over to her and said, "Good morning, Stella. How are you?"

"I'm fine, Jerry. How are you?"

"Real good now that we're getting started out here. What can I do for you?"

"If you've got a few minutes when you leave here, would you stop by the house? Clarence has something he wants to talk to you about."

"Sure, I'll stop by. I shouldn't be here but a few more

minutes, and then I can come. Do you know what's going to be here where they're digging?"

"No, I have no idea."

"When they get through with it, it will be about a ten-acre lake."

"Really?

"Yeah, it should be nice."

Stella said, "I'm going to get back. Don't forget to stop by the house."

"Okay, I'll just be a few minutes."

He hated to leave, but there was nothing he could do if he stayed other and watch them work. He thought as he drove down the road, *I wonder what Clarence wants to talk to me about. There's no telling.* He crossed the main road and drove up to the Cummings' house. He got out and walked up on the porch. Stella was waiting on him. And when he got to the door, she opened it for him.

"Come in, she said. Let me get Clarence."

In just a few seconds, she came back with Clarence. Jerry walked over and held out his hand, and said, "Hi Clarence. How're ya doing?" Clarence grabbed his hands and shook hands with what Jerry called a 'dead fish' handshake. Any time he shook hands with somebody that had a 'dead fish' handshake, he would squeeze the other hand extra hard, and that's what he did with Clarence.

"I'm okay," Clarence said. "How are you?"

"I'm great, thank you. Stella said you wanted to talk to me. What can I do for you?"

"Are you happy with that land I sold you?"

"Yes sir, I am. You probably saw the machine over there this morning. We're finally getting started on the development I want to build. Why do you ask?"

"Would you be interested in some more?"

"I might. What have you got in mind?"

"There's a real pretty section that joins what you bought,

235

and I might be interested in selling it to you if you want it."

"How many acres, and how much do you want for it?"

"There's somewhere around a hundred and fifty acres, and I'd sell it to you for the same price per acre that you paid for your three hundred acres. This is better land than what you bought because it has a large creek and two ponds on it."

"I'm always looking for some good building land, but I borrowed a million dollars to buy the three hundred acres, and now you're talking about another half million. I don't know if Frank will loan me another big amount or not."

"You know what?"

"What?"

"Frank came out here week before last, and we were talking about you, and I got the idea that he would give you anything you wanted."

"Clarence, we're talking money here, and Frank's a banker. Giving me some things is one thing, but you can't count money in that."

"That's not the way I understood it."

"Let me ask you something. Are you trying to sell the hundred and fifty acres for the same reason you sold the other?"

"Yeah, the medical bills are running more than we thought they would."

"Clarence, I wish I could help you in some way other than taking your farm, but I don't know what it would be. Can you think of some way I could help you?"

"Not unless you can give me a pot of money. I'm just lucky I have the farm. If you don't buy it, I guess I'll try to find somebody else to sell it to."

"Tell you what. Let me talk to Frank. It will probably be years before I can use it, but I'd hate for some low-end builder to come in and build a bunch of project houses on it. That would really hurt the sales of my houses. Let me see what I can do, and I'll get back to you. Have you got time to take a ride and show it to me?"

"Yeah, I can go with you."

They got in Jerry's pickup, and when they got to the main road, instead of going straight across, Clarence had him turn right. In about a quarter mile, he had him turn left, and they drove up what looked like an old wagon trail. The land was beautiful, maybe even more beautiful than the other three hundred acres, and Jerry knew he wanted it. When they got to the large creek, it was just a hop and a skip from where he was building the lake. He thought that maybe there would be some way to connect the two.

"This is pretty, Clarence. I'll call Frank when I get back to my office. There's something I want to ask you to do."

"What's that?"

"If I buy this land, I ask that you not sell any adjoining land for anything other than farming."

"Why do you want that?"

"Because the houses I'm going to build will all cost at least a million dollars, and if somebody is going to spend a million dollars for a house, they don't want something next to it that will not compliment it. How would you like to buy a house for a million dollars and then six months later have someone come in there and put up some mini warehouses or a car lot. You wouldn't like it, would you?"

"No, I don't guess I would."

"Well, will you agree to do that?"

"Yeah, I guess so."

"Good 'cause if I buy it, I'm going to have that put in the agreement."

When they finished looking at it, Jerry took Clarence back home and told him he would call him and let him know what he was going to do. Stella was at the door and waved at him as he left.

When he got back to his office, he called Frank.

"Frank, I don't know if I'm crazy or not, but I want to run something by you."

"What's that, Jer?"

"Clarence Cummings wants to sell me another hundred and fifty acres. This is beautiful land with two ponds and a large creek. He wants the same per acre as the three hundred acres. What do you think?"

"What do you think?"

"I think I would really like to have it, but I already owe you a million dollars, and if I buy this, I'd have to borrow another half a million, and you might not even want to loan it to me. I trust your advice, and that's why I'm calling you."

"Do you want me to give you my honest opinion?"

"Yes sir, I do."

He wished Frank hadn't asked him that because he knew he would advise against it, and he really did want that land.

Frank said, "Well, Jerry, I think you ought to call Clarence and tell him you'll buy it, and then you can come by here and get the money."

"Are you serious?"

"I'm dead serious."

"Do you want to go out and look at it?"

"I guess I should, since I'm loaning you a half million dollars on it."

"When do you want to go?"

"How about tomorrow morning?"

"That works for me. About ten o'clock?"

"That's good."

"Okay. I'll pick you up."

Frank and Jerry had become very close as business associates, and now they were becoming close as friends. The ride to the Cummings land was enjoyable, and Frank was very impressed with the acreage. He asked Jerry, "What do you see for this land, Jer?"

"The first thing I see is a beautiful lake. I had planned to have a ten acre lake on the three hundred acres, but now that I'm getting this, and the nearness of this creek to the lake, I'm thinking that I'll increase the size to maybe fifteen or eighteen acres. I see homes on the property that are second to none. I have been planning on maybe eighty homes, but now, I might increase it to a hundred. That will leave about forty or fifty acres that won't have anything on them, and maybe sometime I'll need the land for something."

"Do you think you'll have any trouble selling a hundred, million dollar homes?"

"There's a lot of money in the Atlanta area, and a hundred first class, state of the art homes should move pretty quick."

"I agree. If they're any nicer than the ones at White Rock, I may buy one, myself."

"They're not going to be nicer; just larger."

As they were leaving the land, Jerry asked, "Would you like to stop in and say hello to Clarence and Stella?"

"Yeah, let's do," so when they got to their driveway, they turned in and drove up to the house. They went in and visited with Clarence and Stella for a few minutes, and they seemed to appreciate their visit.

As they were leaving, Jerry said, "Clarence, does that creek on the property have a name?"

"No, why?"

"Well, I'm going to do some things with it, and I thought it would be neat if it had a name. Since it doesn't have one, I think I'll call it Stella's Creek. Is that alright with you, Stella?"

She grinned from ear to ear and asked, "You're going to name the creek after me? Why?"

Jerry, being the old smooth talker of the past said, "Well, it only makes sense that we name a beautiful creek after a beautiful woman."

Stella went over and put her arms around him and said, "Thank you."

"You're very welcome. Frank, are you ready?"

On their way back to town, Frank said, "Jer, that was a nice thing you did back there."

"What did I do?"

"Naming the creek after Stella. She's a good woman, and living with a man like Clarence, I'm sure she doesn't get any outside praise or compliments, and I could tell she was thrilled over that, so I'll say thank you, on her behalf."

"Frank, can you get the hundred and fifty acres surveyed for me?"

"Yeah. Are you in a hurry?"

"Kinda. This is the same deal as the three hundred acres. I asked Clarence if it was, and he said yes. The medical expenses are running higher than they thought they would. How many acres do they have? Do you know?"

"I think they originally had over nine hundred, but since you bought four hundred and fifty of that, they have between four fifty and five hundred left."

"I wonder if they'd like to sell the rest of it."

"I seriously doubt it. The farm has been in Clarence's family for generations. Why? Are you interested in it?"

"I don't know. Just thinking. Are they farming it now?"

"I think they may be raising and selling a few cattle, but now that Clarence is up in years, I don't think he's able to raise any crops. One of his sons lives out West somewhere, and the one who lives just over the line in Alabama is almost a full-time nurse for his wife, so he can't be much help."

"You know what, Frank? I won't make him an offer, but I think I'll tell him that if he ever decides to sell the rest, to please give me first refusal, and that I won't build anything on it. I'll keep it as a farm."

"He might decide to let you have it, but at some point, he's going to have to quit shelling out so much for his son and begin looking after himself and Stella."

Jerry asked, "When have you seen Stony?"

"I saw him at the hospital the other night. Why?"

"Then I guess you haven't heard the big news."

"No, I haven't."

"Stony and Deena are getting married."

"Get outa here. Stony getting married?"

"Yep. Have you met Deena?"

"I met her at the pig pickin and then again, at the open house. She's a beauty."

"She's a fine young lady."

"When did all this come about?"

"They announced it to their parents last week, and then they told Tracy and me last night. I don't guess they've had time to tell everybody else yet. They're planning to get married in about four months, when Deena graduates from nursing school, and they want to rent one of the apartments we're building."

"Will you have some ready by then?"

"We should have the first two building ready and possible the first four."

"It seems like you just started on them. Time flies, doesn't it?"

"It sure does. I told Stony that I didn't see any reason why they couldn't get one. He's starting to make more, now, and Deena will make good when she gets a job as a registered nurse, so the rent shouldn't be a strain on them."

When they reached the bank, Frank got out, and Jerry went to his office to see if he was needed before he left for White Rock. He had lost so much time, that morning, taking Frank to Cummings Acres that he might not even have enough time to go out there. He had several messages when he got there, and while he was talking to one person, his cell phone rang. He told the person he was talking to that he would call him back, and he answered his cell. It was Sheila Higgs, the realtor at White Rock.

"Hi Sheila, what's up?"

"Hi Jerry. Jerry, there's a suspicious looking car parked out here with a man in it. It was here yesterday, and it's back today. The man in it is wearing a shirt and tie, and he just sits

241

there. I haven't seen him get out at all."

"Where is it, Sheila?"

"You know that large house that we sold just a couple of weeks ago? The one in the long curve?"

"Is that the one where that guy paid you cash?"

"Yeah, that's the one. His name is Hernandez."

"Have you seen anything strange going on there?"

"Not a thing. His wife or girlfriend or whoever comes out and waters the flowers, and fools around in the yard, but I've never seen anybody else since Mr. Hernandez bought the house; not even Mr. Hernandez."

"Do you want me to come out there, Sheila?"

'I don't know if that's necessary. The man is not doing anything. He just sits in the car. It's creepy."

"I know, but we need to know why he's there. I'm leaving right now to come out there, and if he leaves before I get there, call me so I won't come all the way for nothing. If I don't hear from you, I'll see you in a little while."

"Thanks, Jerry."

On the way out to White Rock, he racked his brain, trying to figure out why the man was parked in his development, but nothing came to him. Sheila didn't call him back, so he knew he was still there, and he was getting near to the development. When he got to the street, he turned in and drove straight, past most of the homes that were now occupied, until he saw a grey car with a man in it parked on the side of the street, facing in the direction that he was coming from.

Jerry pulled over, nearly up against the front bumper of the car and sat there for a minute, contemplating exactly what to do. He got out of his pickup and walked up to the driver's side of the car, and the man rolled the window down.

When he got to the open window, he asked the man, "Can I help you?" at which time the man held up a badge wallet with a badge that said Drug Enforcement Agency.

The man asked, "Who are you?"

"I'm Jerry Martin. This is my development. Who are you?"

"Special Agent Roger Carpenter. I need for you to leave right now. This is a Federal Surveillance."

Jerry asked, "How long do you plan to be parked out here?"

Special Agent Carpenter said, "As long as it takes."

Jerry said, "Well, I hope it doesn't take too long. I've got workmen out here, and they pass right by here, and I'd hate for any of them to get hurt."

He went back to his pickup, got in, and drove past the DEA agent on up the street to the house Bobby Kunkle was working on.

When Bobby saw him, he said, "Hey, Boss. How're you doing?"

"Good. Listen, Bobby, you get here early don't you?"

"Yes sir; normally about seven o'clock."

"Have you noticed that grey Impala parked down the street?"

"Yeah, I saw it when I passed by it earlier today. Why is it parked there; do you know?"

"Kind of. I stopped and asked the man why he was there, and he's a DEA agent surveilling the Hernandez house. I don't know why, but when I was talking to him, he told me to leave right then. I'd like for you to kind of keep an eye on him and keep me posted on anything that happens over there."

"I'll do it."

"By the way; congratulations on Deena and Stony's engagement. They're both lucky to get each other."

"Thank you. I think they're both lucky, too. I'll tell you, if Stony had come around ten years ago, I would have run him off, but he has grown into a very good man, and I'm going to be happy to have him as a son-in-law."

Sheila Higgs had set up shop in one of the houses that was still for sale, and when Jerry left Bobby, he went to see her. "Hi Sheila."

"Hi Jerry, did you find out why that man is parked out there?"

"Not exactly. He's a DEA agent surveilling the Hernandez house for some reason. I assume it has something to do with drugs, but you don't have anything to worry about."

"Thanks for coming out, Jerry. Right before I called you I showed this house, and the people are very interested. I won't be surprised if they come back and say they want it."

"Great. We had better get some more ready, hadn't we?"

"I'd say so. They're selling about as fast as you build them."

"I've got to go, Sheila. Bobby Kunkle will keep an eye out for our friend and call me if anything happens that I need to know. I may be back tomorrow. I'll see you."

"See ya, Jerry."

When Bobby went to White Rock the next morning, there was a burgundy Dodge Charger parked where the grey Impala was parked the day before, and then, when he went back by there around eleven o'clock, the grey Impala was back.

Since no one called him from White Rock, Jerry went to Cummings Acres and watched them grade the streets and dig and bulldoze the lake. He took a set of surveys with him along with several artist drawings of houses for which he had the plans. He visualized the houses on different plots and when he was sure about where a particular house would go, he would write the plan number on the survey.

While he was in the midst of doing that, he heard a car coming up the trail, and when he looked, it was a strange car. It stopped a little way away from his pickup, and when the driver got out, it was Stella Cummings. "Hi Stella, I didn't recognize your car," Jerry said.

"Hi Jerry. What are you doing?"

"I'm just doing a little planning. I'm trying to figure out where different houses will be. What are you doing?"

"Clarence is gone for a while, and I saw your truck turn in, so I thought I'd come up and see you."

"Well, I'm glad you did. How's your daughter-in-law doing?"

"About the same. She's just about eat up with cancer, and they keep putting her in the hospital, and I don't know why. Every time they put her in there, it costs thousands of dollars, and they don't have any insurance."

"I'm sorry."

"Don't be. They got themselves into that situation; not the cancer, but the no insurance deal. My son was too tight to pay for insurance, and look what it got him. His Mama and Daddy are bailing them out."

"Does Clarence feel the way you do?"

"Yeah, but maybe not as strong as I do. Jerry, what do you do in your spare time?"

"I don't have a lot of spare time, but when I do, I usually spend it at home with my wife and our five year old son. He'll be six pretty soon. What do you do?"

"Nothing. I don't have much of a chance to do anything. Clarence expects me to stay right there the whole time he's at home, and that's most of the time. He's so jealous, he thinks I'm going out to find a man if I ever get out of the house."

"Is he right?"

"I don't think so. Maybe." She took a couple of steps over to him, put her hand on his arm, and said, "If I ever ran into somebody like you, I might think about it." When she put her hand on his arm, she inadvertently put it on his watch and then slid it off the watch and onto his arm.

He said, "You can get yourself in trouble like that."

"I know, but it might be worth it."

Stella looked to be in her mid to late fifties and was very attractive, and Jerry knew he had better back away from that situation in a hurry. He said, "Stella, it was great to see you, but I've got to get back to town. I'll be coming out here a lot, now that we're getting started on the development, so feel free to come over any time, okay?"

"Okay, Jerry. I'll come over when Clarence is gone sometimes. You'll probably have to run me off."

"I won't run you off."

"Promise?"

He looked at her and paused before saying anything and then said, "Promise."

They both got into their vehicles at the same time, and he followed her down the road. She waved as she crossed the main road, and he waved back. On his way back he thought, *what did I nearly get into out there. Lord, thank you for keeping me strong enough to resist that temptation. I sure don't need to get into a situation involving a woman. I've had enough of those with Barbara Mills and Melissa Morris, and you were good enough to give me the strength to resist them. You have been so good to me, I don't ever want to disappoint you. Thank you again, Father.*

The day was nearly gone, so instead of going back to his office, he turned and went home. After what almost happened with Stella earlier, he wanted to see Tracy and melt into her sweetness. They had a great evening together. She studied for her real estate course and he watched TV and played with B.J..

Just as he was getting ready for work the next morning, Bobby called at six forty-five. "Hey, Bobby, is something wrong?"

"Jerry, I'm trying to get to the White Rock house I'm working on, but they've got the road blocked. There are about five or six cars with blue lights flashing and what looks to be a Swat-Team truck at the Hernandez house. What should I do?"

"Did any of your men get through?"

"I don't think so. I'm usually the first one here, and the road was blocked when I got here. There are a couple behind me."

"I've seen things like that on television, and they don't

usually last too long, so hang there for a little while, and they'll probably let you by before too much longer. It's a little before seven now, so they must have raided the house around five or six o'clock. I'm glad old Hernandez paid for his house."

"He paid for it?"

"Yeah; in cold, hard cash."

"Man, I wish I could do that."

"Well, start selling drugs and maybe you can, but be ready to wind up like old Hernandez."

"Okay, Boss. I just wanted to let you know about this. Maybe we can get to work pretty soon."

"I hope so. Thanks for calling, Bobby."

He finished getting ready and soon left the house. He hadn't been in his office long before he got a call from Melissa. "Good morning, Sunshine. What's up?"

She asked, "Have you seen the morning paper, yet?"

"No, why? Did you get arrested or something?"

"You're funny. Ha ha. No, I didn't get arrested, smarty pants. I just wanted to tell you that Denise Tabor was sentenced yesterday."

"Really? What did they give her?"

"She got one year on the assault charge and one year on the battery charge, and they are to run concurrently. The paper said that she was given credit for the two months she has already served, so the sentence is actually just ten months. It also said that she will probably just have to serve about four more months. It said that Cliff Jackson tried not to prefer charges, but the judge wouldn't allow it due to the severity of the attack on him."

"I wonder how I go about getting my wrench back."

"I don't know. You may have to call the District Attorney. His office prosecuted her."

"You're probably right. What are you up to?"

"Same old boring stuff. Uncle Frank is keeping me pretty busy typing contracts and notes and things."

Bud Fussell

"You need to find yourself a man to take you away from all that."

"I've already found one."

"I'll see you, Melissa."

"Before you hang up, let me ask you a question. When will the apartments you're working on be ready to rent?"

"The first four buildings should be ready in late May or early June. Why? Are you going to get one?"

"I'm thinking about it. Okay, I'll see you."

Chapter Twenty

Three Months Later

Deena's graduation was coming up the following week, which meant her wedding would be in four weeks. She already had a job to go to, but she arranged to not have to go to work until she and Stony got back from their honeymoon. She would be working in the Emergency Room at the hospital, and she was both excited and nervous about it.

She and Kitty had really been busy for the past three months, and as the date got closer, fuses started to get a little shorter.

The apartments were almost ready and she and Stony had decided on the one they wanted. It was on the ground floor in building two about fifty yards from the swimming pool and about a hundred yards from one set of tennis courts. With Bill's permission, an extra effort was being made to be sure there would be no holdup on their apartment.

They still didn't have any furniture, and she and Kitty were so busy planning, she and Stony didn't have much time to look for any. They did see some that they liked and just hoped it would be there when they got ready to buy it. Stony thought that if he could get Deena pinned down to a definite decision on it, he would put down a deposit and have the store hold it, but that was one of the things causing short fuses.

Kitty had sent out announcements a couple of months ago, but the invitations hadn't been mailed yet, and that was one of the next things on the list. Most of them were to go to Deena's friends because she had more friends than Stony. Of course, his friends were to be invited too; there just weren't as many. Some overlapped because he and Deena's dad both worked for Jerry, and they had mutual friends.

One day, Stony was talking to Jerry, and they were talking

249

about inviting people to the wedding, and Jerry asked, "Are you sending one to Monty Shepherd?"

"No sir. I hadn't thought about sending him one."

"Well, I would definitely send him one. You were a hit with him when we went to Florida, and I think it would hurt his feelings if you didn't invite him."

"Okay, I'll have him put on the list. Do you know his address?"

"I have it in my phone." He looked it up and gave it to him.

When he got to Deena's that night, he told her he wanted to send Monty an invitation, and she said, "Just in time. They're all being mailed tomorrow. I'm surprised you're sending him one."

"I was talking to Jerry about sending invitations, and he asked me if I was sending one to Monty, and I told him no. He told me I should because I had made a hit with him, and he thought his feelings would be hurt if we didn't send him one. Where do we stand on everything now?"

"Mom is amazing. She has just about everything ready, except, I still don't have my dress. Mom has her's, and the bridesmaids all have theirs. Everybody has theirs except me. I think I'll just wear jeans."

"That's what you should do, and I'll wear shorts. How would that be?"

"If we don't ever want to face any of our friends again, I guess it would be alright."

Stony said, "Honey, I know you've been real busy and still have a lot to do, but I need to put down a deposit on some furniture, if we're going to have any, and I want you to be sure about some of the things we've looked at. When do you think you might be able to go with me to look?"

"Since the invitations are going out tomorrow, I should have some time. Do you want to go tomorrow after you get off?"

"I'd like to. Yeah."

"Okay, we'll go tomorrow."

While Jerry was in his office the next morning, a man went in and asked for Jerry Martin. Beverly walked him back to Jerry's office and told him the man wanted to see him. Jerry got up and asked the man, "What can I do for you?"

"Are you Jerry Martin?"

"I am."

"I have something for you," and he gave him a subpoena that said, 'State of Georgia vs. Julian David Tabor.' The trial was to take place the following Monday at nine o'clock. He thought, *with all I've got going on, all I need is to spend time at a darned trial.* Then he thought, *maybe it won't be too bad. J.D. pled guilty, so there shouldn't be much to it. I don't know why they want me, but I guess I'll have to go.*

Construction was in the final stages at White Rock and most of the men that had been working out there were being brought to the apartments on a temporary basis.

Now that the streets were graded and paved at Cummings Acres and the electricity and water lines had been run, Jerry was taking Bill's suggestion and would have Stony lay out the first ten houses. After they are laid out, it will be time to move the White Rock workers over there, and Jerry thought there needed to be a construction office on site.

He went to a trucking company that had several trailers for sale and found a relatively nice forty-footer. He bought it and arranged for the trucking company to pull it to a sign painter where it would have the Martin Builders name painted on it. He then arranged for a mobile home dealer to pull it out to Cummings Acres for him and drop it where he wanted it and then level it up. As he did when he first bought a trailer for the office at the mall, steps had to be built, electricity and lights had to be run, and work tables built inside on which to work with blueprints and other things.

Just as soon as those things were done, Cummings Acres was ready to be changed from a farm to a lavish residential neighborhood. Jerry met Stony at the apartment site, on the day they were to begin, and they rode out together with the Precision Lay-out Pro.

The first thing they did was to go inside the trailer and lay out blueprints so Stony could familiarize himself with the house, its location relative to the street and property lines and other information needed to ensure that the house was laid out in the correct place. Jerry had learned how to operate the Lay-out Pro when he bought it, but his expertise wasn't as good as Stony's even though Stony had only used it on the apartments.

Bill had actually understated Stony's efficiency when he talked to Jerry about having him lay out the homes. Even though they got a late start that first day, he was able to get two houses completely laid out. Jerry was tickled because they could start building immediately, instead of having to wait two or three days for the lay out to be completed. On their way back to the apartment site to pick up Stony's car, Jerry asked, "How was your first day as foreman?"

"Gosh, I forgot about that. It was great."

"Well, I've been thinking about a little perk for your job."

"A perk? What could be a better perk than just being a foreman?"

"I want you to take off at noon, Friday, and go down to Hardy Ford and see what they have in the way of F-150's. If they have one you like, call me, and I'll go look at it, and if I think it's what you need, we'll buy it, and you can have it as a company truck. You can treat it like it's your own."

"Wow! Thank you so much, Jerry. That's great."

It was Wednesday when Jerry told him about the truck, and by noon Friday, he had laid out five houses. Jerry had told him he wanted ten laid out, so it would take until sometime the next week to finish that many, and they would have men all over the place, building what a lot of people would call mansions. Each house, when finished, would have anywhere from four thousand to seven thousand square feet, depending on the accouterments in each house.

He was so excited about getting a new truck, that he had a hard time concentrating on what he was doing Friday morning. At twelve sharp, he said so long to everybody and left for Hardy Ford. When he got to the dealership, he began looking, and an overbearing salesman came out to wait on him. He told the salesman that he was looking for something his company could furnish him as a company truck, and when he said that, the salesman told him if he found something he liked to call him, and he went back inside. Stony figured the salesman knew that when company vehicles were sold, most of the time, the ones who bought the vehicle went to the sales manager or general manager and cut out the sales commission.

He found two that he liked. One was white and was really pretty. The other one was grey, and not quite as pretty, but he figured Jerry would choose the grey one because the white one would stay dirty all the time. He hoped he would choose the white one, but he would be thankful for either one.

He called Jerry when he left Hardy Ford, and Jerry told him to meet him out there the next morning. They met and Stony showed him the two pickups he picked out. Jerry asked him, "Which one do you like the best?"

Trying not to say the one that Jerry didn't like as well, he said, "I like them both."

"Well, if we were to drive one of them out of here this morning, which one would you get in?"

"The white one."

"Okay, then we'll get the white one. I called Jim Hardy and told him we were coming, and he made arrangement with somebody inside to do the paperwork for us, so let's go in and sign the papers.

Everything worked out fine, and Stony drove away with a brand new F-150 pickup truck. Jerry told the man at the dealership to fill it up with gas, so he wouldn't have to worry about it.

Before Jerry left him, he said, "Stony, I forgot to tell you that I won't be there Monday morning. I've been subpoenaed to appear at J.D. Tabor's trial, and I'm sure it'll take most, if not all, of the day. You've got plenty to do, don't you?"

"Yes sir. I've got plenty to do. I've only laid out five of the ten that you said you wanted, and it will take me two or three days to finish them."

"Okay. You have a good weekend, and I hope to see you Tuesday morning."

"I will and thank you for the truck."

"You're welcome. See ya."

Naturally, the first place he went was to Deena's. He really hadn't paid any attention before, but when he got to her house and saw Bobby's truck, it was an F-150 as well, except it was red, and it dawned on him that Jerry was furnishing Bobby a truck, too. Bobby's was a model year older than his, but unless a person knew their trucks, nobody would be able to tell the difference.

He tooted the horn and got out and went to the door. Deena answered it, and he told her to come out and see his new truck. She did and was almost as excited as he was. They got in and took a spin around the neighborhood and were like two teenagers.

They decided they would go eat and then go to a movie that night, so Stony left Deena and went home to help his parents do some things at their house that afternoon, and then he would go back to pick her up in time for their date.

Frank and Melissa had also been subpoenaed to J.D.'s trial, and when Jerry got to the courtroom, they were already there, so he sat with them. Frank was on the end seat with Melissa next to him, and he didn't offer to scoot over, so Jerry had to climb over and sit next to Melissa. When he and Frank had something to say to each other, they had to lean over Melissa, and finally, she asked Jerry, "Do you want to sit here? Come on; let's change seats."

"Okay. Thank you," and they swapped seats. That suited her better, anyway because she could press her leg against his easier than she could when sitting next to Frank.

Sharply, at nine o'clock, the clerk called court to order. He said, "Court is now in session. The Honorable Judge Dale Lee presiding."

The Judge said, "In the matter of the State vs. Tabor, Mr. Tabor, how do you plead?"

J.D.: "Guilty, your Honor."

Judge: "Counsel, have you reached a settlement?"

D.A.: "Yes, your Honor. In response to Mr. Tabor's cooperation, the people are satisfied with the minimum sentence required by law."

Judge: "Mr. Tabor, do you know that by pleading guilty you lose the right to a jury trial?"

J.D.: "Yes, your Honor."

Judge: "Do you give up that right?"

J.D.: "Yes, your Honor."

Judge: "Do you understand what giving up that right means?"

J.D.: "Yes."

Judge: "Do you know that you are waiving the right to cross examine your accusers?"

J.D.: "Yes."

Judge: "Do you know that you are waiving your privilege against self-incrimination?"

J.D.: "Yes."

Judge: "Did anyone force you into accepting this settlement?"

J.D.: "No."

Judge: "Are you pleading guilty because you in fact committed these crimes that you are charged with?"

J.D.: "Yes."

Judge: "Mr. Tabor, here's your sentence. In keeping with the recommendations of the District Attorney, you will be sentenced to the minimum on each charge They are as follows. On the charge of concealing a body; one year. On charge one of attempted murder; seventy five percent of one hundred and eighty months or eleven years and three months. On charge two of attempted murder; seventy five percent of one hundred and eighty months or eleven years and three months. On the charge of Criminal attempt to commit arson; one year. All these sentences are to run concurrently and will amount to eleven years and three months. There is a chance that you can be released earlier for good behavior.

"Mr. Tabor, eleven years is a long time, but had you not cooperated with law enforcement, and if you had been found guilty by a jury, you could have been sentenced to what would have effectively been a life term, so be grateful for what you have.

"Is there anything else?"

Both attorneys said, "No, your Honor," and the judge said, "Court is dismissed."

As they were leading J.D. out of the courtroom, the defense attorney caught up with him and asked the deputies to wait just a minute. They did and the lawyer told J.D., "I look for you to get out in less than five years if you are a model prisoner, so behave and don't give them any reason to write you up for anything. Five years is a long time, but you're still a young man, and you can have a long, good life after you get out. Good luck to you."

Jerry stood up and told Frank, "That was interesting, but a waste of our time; don't you agree?"

Frank replied, "I agree. Melissa, let's go to work. Jerry, I'll see you."

It was only a little after ten, so there was still time to save the day. Jerry went to his office and stayed until lunch, and then went out to Cummings Acres.

When he got there, Stony was finishing up laying out the sixth house and getting ready to begin the seventh. "Boy, you're going to town, aren't you, Padna?"

"Yes sir. I love working with this Lay Out Pro, but I'm ready to finish these ten so we can get started on building them."

"The trucks will be here this afternoon to start on the footings. You'll be through laying out the ten by Wednesday, won't you?"

"Oh yeah."

"I'm going to start Bobby on his five tomorrow."

"Really? I was going to race him to see who could finish their five first."

"Well, you still can, but you'll be starting from behind. You're starting behind a couple of days, and then when you go on your honeymoon, you'll lose another week or ten days, so I guess you'll have to wait on the next set."

"I'll tell you something, Jerry. If you'll let me pick my men, we'll still beat Bobby."

"You can pick your men, but counting your honeymoon, you'll already be about ten days behind. I don't see how you can catch up."

"If you'll let me have the men I want, just watch. That'll be no hill for a climber. I'll be through laying out these ten on Wednesday, and if you'll have my men out here first thing Wednesday morning, I can get them started while I finish laying out the last one or two. I'll give you a list of who I want."

"Alright, I'll let you have the men you want, and I'll have them out here Wednesday morning. Now how are you wanting this competition to work; the one who finishes the first house wins?"

"No, no. The one who finishes the first five wins. I'll be starting out behind ten or eleven days, and I might not be able to catch up on the first house, but we'll smoke 'em on the next four."

"What will the prize be?"

257

"I don't guess there will be a prize. Bragging rights should be enough."

"Alright but be careful about bragging rights. Remember, Bobby is going to be your father-in-law pretty soon."

"I know, but Bobby and I are cool."

He worked hard to finish laying out the seventh house that afternoon, and he was confident that he could do two the next day and finish the tenth one by noon Wednesday. Then, he reasoned that if he had to get his men started Wednesday morning, it might be late Wednesday before he could finish laying out number ten, but that would be alright; he would still beat Bobby.

Jerry purposely didn't go out to Cummings Acres the next morning because he knew Stony was going to get a surprise, and he didn't want to interfere with it, so he went to the apartments and stayed until lunchtime.

Stony went to work at the regular time and really turned it on. He was hoping that he could get eight and nine finished and a good bit on ten. He worked feverishly until his phone rang about eleven o'clock. He looked at the caller ID and it said SHEPHERD AP. He answered it and on the other end, the voice said, "Stony, this is Monty Shepherd. How are you doing?"

"I'm fine, Mr. Shepherd. How are you?"

"I'm fine. I'm sorry I didn't call you earlier, but I've been in Munich, Germany, and just got back yesterday. Listen, congratulations on your upcoming wedding. It's just about three weeks away, isn't it?"

"Yes sir. Actually two weeks and four days, but who's counting?"

Monty laughed and asked, "Do you and your bride already have your honeymoon planned?"

"No sir. We've talked about going to several places, but she won't start working until we get back from where ever we go, and everything is so expensive, we're going to watch our pennies and not do anything too extravagant."

"Well, maybe I can help a little. Stony, I have a really nice place in Florida, if you like Florida, and I'd be happy if you and your wife would go down there for your honeymoon. I wouldn't want you to have to drive, so I'll have my plane fly you down and then pick you up and bring you home when you're ready. Does that sound like something you would be interested in?"

"Mr. Shepherd, I don't know what to say. I've been trying to get used to all the things God has been doing for me and now this. Yes sir. I would be very interested in going to your place in Florida. This is an answer to another prayer."

"Oh, by the way; There's a Suburban at the house, and you're welcome to use it while you're down there."

"I'm speechless. I just don't know what to say except thank you so much."

"You're very welcome. I've been talking to Jerry, and he tells me that you led one of your buddies to Jesus. Good boy."

"Thank you. He was the one that was with me when we broke into Jerry's houses when we were teenagers."

"That's what Jerry said. I'm proud of you, Stony, and I know God is. Listen, I know you're working, so I won't keep you. I just wanted to make you the offer of my place. Call me or have Jerry call me next week and give me the date and time you want to leave. Is the wedding at night?"

"Yes sir. It is."

"Well, you probably won't be ready to leave before ten or ten thirty, but whenever you're ready, we'll take you. Just let me know when, and I'll have the man who looks after my place pick you up at the airport, so all you have to do is go down there and enjoy yourselves."

"Mr. Shepherd, I'm just an unimportant carpenter, and I don't have anything to offer you, but if there is ever anything I can do for you, I hope you'll let me know."

"There is one thing."

"Just name it."

"I'd like to have you go with Jerry and me to speak to another FCA meeting when we go. Will you do that?"

"Yes sir. I will."

"You can add your friend's conversion to your story."

"Okay, I will. Thanks again, Mr. Shepherd."

"You're welcome. I'm sorry I won't be able to get there for your wedding. I'm very anxious to meet your bride, but maybe I can soon."

As soon as they hung up, Stony sent a text to Deena. He knew she was in class and couldn't talk, but he wanted her to get the message to call him as soon as possible.

He went back to work and worked like a demon to get the lay outs done. There were so many good things happening to and for him, he had a hard time believing they were happening to him. He only took a ten-minute lunch break because he didn't want to lose any more time than he lost while on the phone to Monty.

About one thirty, Jerry drove up and got out. He walked over to Stony with a big smile on his face. When Stony saw him, he smiled, too. Jerry asked, "Did you happen to get a phone call this morning?"

"Boy, did I. I still can't get over it."

"What did he say?"

"He offered to fly Deena and me down to his place in Florida and then pick us up when we get ready to come home, and we can use his Suburban while we're down there. Jerry, I didn't know what to say."

"I hope you said you'd go."

"I did."

"How's your truck driving?"

"Just like a Cadillac. Jerry, I don't know what's going on. There are so many good things happening to me right now. You gave me a good job and then gave me a promotion. You let me have a brand new truck to drive. Monty Shepherd is giving Deena and me a dream honeymoon and best of all, I'm getting ready to marry a beautiful, good, Christian woman. I owe you a lot for it, in fact; most of it, but I think God made it happen, and I don't know how to thank Him."

"Just keep being a good example like you were for Reed Thomas. You know, God says that one soul is worth more than the whole world, and you're the one who introduced him to Jesus, so I'm sure God is very proud of you."

"Stony said, "And you introduced me. I'm sure He's proud of you, too."

Jerry blushed a little and said, "I guess we had better get to work."

"I guess we had better, or I'm not going to be through laying out all ten houses."

"Before we do, what else did Monty say?"

"He said he wanted me to go with you all when you go speak to another FCA club."

"What did you tell him?"

"I told him I would."

"Good boy. Now, let's get to work."

Stony went back to work with a feeling of euphoria and worked hard until Deena called. "Hey, Good-looking."

"Hey. I got your text. What's up?"

"You're not going to believe it. You remember who Monty Shepherd is, don't you?"

"Yeah, I remember."

"Well, he called me this morning, and he wants to furnish our honeymoon for us. He has a big layout in Florida, and he said we could use it, and guess what."

"What?"

"He's going to have his plane fly us down, and then when we get ready to come home, the plane will pick us up. And here's something else. He has a Suburban down there, and we can use it while we're there. The only thing we'll have to pay for is our food."

"That's wonderful. I just hope you don't get cold feet."

"Haha. If anybody gets cold feet, it'll be you. Listen, I've got to go. I'll see you tonight. Love you."

"You, too."

Late that afternoon, Jerry called him and said, "Bill Case called and said your apartment is ready for you to move in."

"Great. We have some furniture being held at the furniture store until we're ready for it, so we'll arrange to have it delivered. Deena gets out of school early on Tuesday and Thursday, so she can be there when the truck comes. Thank you, Jerry."

"You and Deena will need to sign a lease, Stony. I think Melissa handles that; I'm not sure, but whoever handles it, I'll have them leave it on the bar in the kitchen, and after you've both signed it, I'll have her pick it up or you can bring it to me. We'll figure it out."

"How do I make out the check? Thomas-Martin Properties? And is it twelve hundred dollars?"

"Just wait on the check. I'll talk to you about it."

By the time he finished talking to Jerry, it was five o'clock and time to knock off for the day. He was afraid to leave the Layout Pro in the construction trailer/office, so he put it in his pickup and took it with him.

He went straight from work to Deena's where she was all smiles. She told him, "I'm really looking forward to going to Florida, but I'm nervous about flying. I've never been on an airplane before."

Stony tried to reassure her, and he said, "I never had until I went with Jerry and Monty to Gainesville, and now I feel as if I'm an old hand at it. I think you'll like it."

"Stony, we need to talk about the wedding. Have you arranged for your tux yet, and do you have all your ushers lined up? You know, it's only two weeks now."

"You know something, Honey? I'd really like for Jerry to be my best man, but I will feel guilty if I don't ask my Dad. What would you do?"

"I don't know. That's a tough one. I don't really know your Dad, but I do know Jerry. From what you say, you're not very close to your Dad, so I guess if it were me, and I was sure it wouldn't hurt my Dad's feelings, I'd ask Jerry."

"That's kinda the way I feel about it. I'll ask Jerry tomorrow and see if Dad will agree to be an usher."

"What if he doesn't want to be an usher?"

"Then I'll ask somebody else."

"Well, you'd better hurry. We don't have too much time."

"Listen, while I'm thinking about it, our apartment is ready. When can you meet the furniture truck out there?"

"I get out of school early Thursday. I can meet them then."

"Okay, I'll call them tomorrow. What time? About three o'clock?"

"Yeah, that will be good."

"Now, let's talk about the rehearsal dinner; that's usually something the groom's family takes care of. Has your Mom said anything about it?"

"Not a word. If we have one, I guess I'll have to pay for it. Who all goes to one?"

"Usually the wedding party, the parents of the bride and groom, and any out of town guests."

"What should we have?"

"Anything you want. I remember when my friends Steve and Buffy Russell had theirs, they had a pig pickin, and it went over great. You might want to do something like that."

"That would probably be cheaper than a sit-down dinner wouldn't it?"

"I'd say it would be a lot cheaper."

"Then let's do that. Where will we have it?"

"Maybe we can get Douglas Park. They have shelters in case of rain, and it's a good place to have something like that."

"I'll call and try to reserve it tomorrow. Beverly, Jerry's secretary handled Jerry's pig pickin, so I think I'll call her for some suggestions."

"Okay. Sounds good."

"Honey, I think I'll leave you early tonight and go home and feel my Dad out about being in the wedding. Do you mind? If he doesn't want to, then I'll ask Jerry.""

"Of course not. I think that's a good idea."

When he got home, his Mom and Dad were surprised to see him because he didn't usually get home until after they went to bed. They talked about different things; mainly the wedding, and then he said, "Dad, I was wondering if you'd like to be my best man. What do you think about it?"

"I don't know. Wouldn't it be better if you had one of your friends?

"Does that mean you'd rather not?"

"I just think it might be better if you asked one of your friends."

"Okay, I'll ask Jerry. I'm sure he'd like to do it. How about being an usher? Would you want to do that?"

"Same thing. It would be better if you got one of your friends."

"Okay, Dad. Are you even coming, or does Mom have to come by herself?"

"Oh yeah, I'll be there."

"That's good."

He sat with them and talked for a while, mainly to his Mom, and about ten o'clock he said, "I think I'll go to bed. Goodnight."

"His Mom said, "Goodnight," and his Dad just grunted something.

When he got to his room, he called Deena. "Hi."

"Hi. I asked Dad about being best man and he doesn't want to, and then I asked him about being an usher, and he doesn't want to do that either, so I guess I'll ask Jerry, and I'm not sure who I'll ask to be an usher; maybe Kyle Tillotson."

"Did you mention the rehearsal dinner?"

"No, I'll take care of it myself."

"I can help you."

"Okay. I'm going to bed now, I just wanted to tell you that Dad won't be in our wedding."

"Does that bother you?"

"No. Well maybe a little, but I'll live through it."

"We'll live through it."

"That's right. We'll live through it. I love you, Goodnight."

"Love you, too."

When he called Jerry the next morning, Jerry said he would be honored to be his best man and asked if he didn't want to ask his Dad. He told him he did, and his Dad didn't want to, and he told him he would rather have him (Jerry) anyway.

He also called Douglas Park and was able to reserve a place that had a shelter in case it rained, and finally, he called Beverly to ask about someone to cook the barbeque. She suggested that since there wouldn't be a whole lot of people, that they just cook pork shoulders instead of a whole hog, and that suited him just fine. She offered to make the necessary arrangements, and that really helped him. He told her he would bring a check by the office when she found out how much it was.

The next night, he and Deena made a list of who they were going to invite to the rehearsal dinner, and although Frank and Marilyn weren't in the wedding party, they were almost like parents to Stony, so he invited them.

The next two weeks were going to be crushers. Deena's graduation was Saturday at five o'clock, and that would only leave one week until the wedding. He tried to work extra hard, but he had a hard time concentrating because of it. He remembered about letting Monty know about the time for them to leave on the wedding night, and he asked Jerry if he would call him.

Finally, the day of the rehearsal and rehearsal dinner

arrived. Beverly was a lifesaver because she not only arranged for the barbeque, she got the knives, forks, and napkins, and she came to the dinner and served the guests. That was something Stony hadn't even thought of. Also, she was able to get the barbeque cooks to make apple cobbler for guests, so the entire affair went very well, mainly because of her.

Tradition wouldn't allow the bridal couple to see each other the next day, and Stony needed support, so he called Reed, and they went to the mall and spent some time. Deena had her Mom for support, and they had all kinds of girly things to do.

The wedding was to be at five o'clock with the reception following in the Fellowship Hall of the Church. To be sure they had plenty of time, Stony arranged for Monty's plane to be ready to take off at ten-thirty. Flying time was going to be one hour and thirty minutes, and Monty's man was to be at the airport at midnight to meet them.

Deena was a beautiful bride as were her bridesmaids. Kitty Kunkle was a knockout in her dress, and Bobby was very handsome in his navy suit.

Stony looked like a million dollars in his tuxedo, and his attendants were handsome in theirs.

The ceremony was pretty much traditional; everything coming from the Bible, which was what both sides wanted. The reception was mostly punch, mints, peanuts, and wedding cake, but everybody seemed to enjoy it.

As the reception was winding down, Jerry called Stony and Deena over to where he and Frank were standing. When they got to them, Jerry said, "Stony, I guess you've been wondering what Tracy and I were going to give you for a wedding present. We thought about several things and decided that until Deena starts working, something financial might be better, therefore, we're taking care of your first months rent in your new apartment. Deena and Stony both hugged him and Tracy, thanking them and assuring them that their gift was the perfect gift.

When their excitement waned a little, Frank said, "Stony, you've been almost like our son, so Deena, I guess that makes you almost like our daughter. Jerry and I talked about what to give you, and we both came to the same conclusion. What you need right now is not a toaster or a blender. You can use something financial, so Marilyn and I are matching Jerry and Tracy and we're giving you your second months rent. We felt that these two months rent can help with paying some on your furniture or something else that you need."

The hugging and thanking began all over again, and tears came into the eyes of all six of them. As he and Deena started walking away, Stony turned around and said, "Thank you again. This is such a big help. I love you all."

Reed had driven Stony to the Church, and Jerry wanted to take the newlyweds to the airport, so a little after nine, the crowd had thinned out considerably, Jerry said, "What do you say we go to the airport?"

"Stony said, "That's fine. Let us tell our parents bye, and we'll be ready. They went over to his parents and told them they were leaving and Nancy said, "Deena, I'm happy to have you as my daughter-in-law. Come see us when you get back." They turned to his Dad and said, "Bye, Dad. I'm glad you came."

His Dad said, "Bye. Have a good time."

"Okay. I'm sure we will. We'll see you in about a week."

Then, they went to Kitty and Bobby. Stony said, "Well folks, we're off to the Sunshine State."

Bobby said, "You all have a great time. We'll see you in what, a week?"

Stony said, "Yeah, we'll be back next Sunday night." Then he said, "Kitty Kunkle, I haven't had a chance to tell you, but you look beautiful."

"Thank you, Stony Gray."

After Deena hugged them both, Stony shook Bobby's hand and hugged Kitty. As he was breaking away from her, he

smiled and said, "I love you, Kitty Kunkle."
"I love you too, Stony Gray."

Chapter Twenty-One

After they had told everybody goodbye, the four of them piled into Tracy's Lexus and headed for the airport. They got there at ten-ten, and the plane hadn't arrived yet, so they sat in the car and talked. At ten twenty they saw a plane coming in, and when it got closer, they could see the Shepherd Apparel lettering on the side above the windows.

Deena asked, "Is that the plane we're going to fly in?"

Stony said it was, and they got out of the car. Jerry popped the trunk and Stony got their luggage out. They had a lot, so Jerry helped with it. When they got to the door leading out to the tarmac, the pilot met them. "Hi folks. Mr. Martin, how are you?"

"I'm good. It's good to see you again."

"Hi Stony. Remember me?"

"I sure do. It's good to see you. This is my wife, Deena."

"Hello Deena. It's nice to meet you. Are you ready to fly like a bird?"

"I'm not sure. I've never flown before."

Remembering that Stony flew with him on his first flight, he said, "Just hang on to Stony. He's an old hand at this now. I think you're going to enjoy the flight. It's a beautiful night, and the weather is perfect. We'll be in the air somewhere around an hour and a half, so just kick back and enjoy the ride. We're ready if you are."

Stony said, "We're ready." He shook Jerry's hand and hugged Tracy. Deena hugged them both, and they told them bye. Tracy and Jerry watched them take off and Tracy said, "I wish we were going with them."

Jerry said, "Yeah, right. I'm sure they wish we were with them, too."

When the plane was out of sight, they went to the car and went home.

Bud Fussell

The Gulfstream landed in Florida almost exactly at midnight. Robert, Monty's caretaker was there to meet them and take them to the compound. It wasn't far from the airport, and when they got there and went inside, neither of them had ever seen anything so luxurious, even for a beach house.

Robert gave them the keys to the house and to the Suburban and told them if they needed anything, that his number was on the board over the bar in the kitchen, and he would probably come over the next day to help them familiarize themselves with everything. They told him goodnight and then explored the huge house. When they got to the master bedroom, Stony said, "I think I'll sleep in here. Which room are you going to be in?"

"You're funny. I'm going to be right with you, unless you don't want me to."

"Honey, I've been wanting to sleep with you for the last six months, and you're not going to get away from me now. Are you ready for bed?"

"I definitely am.

She got some things out of her suitcase and went into the bathroom to change. Stony stripped down to his boxers and got in the bed with the covers over him. In a few minutes, she came out of the bathroom, and Stony told her to leave the door cracked so a little light could come in around the crack in the door. He could see her, and she had on a really sexy peignoir set.

She dropped the peignoir on the floor and slipped into bed with her slinky gown on and moved up against him. They embraced, and in a few minutes, they decided that the six month wait was well worth it.

Both of them were used to getting up early, so they woke up early Sunday morning. Each one got up and went to the bathroom and then went back to bed, not wanting to separate themselves from the other.

About eight thirty, they decided to get up. Deena went into

the kitchen to see if there was any coffee, and she discovered a Keurig Coffee maker. They dressed and sat outside on the patio while they drank their coffee. In a little bit, Stony asked, "Are you hungry?"

"Starved. Are you?"

"Starved. Let's go see if we can find some place that serves breakfast. Want to?"

"Yeah, let's do it."

They put some shoes on and drove the Suburban up the street until they came to a place named Corner Diner. There were several cars in the lot, so they figured it must be good, and they went in. Both of them had a huge breakfast, and after they finished, they drove around a little, looking for other restaurants where they might eat lunch and dinner while they were down there.

Deena asked, "Do you want to buy groceries and eat in most of the time, or do you want to eat out every meal?"

"What would you rather do?"

"Why don't we buy stuff for breakfast and lunch and go out for dinner?"

"Sounds like a plan, now, let's find a grocery store."

"There's one," and they pulled in a Publix parking lot."

After they bought groceries, they went back to Monty's and changed into their bathing suits. They looked around and found some beach chairs and took them to the beach where they stayed for a large part of the day, only taking an occasional break to get a snack or to go to the bathroom.

At one point, Deena said, "This is like Heaven, isn't it, Honey?"

"It sure is."

The rest of the week was like Heaven to the couple. They did exactly what they wanted to which was practically nothing. Breakfast was always early and then lunch. They would usually go to bed either mid-morning or mid-afternoon and sometimes both. One evening, after they had dinner, they went to a movie, but that was all the outside entertainment they had; not because there wasn't anything to do; they just didn't want to do anything else.

On Friday, Robert came over and told them, "Monty called and said he needs the plane back in Chattanooga by mid-afternoon, Sunday, because it has to be somewhere up north on Monday morning. He said to tell you that he's sorry to cut your Sunday short, but it's necessary. He said to tell you that the plane will be here at noon Sunday, which means that I'll pick you up and take you to the airport at eleven-thirty. Okay?"

Stony said, "That's okay. If he said he needed it today, it would be alright. We just appreciate what he's done for us. We'll tell him, and when you see him or talk to him, please tell him how much we enjoyed our time down here, will you?"

"I'll be sure to."

They finished out that day, and then on Saturday, they went to a seafood restaurant they had found for a last delicious platter of seafood. Stony had shrimp, and Deena ate stuffed flounder. They hated that it was their final trip because it was so good, but they were thankful they had found the place and had been able to enjoy it while they were down there.

After they got home from the restaurant, they packed some of their things, so they wouldn't have to do everything Sunday morning, and then they went out on the patio and sat until bedtime. While they were on the patio, Deena called Kitty and told her they would be home around one-thirty the next day and asked her if they could pick them up.

On Sunday morning, Robert got them to the airport just in time to catch the plane for a noon take-off.

Jerry had been filling in for Stony while he was gone, and he was really glad to see him when he got back. When Stony showed up for work Monday morning, Jerry felt like a free man.

About mid-morning, Jerry dialed Frank, and when he

answered, he said, "Frank, whatta ya say?"

"Just living the dream. What's up?"

"Do you have a day this week that you have some free time? I'd like to just sit down and talk to you for a while. I'll buy your lunch, if you'll let me."

"Hold on, Jer. Let me check my appointments." In just a minute, he came back and said, Wednesday looks good. How about with you?"

"Wednesday's good. Do you want me to come over there, or do you want to go to lunch?"

"How about me coming to your office. That way, I can get away from the phone."

"I'd love that. Come any time you want to."

"I'll be there late morning."

"Okay, I'll see you."

Frank got to Jerry's office around eleven o'clock Wednesday morning. He sat down and they made the usual small talk; the weather and other important subjects. After they had solved those problems, Frank said, "What did you want to talk to me about, Jer?"

"Nothing specific. For the last several days, I've been reflecting about my life and all the good things that have been happening, and you've been a large part of them. When Stony came back to work Monday morning and took over building five houses, I realized how thankful I am for having him in my company and in my life.

"And then I got to thinking back about seven years when Stony and Reed got into the houses I was building. For some reason, I wasn't overly upset like you'd think I would be, and I had empathy for those kids. I remembered my Dad had to bail me out of trouble more than once. I never did do anything to destroy somebody's property, but I did my share of mean things, and now that I look back, I feel sure God had something to do with that whole thing."

Frank asked, "What do you mean?"

"Think about it. If they hadn't got into my houses, and if I hadn't got the judge to let them work off their sentences by working for me, it's unlikely that I would have ever met you again after that night. If I hadn't done that, it's highly unlikely that you would have loaned me twenty five or thirty million dollars the way you did. It's highly unlikely that you would have ever let me build your apartments, and it's extremely unlikely that you would have picked me to build Skint Chesnut. As important as those things are, I don't think they're the most important."

"What do you think is the most important?"

"I think the most important things, and that's plural; I think the most important things are when I was able to introduce Stony to Jesus, and when Stony was able to introduce Jesus to Reed. None of those things would have happened had they not broken into my houses that night seven years ago.

Frank said, "I see what you mean."

"But that's not all. Things have happened this last year that are both directly and indirectly connected to that night."

"Such as?"

"Let's go back to earlier this year when you hired me to renovate the Chrisman House and then come forward to the day that J.D. Tabor tried to kill Melissa. If I hadn't known you, I wouldn't have been there to save her. If it wasn't for that night, Stony would never have met Deena. There have been so many diverse things that have happened because of that one night, if someone ask me what I would call all of it, I'd have to call it diversity because there's such a wide variety of things, and I give God the credit for all of it."

"I think diversity would be a good name for it. I've thought of a lot of those things you mentioned, but not in as much detail as you have, and I appreciate you telling me all this."

"You're welcome. Now, let's go to Old Smokey's and I'll buy your lunch."

274

www.ingramcontent.com/pod-product-compliance
Lightning Source LLC
Chambersburg PA
CBHW060901250626
47159CB00008B/2831